Re:ZeRo
-Starting Life in Another World-

"What are you
doing staring
at my servant,
you imbecile?"

"What are...!
G-get off!
Emilia-tan's
gonna get the
wrong idea!"

Characters

Re:ZERO Starting Life in Another World

The only ability Subaru Natsuki gets when he's summoned to another world is
time travel via his own death. But to save her, he'll die as many times as it takes.

Crusch

Head of the House of Karsten.
A beautiful woman, dressed in
male attire. Her knight
is Ferris.

Ferris

Ferris

An envoy from the royal capital who
visits Roswaal Manor. Has cat ears.

Wilhelm

Wilhelm

Driver of the dragon carriage that brings
Ferris to Roswaal Manor.

Priscilla

A girl Subaru meets in the royal capital.
Distinguished by extravagant clothes
and a haughty disposition.
Her knight is Al.

Al

Wears a pitch-black helm and
clothing that makes him look
like a bandit.
Curious fashion sense.

Anastasia

Anastasia

Chairwoman of the Hoshin Company,
the greatest power in Kararagi.
Her knight is Julius.

Juli

Julius

One of the Knights of
the Royal Guard of the
Kingdom of Lugunica.
"The Finest of Knights."

Re:ZERO -Starting Life in Another World-

The only ability Subaru Natsuki gets when he's summoned to another world is
time travel via his own death. But to save her, he'll die as many times as it takes.

CONTENTS

Re:ZeRo

-Starting Life in Another World-

VOLUME 4

TAPPEI NAGATSUKI
ILLUSTRATION: SHINICHIROU OTSUKA

YEN ON

NEW YORK

RE:ZERO Vol. 4

TAPPEI NAGATSUKI

Translation by ZephyrRz
Cover art by Shinichirou Otsuka

RE:ZERO KARA HAJIMERU ISEKAI SEIKATSU
© TAPPEI NAGATSUKI / Shinichirou Otsuka 2014
First published in Japan in 2014 by KADOKAWA CORPORATION, Tokyo.
English translation rights reserved by YEN PRESS, LLC under the license from
KADOKAWA CORPORATION, Tokyo, through Tuttle-Mori Agency, Inc., Tokyo.

English translation © 2017 by Yen Press, LLC

Yen On
1290 Avenue of the Americas
New York, NY 10104

Visit us at yenpress.com
facebook.com/yenpress
twitter.com/yenpress
yenpress.tumblr.com
instagram.com/yenpress

First Yen On Edition: June 2017

Yen On is an imprint of Yen Press, LLC.
The Yen On name and logo are trademarks of Yen Press, LLC.

Library of Congress Cataloging-in-Publication Data
Names: Nagatsuki, Tappei, 1987– author. | Otsuka, Shinichirou, illustrator. |
ZephyrRz, translator.
Title: Re:ZERO -starting life in another world- / Tappei Nagatsuki ; illustration by
Shinichirou Otsuka ; translation by ZephyrRz.
Other titles: Re:ZERO kara hajimeru isekai seikatsu. English
Description: First Yen On edition. | New York, NY : Yen On, 2016– |
Audience: Ages 13 & up.
Identifiers: LCCN 2016031562| ISBN 9780316315302 (v. 1 : pbk.) |
ISBN 9780316398374 (v. 2 : pbk.) | ISBN 9780316398404 (v. 3 : pbk.) |
ISBN 9780316398428 (v. 4 : pbk.)
Subjects: | CYAC: Science fiction.
Classification: LCC PZ7.1.N34 Re 2016 | DDC [Fic]—dc23
LC record available at https://lccn.loc.gov/2016031562

ISBNs: 978-0-316-39842-8 (paperback)
978-0-316-39844-2 (ebook)

1 3 5 7 9 10 8 6 4 2

LSC-C

Printed in the United States of America

PROLOGUE

A FOOL AND HIS STUBBORNNESS

—How many times had he been slammed to the ground?

He felt the hard, flat earth beneath him. A mix of blood and gravel made a mess of his mouth. His entire body burned like it was on fire. After so many blows to the head, his thoughts felt foggy and out of focus. His left eye had swollen shut.

He heard a voice from somewhere high and distant, from someone looking down at him.

"—I believe it would be futile to continue further?"

Subaru remained flat on the ground, limbs splayed, as he looked in the direction of the voice. He saw the violet-haired young man swaying the tip of the wooden sword in his hand.

His mostly white ceremonial uniform did not have a single speck of dust on it, nor was he out of breath, nor even sweating. Only the bloodstained weapon he held detracted from his elegant mien.

"If you take back what you said and bow your head before me, I will leave it at that. Do you accept?"

It was the young man who had inflicted such pain on Subaru's body, relentlessly striking until he mercilessly drove Subaru to the ground. Each time he did, he would deliver his order for surrender again, as if some kind of rule demanded it.

But Subaru's reply was set in stone.

"...I'm not wrong... I'm not...bowing my head."

Even with blood trickling from his nostrils in an unsightly fashion, Subaru leaned on his wooden sword and rose again. He coughed violently to spit out the blood clogging his throat.

The difference in strength was clear. Everyone knew who the winner and loser would be. It'd take a miracle for Subaru to get a single blow in, let alone win.

But he thought, *Yeah, like I care.*

"...*You* should take back what *you*...!"

Subaru bit back the pain in his mouth and cut off his last biting words before charging forward too slowly, too late. He poured all his strength into one desperate blow.

"You can put everything on the line and it will never be enough. That is the difference between us, unchanged from birth."

He smoothly parried the oncoming blow, and, after Subaru lost his balance, the young man slammed him hard in his chest. Subaru's breath deserted him, and the next moment, when his vision flickered, a blow to his face sent him tumbling backward onto the ground.

The pain was tremendous. Amid agony so strong he forgot to breathe, Subaru stared up toward the heavens through his right eye. He saw the azure sky, high and distant, but nothing beyond it.

It was so blue it made him sick. Subaru forced himself back to his feet and peered ahead, enduring bloodcurdling pain with nothing more than his inexhaustible anger.

But it was as if that anger was a diversion from whether he was in the right or the wrong in the first place.

CHAPTER 1
RETURN TO THE ROYAL CAPITAL

1

"And last, stretch your arms high in the sky for the big finish—
Victory! —Victory!" He listened to the giddy voices as he wiped the
sweat off his brow.

Subaru raised both hands high as he spoke his trademark phrase.
A chorus followed, ending another morning's workout.

The people who joined him in his exuberant radio calisthenics were residents of Earlham Village, the one closest to Roswaal
Manor. Probably half the village was present.

Subaru's cheeks softened without him realizing it at the sight of
the familiar buoyant faces. He wordlessly lowered his gaze a little,
unable to watch them for a few moments.

Subaru had suggested teaching Japanese radio calisthenics to help
the village, where scars from the recent demon beast crisis were still
fresh. This had improved his reputation among the otherworldly
residents and exploded into a village-wide movement. At first,
Subaru had been worried about the lack of participants. But seeing
the children who had been victims of the demon beast attack enjoy
themselves made him feel it was all worth it.

The customs of his homeland were not to be underestimated. Radio calisthenics weren't the only popular tradition…

"Okay, you brats, line up! It's stamp time!"

Subaru raised his voice while taking out a raw potato with one end sliced flat. Subaru dipped the flat end into an ink container, then pressed it onto the sheets of paper that the queued-up children held out eagerly. The very in-demand "potato stamp" recorded that day's fruits of labor.

"So how about it? In another week we'll start the long-awaited, much-requested event, Monday Puck. The highlight will be those floppy ears."

"The kitty's so cute!" "He's wonderful!" "He's adorable!"

He'd stolen the potato-stamp idea from radio calisthenics during summer break back home. A lot of kids had fun guessing what was going to be on that morning's stamp. Subaru thus used his oddly dexterous fingers to engage their young minds.

After a time, his pleasant chat with the villagers came to a close. Subaru waved to them and went on his way. He approached a tree at the edge of the village square, wearily calling out to the girl leaning against the trunk in the shade.

"Ahh, that wore me out. Anyway, sorry to keep you waiting, Emilia-tan."

"No, it's all right. I see you worked hard, Subaru." Emilia smoothed her silver hair with a charming smile, readjusting the hood she wore low over her face. "The villagers seem much happier these days, and it's all thanks to you, Subaru."

"It's no big deal. I just showed them how to do some healthy exercises that get the blood flowing. But I feel bad making you come with me every morning, day after day."

"That's okay. You're not in tip-top shape yet, and Ram and Rem can't come because of their work at the mansion. Besides, I really don't mind doing this."

"As in, you don't mind spending your mornings with me?"

"Pfft, not that. More like…I like being even a tiny bit involved with the villagers I never used to come in contact with. I think maybe...I drew a line between us until now."

He could make out a small blush on Emilia's face under her hood. The lovely sight warmed Subaru's cheeks before he even realized what was happening.

Lately, Emilia had often gone with him to the village as soon as she finished her daily chitchats with the minor spirits, returning together after Subaru completed the morning workout routine. For about fifteen minutes, he and Emilia would walk side by side on the way from the village back to the mansion. Subaru treasured these rare moments more than anything.

"I have to say, though, you really get along with the villagers, Subaru. You're probably more famous than Ram and Rem by now."

"Well, I am kind of the hero who saved them. Plus, I'm the ultimate gentleman who never asks for thanks, never brags about my deeds... I'm sure you'll fall in love with me all over again!"

"I wasn't in love to begin with, mind you... Also, I think your assessment is slightly off." Emilia put a finger to her lips, tilting her head slightly with a conflicted look. For his part, Subaru was a little dejected at her brushing off his favor so easily. She continued, "I think that the villagers see you as oddly perceptive rather than a hero who saved everyone. I mean, you know some very mysterious things."

"So they're treating me like a well-educated professor, huh... But, um, besides aerobics, I don't know all that much..."

"There's the games you play with the children, potato stamping... Also, mayonnaise."

Emilia clapped her hands together as her eyes sparkled. She'd become a huge fan of the experimental mayonnaise Subaru had made at the mansion. Subaru, a natural-born mayo lover back on his world, had reproduced mayonnaise to put some zest in his meals; the sauce was apparently a smash hit with Emilia and the villagers.

"I think they're underselling my hard work a bit, if they think mayonnaise and rescuing children from demon beasts are on the same level. I mean, I put my body on the line and everything..."

He'd gone into the forest to save the children, and got bitten all over. When Rem went out to save him from certain death, he protected her and got bitten, and he was about to be bitten some more when Roswaal showed up to save him...

"Huh?! Come to think of it, I did, like, almost nothing!"

Thinking back on his exploits, they amounted to considerably less than he'd originally thought. Perhaps it was better to say that he'd been involved in many exploits, but his individual efforts had accomplished close to nothing.

"Sheesh. Don't worry about silly little things like that."

"But, Emilia-tan..."

"Everyone knows you worked very hard, Subaru. Roswaal, Ram, and especially Rem, right?"

Subaru's expression remained pathetic in spite of Emilia's encouragement. She ran a few steps ahead of him and turned around. The sudden movement sent her hood falling back, letting her long, silver hair flow down her back, sparkling in the morning sun.

"And me, too."

"—Huh?"

"I know very well how hard you worked. That's why we will have no moping. Understand?" Emilia tilted her head and asked, "Your answer?"

The dumbfounded Subaru vigorously nodded his head. His reaction prompted a beaming smile from Emilia.

"What was that? You were moving like a broken toy. You're always like that."

"Er, this time it wasn't on purpose... And besides, you're a hundred times more unfair. No matter how much I struggle, I just keep falling back in love..."

"Yes, yes. I think you have very bad habit of glossing things over, like just now."

Emilia wore a charming smile, oblivious to the sincerity of his words. Watching her put her hood back on and walk beside him once more, Subaru thought again that he'd never find a better girl than this.

The gate of Roswaal Manor had come into view during the course of their conversation. A few meager minutes remained until they arrived—and the regretful end to his morning bliss.

"There's a...dragon carriage parked in front of the mansion."

When Emilia paused beside Subaru and murmured, he stopped, too, looking in the same direction. There was indeed something like a horse-drawn carriage parked at the gates. It was "something like" because the vehicle was clearly not horse-drawn.

After all, the creature pulling the carriage was a lizard as large as a horse.

Subaru was so surprised at its sheer size, compared to lizards back home, that he wound up clapping his hands together.

"Oh, right, I saw those passing through the royal capital here and there. Dragon carriages, you say?"

"...? Yes, the land dragon pulls the carriage that's behind it, so it's a dragon carriage. Wait, don't tell me it has a common name I don't know?"

"No, no, I'm the one who knows nothing about it. I'm sure you're right, Emilia-tan. Have confidence in yourself."

"Really? You're not teasing me? You're not going to embarrass me by letting me use the wrong words in the wrong place, are you? If you're pulling my leg, I'll clobber you!"

"Nobody says *clobber* anymore..."

When Emilia raised a hand in mock anger, Subaru clutched his head and pretended to recoil. Their antics continued as they made their way forward, arriving in front of the dragon carriage.

"Whoa... Damn, this is impressive. It's, like, so huge it's unreal."

He'd seen these several times back during his time in the royal capital, but this was his first good look at one up close. The lizard that Emilia had dubbed a land dragon was indeed as large as a horse, but thinner and lighter. It looked like it'd beat a horse in a footrace.

As the two approached, a man stood up from the dragon carriage's box seat and announced, "My, my. Please look out below."

Before the startled pair's eyes, the man agilely leaped from the top of the seat to stand on the ground below. Subaru's breath caught a bit when he noticed he'd barely made a sound upon landing. The box seat was around Subaru's eye level—not a height to casually leap from.

The old man bowed and spoke with eloquence befitting an aged gentleman.

"Welcome back. Please excuse me for currently occupying the front of your gate."

He politely stroked back his solid white hair before donning an immaculately tailored black suit. Though advanced in years, his body was obviously honed into fine condition, and his aura made Subaru subconsciously stand up straighter.

If this man was indeed the driver, and therefore a servant, the master he accompanied had to be quite the person. Thinking this, Subaru shifted his gaze back to the dragon carriage.

"The envoy is already inside the manor and possibly engaged with Marquis Mathers."

The aging gentleman seemed to read their minds and answered their question preemptively. Subaru was unexpectedly at a loss for words as Emilia, standing beside him, stepped forward and faced the old man.

"Envoy...? Could this be...?"

"As you have no doubt surmised, Lady Emilia, this concerns the royal selection."

At the term *royal selection*, Subaru's head snapped up. The way Emilia's expression tensed had Subaru furrowing his eyebrows, suspicious about this turn of events. The man continued, "I believe the envoy has an official message for you. Please return to the mansion to receive it in person."

"...Am I being summoned?"

"Please ask the messenger personally."

The old man's discreet reply caused Emilia's face to harden as she lowered her head. "—Let's go." She began walking without even looking back at Subaru.

He broke into a short jog to catch up. At the last moment, he glanced back, and saw that the driver was still bowing low, silently watching them go.

2

"Welcome back, Lady Emilia."

After the driver saw them off, the two arrived at the mansion's foyer and were greeted by a girl in a maid outfit—Rem.

Strangely, emotions were absent from her high-pitched voice, replaced with calm formality. It was Guest-Greeting Mode, something Subaru hadn't seen much in the mansion lately—she'd been showing her smile to Subaru especially.

"Thank you. I'm sorry for leaving the mansion. It seems that we have a guest?"

"An envoy from the royal capital is visiting. Master Roswaal is engaged with the guest. Do you wish to join them?"

"Of course. It's my problem, so we can't have me out of the loop."

Rem nodded in response. Emilia began up the stairs. Subaru walked by her side, joining the conversation like it was a normal thing.

"All right. Just because the pressure's on doesn't mean I can let it get to me. I better pull myself together and not do anything stupid."

He was pumping himself up. But seeing Subaru so enthused, Emilia halted.

"Err, what is it, Emilia-tan? Suddenly all stressed out? Need a massage?"

"Err... Sorry, Subaru, this is an important meeting, so..."

"...I know that. That's why I'm getting my head in the game and..."

Emilia was finding it hard to let him down easy, so Rem dispassionately cut him off for her. "Sister is already attending in the reception room. There is no place there for other servants. Understand?"

Subaru took in Rem's words and looked back at Emilia.

"You're kidding, right? I'm the one who's out of the loop?"

"Sorry, Subaru. Rem, lead the way."

"Yes. Subaru, please return to your room."

After Emilia's small apology, Rem spoke kindly to Subaru even while in Work Mode. Rem walked off to the upper floor with Emilia behind her. Subaru stayed in place and clicked his tongue.

"Well, I don't know much about this world, so I probably wouldn't be of much use anyway…"

He wondered if it was selfish that he still wanted to be a part of this.

It had been approximately one month since Subaru had been summoned into another world. During that time, Subaru had taken it upon himself to favorably alter the destinies of the people with whom he'd become involved. Emilia was the first, but his rapport with the people in the mansion and the village was proof he'd done some good.

In light of that, he was disappointed he hadn't been included in such an important issue. "I'm being left behind here—literally and metaphorically." Of course, he accepted that his limited talents were the main reason why.

"But accepting that and giving up are two different things. What should I do, huh?"

Subaru Natsuki wasn't meek enough to simply wander back to his room and sulk in bed. He sank into thought, trying to cook up an approach to deal with the situation his way.

Finally, Subaru's face twisted into an evil grin as he thought of something and snapped his fingers.

"*—Ding.*"

3

"Isn't it boring waiting out in front all this time? Maybe take a breather?"

The old man on the box seat widened his eyes in surprise as Subaru came with some tea. The dragon carriage was still parked by the front gate of the mansion.

"Forgive my rudeness. This is somewhat unexpected, and so,

please watch out below again." With that, the aged gentleman leaped down from the box seat. Just as before, his landing was nearly silent. He continued, "I shall do as you suggest. Certainly, my throat has become slightly parched."

"Well, then, here you go. I didn't know what you liked, so I just brought the most expensive tea I could find."

The aged gentleman had a mild smile on his face as he accepted the tray. The expression deepened the age-appropriate wrinkles around his mouth, Subaru noticed, studying him intently now that he was close, when…

"Whoa, what the…?"

Suddenly, a light impact from the side took him by surprise. He quickly found the culprit—the land dragon was poking its snout into Subaru's shoulder. The jet-black creature regarded Subaru with sharp, reptilian eyes.

Its gaze felt strange, but not uncomfortable. Perhaps he simply didn't feel any hostility in those gentle eyes.

The gentleman quickly addressed Subaru. "M-my apologies. This land dragon is the finest one in our house, but…"

"Ah, no, don't worry about it. Actually I feel lucky to get so up close and personal."

"I am relieved to hear that. I must say, it is rare for it to react in this manner." After apologizing for the animal's discourtesy, the aged gentleman turned his blue eyes on Subaru as well.

The boy's body tensed, as if he were suddenly at knifepoint.

The gentleman continued. "—If I may ask, are those battle scars?"

"These? Well, a bunch of things happened, but I wouldn't go as far as calling them battle scars…"

"They are from the claws and fangs of beasts. That is why you are favoring your left side, yes?"

"……"

Subaru was surprised the old man could tell exactly what had left the white traces exposed by the rolled-up sleeves of his track jacket. It was true that Subaru had been favoring his left side ever since he had been injured.

"—I am deeply sorry for my repeated offenses. It may not be a question you wish to answer." Apologizing in response to Subaru's silence, the aged gentleman took a cup of black tea and brought it to his lips. He commented, "A fine taste. It has a considerable kick to it, I think."

"...Well, I didn't exaggerate. It seriously is the most expensive tea in the mansion. I'll have a pink-haired maid on my case if I get caught for this..."

That was no hyperbole, either. Ram would have quite the lecture waiting for him if she found out he used the "Do Not Touch" top-class tea without permission.

The aged gentleman kept one eye closed as he appraised Subaru with the other.

"Now then, what do you want from this old fossil after buttering me up with such wonderful tea?"

Faced with the man's calm demeanor and shrewd discernment of his ulterior motive, Subaru could only tense up. As a youth, he knew he was sorely outmatched in this war of words, so he promptly raised the white flag.

"Ya got me. My name is Subaru Natsuki. At the moment, I'm an apprentice servant here at Roswaal Manor. I'd at least like to ask what your name is."

Acknowledging his status as a novice, he hoped to get his senior to offer a shred of mercy.

Seeing Subaru meekly bow his head, the aged gentleman relaxed his expression.

"My, that is polite of you. I am called Wilhelm. I currently serve the House of Karsten, and that work has brought me to this place."

"Wilhelm, is it? Thank you very much... I'd be really grateful if you could at least tell me what brings you here... Ah, er, would you like to come inside?"

"I believe that the envoy is speaking about the matter?"

"Well, yeah, but they won't let me in on that. It's no fun to be left out of an event and not advance the story, so I figured I'd approach it my way."

He knew this was not a man to spill secrets about important matters. But gradually growing on people was Subaru's specialty. He wasn't just a delinquent without any talent for reading the mood.

For a brief moment, Wilhelm was at a loss for words at Subaru's ambitious behavior.

"You remain levelheaded at unforeseen developments, and when your motives are exposed, you do not cower but only grow more defiant— Such a personality will assuredly incur displeasure."

"…So you're saying I can't even take a hint?"

"As I do not know your position within this manor, I cannot carelessly run my mouth. I hope you understand."

Wilhelm's expression sharpened for a brief moment, then softened as he politely brushed off the impudent request. If things continued this way, Subaru would just wind up making Ram angry.

"I will say, you do seem very close to Lady Emilia. It does not look like you are a mere servant."

"R-r-really? Emilia-tan and I don't look like an odd pair to you?"

"'Tan…'?"

Wilhelm raised an eyebrow at the odd manner of address. Then, he smiled thinly as he realized the nature of Subaru's feelings.

"You walk a treacherous path indeed. She may become the next queen of Lugunica one day."

"Right now, we're just a super-cute girl and a dull servant boy. With the infinite future ahead, you never know what'll happen. When you asked your wife to marry you, Wilhelm, did you think she was the loveliest woman in the whole world?"

"My wife—"

Subaru's radical assertion made Wilhelm slip for a brief moment. He immediately nodded.

"I see. Certainly, it is just as you say. I think of my wife as the most beautiful in the world. I felt like everyone was staring at her, and I needed to woo her while I could. Pathetic, yes?"

"You see? I'm like, if she has to end up with someone, might as well be me, even if I'm 'unworthy.' It might take a lot of persistence, but that's my win-win ideal."

"You certainly act according to some very amusing logic. Fascinating, really. However, in the end I am a mere driver. I do not think I shall be of much service."

"I wonder. If you could tell it was Emilia-tan under her hood, I don't think the 'I'm just a driver' excuse works very well."

"_____"

Subaru's flippant statement wiped the expression from Wilhelm's face and silenced him. "The robe Emilia-tan wears is supposed to stop bad magic users from figuring out who she is. Plus, because of some stuff recently, a hooded mantle was added that makes it even stronger... People can't see who she is unless she wants them to, or they can break through the magic."

The robe, put together with Roswaal's magic, was an effort to nip trouble in the bud before Emilia's half-elf background could cause it. It was to protect her from the unfair handicap she had to bear, being born in her world.

"—And you realized all that from the beginning. Very cunning."

"Oh no, it was total dumb luck. When I was pouring the tea inside the mansion, I was like, 'Wait, wasn't that kinda odd?'"

The color of Wilhelm's gaze changed as he watched Subaru smile very casually. At the very least, he probably figured Subaru wasn't just a tea fetcher.

"I suppose I cannot call myself a mere driver, then... As you surmised, I am indeed related to the royal selection—or related to someone related, I should say."

"Related to someone related... That's pretty much the position I'm in here."

"You and I are different, I believe, because my reason for involvement is not so romantic."

"Well, of course not, when you're married to the most beautiful woman in the world. I think Emilia-tan would beat her out for cuteness, though."

"No, even in loveliness, my wife has no match."

Subaru had meant to make light of things, but the firm reply left him without a comeback. Wilhelm's cheeks seemed to slacken again as he successfully drove the riposte home.

"However—it would seem we are out of time."

"Ah?" Subaru blurted like a dimwit as Wilhelm silently motioned to the mansion. "That's Rem coming out with... Who is that?"

The familiar blue-haired maid was leaving the mansion with someone unfamiliar. Based on Wilhelm's behavior and their previous conversation, he reasoned this must have been the all-important envoy in question.

"I guess, objectively, this fantasy stuff is extraordinary..."

Perhaps he said that without thinking because the object of his attention didn't look like an "envoy" at all. The visitor noticed Subaru's gaze and responded with a teasing smile.

"Hey, it's normal to fall in love with a beautiful person at first sight, but don't you know it's rude to stare?" The speaker was a girl with a lovely face, her flaxen hair cut semi-long. She was tall for a girl, almost the same height as Subaru. However, her figure was terribly delicate, and her every action terribly feminine—everything just screamed *girl* at you.

A white ribbon adorned her hair, and the sparkle in her wide eyes gave her the impression of an adorable cat. Indeed, atop her head were...

"Seeing them in person, I have to admit, cat ears do have a certain magic to them."

"*Meow, meow?*"

As if responding to his murmur, the animal ears, the same color as her hair, quivered. He hadn't had any chances to get up close and personal with a demi-human before. The genuine article was really a sight.

—Subaru had never felt such anguish before at keeping his inner fur connoisseur in check.

As Subaru drifted off into the clouds, the girl turned to Wilhelm as he greeted her.

"Hey, Grandpa Wil. Sorry to make you wait outside like that. It was boring, *meow*?"

"Not at all. This kind individual deigned to engage these old bones in conversation, helping me pass the time pass quite enjoyably."

"*Fumyu?*"

At the old man's reply, the girl put a finger to her cheek and tilted her head. Her catlike pupils narrowed as she observed Subaru. After a supercilious inspection, she clapped her hands together and announced, "Oh-ho. You're the boy Lady Emilia meowntioned."

It was what she did next that caught him completely off guard.

"Uh, eh, ehh?!"

"Don't move. It's time for a little inspection."

Subaru was dumbstruck as the girl wrapped one arm around his neck, embracing him with her slender body. Since their heights were similar, her face pressed up to the side of Subaru's. The whisper of her voice in his ear made his body tingle all over, and he blushed in acute embarrassment. The soft sensation was accompanied by a curiously nice scent. The sudden turn of events froze him solid as he devoted every ounce of willpower to keeping his cool.

"Nom!"

"*Hyaa!*"

His efforts crumbled when he felt a single nibble on his ear.

Laughing at Subaru's adorable yelp, the girl released him from her embrace with satisfaction. He hastily backed up, tumbling down onto his bottom.

"Tee-hee, what a cute reaction. Anyway… The flow of water mana inside your body really is stagnant. If only there was time to do something about that, *meow*."

"Wh-wh-what were you doing?!"

"Checking your body out a little. The bite was complimeowntary."

Her glossy eyes locked on him as she provocatively bit her own pinkie finger. Even knowing that she was teasing him, Subaru was still agitated and couldn't dismiss it as mere humor.

"Oh, don't blush so much. Anymeow, I guess nobody's told you anything, have they?"

"What do you mean? About what?"

"About your body, and the deal, and things like that."

Subaru's eyebrows rose as the girl seemed to be deliberately prancing around the details. Though he found it hard to ignore her peculiar disposition, he had to simply hang on for the ride. "It would kinda help if you could tell me what those things are, you know."

"Oh, what to do? This is an important job, too… Tee-hee."

"Let us leave it at that, Ferris." Wilhelm scolded the girl for her excessive teasing.

She pouted in response. "*Thhbt*. You're too serious, Grandpa Wil. It's no fun."

"I am grateful to Sir Subaru for the tea, and besides, it is time to be on our way."

Wilhelm bowed as he exchanged what somehow seemed like lighthearted banter with the girl. The girl still had a sour look about her, but she seemed to recover her humor as she winked in Subaru's direction.

"Sowwy. You look like you could use some more teasing, but we're meowt of time for today. If we don't get home soon, dear Lady Crusch will be so worried she won't sleep a wink tonight."

"I don't want to ignore that first part, but who's Lady Crusch?"

"A name you'd better remember—she's the lady who'll rule this country someday."

At the last sentence, her carefree demeanor vanished, replaced by total seriousness. Then she gave him the dumbstruck Subaru a little wave. Wilhelm set his empty teacup back on the tray.

"It was a fine drink. Well then, Sir Subaru, may you be in good health."

Wilhelm agilely leaped back up to the box seat and took hold of the land dragon's reins.

"Well, sorry for no introductions but Ferri's real busy. Later!"

"Hey, wait! There's a mountain of things I still want to ask—"

"You should take all that up with Lady Emilia. If fate permits, we'll meet again at the royal capital. Bye meow!"

The girl left him nothing, her smile being the last thing he saw as she entered the dragon carriage. Realizing that his opponent had completely thrown him off balance, Subaru instinctively realized she was his mortal enemy.

As Subaru held back his frustrations, Wilhelm cracked the reins with a brief "Farewell."

The land dragon brayed while the wheels of the heavy carriage creaked into motion. It stomped the ground several times before taking a powerful step, accelerating rapidly the next moment. Before Subaru's eyes, the land dragon burst into a high-speed sprint down the road, kicking up a large cloud of dust as it sped off into the distance.

Subaru, left in abject defeat, had only the scent of the high-priced tea, largely left untouched, to console him.

4

"—And did you fulfill your duties as envoy?"

"Well, of course. I would never fail to do anything my Lady Crusch requests of me. Oh, Grandpa Wil, you're such a worrywart!"

Servant and envoy conversed as the land dragon left Roswaal Manor far behind.

Wilhelm sat on the box seat, guiding the land dragon effortlessly. Behind him, the pale-haired girl poked her head out the window of the dragon-drawn carriage.

In one sense, there were few places more suited to a private conversation.

"But I have to say, Grandpa Wil, I didn't expect you to speak to that boy while you waited. You don't like talking to people, do you?"

"That is a most grave misunderstanding."

"Oh, is it now? Sowwy. —It's just that you like slicing people more than talking to them, right?"

"...That is an even worse misunderstanding."

She had only been teasing, but Wilhelm offered no elaboration. The girl pressed her lips together in a pout, displeased with the stony reaction to her provocations.

"You're no fun. What, it was more fun listening to that boy than your dear Ferris? He didn't seem that special, but you like him that much, *meow*? You think he's actually so strong he's hiding his abilities?"

"Not so. He is an amateur—a cub without a mane. Nor does he have any talent worthy of mentioning. I am certain he is very ordinary."

"So why then, Grandpa Wil? You said you hated riffraff meowst of all."

Everything the girl said painted him in the worst possible light. In response, Wilhelm calmly raised a hand and pointed at his face.

"It's his eyes."

"—Eyes?"

The girl lowered her head as she inquired. Wilhelm simply raised his gaze, thinking back.

"The lad's eyes interested me ever so slightly. They said he has crossed the boundary of death. Many come close to the line, stop, and draw back, but..." Wilhelm lowered his lids in thought as his words trailed off. "Those are the eyes of one who has crossed once, no...several times, and returned. I know of no such being. You might say I was compelled by curiosity."

But the girl blithely dismissed Wilhelm's expression of wonder. "*Meow*, that doesn't make much sense..."

This time, Wilhelm answered with a strained smile. The girl continued, adding, "But if that's true, Grandpa Wil, that boy's won't find an easy path to follow."

The girl narrowed her eyes as she tossed her glossy gaze toward the broad back sitting against the box seat.

"Having the Sword Devil, Wilhelm van Astrea, interested in you is as unfortunate as the Witch having a thing for you."

5

"You're going to the royal capital, right? Well I'm going, too!"

With the guest having gone home, those in the reception room were able to breathe a sigh of relief—an atmosphere thoroughly shattered with a single sentence out of Subaru's mouth.

"You seeee?" Roswaal's grin drew a fatigued response from Emilia. "I suppose I do…"

Subaru wore a sullen expression at being left out of their exchange, which prompted Emilia to let out a sigh. "Just so you know, I'm not going there to play around. This is an important summons…very important."

"It's the royal selection stuff, right? I know, I know, it's a big enough deal to shake the whole kingdom up and everything, but I'm begging ya, take me, pleeease?" Subaru knelt on the carpet and brought his hands together in a desperate plea.

Emilia seemed conflicted as she surveyed the reactions of the others in the room. However—

"Ah, do not mind meee, I would say you are free to choose as you desiiire."

"This aroma… It can't be! Ram's treasured tea leaves?! Barusu is truly capable of anything…!"

Roswaal washed his hands of the situation, grinning all the while. Ram, on the other hand, was preoccupied with shock at a sudden discovery about something, and barely registered Emilia's predicament.

And Rem, the final person, said, "Taking him along is fine, isn't it? It seems that Subaru has acquaintances in the royal capital. He should visit them so they can rest easy." Until recently, Rem could be relied on to offer the most sensible opinions, but now she was solidly in Subaru's corner.

"Ooh, nice assist there! Rem, Reeem, come over here!"

"Yes!"

Answering Subaru's call with a flower-like smile, Rem sat beside him and offered her head. Subaru began to stroke her hair with a clearly practiced hand, making sure he would not mess it up. Rem's obvious pleasure helped Emilia realize she had no allies in this argument.

"In the first place, what do you intend to do by coming, Subaru? There'll be a *really* important meeting about the royal selection, so

I'll have my hands too full to deal with you at all. On top of that, in a real sense, this meeting is different than all the previous ones…"

"That's even more reason to go. I'll cry if I'm not involved at all in the critical moment that might make Emilia-tan into royalty, even if it's way off on the edge of things."

"That's why I can't bring you. If you go with me, you'll try too hard again for sure. I don't want to make you do such a thing. Understand?"

"You're the one who doesn't understand, Emilia. If trying too hard can help you, then I *want* to try too hard, see?"

"I…don't…"

With bewilderment in Emilia's eyes as she murmured, an awkward silence fell over the reception room. It was Roswaal who broke the unpleasant mood with a clap of his hands.

"Yes, yeees, that is far enough. It seems this conversation is not maaaking any headway, so let us wrap things up. I have decided that Subaru shall accompany you to the capital. This is my command to him as his employer."

"Roswaal?!"

Roswaal completely bowled over Emilia's hesitance. As shock made itself plain in her expression, Subaru raised a thumb in approval.

"Yesss! You said it, Rozchi!"

"Howeeever, Subaru is going to the capital strictly for medical reasons. All matters pertaaaining to the royal selection are striiictly separate. Understand?"

"Huh? Medical…reasons?"

Subaru raised his eyebrows at the unexpected addition. He noticed that Rem's face, still resting against his shoulder, tensed slightly. Emilia wore a pained expression as well.

"In the course of your battle with the demon beasts, your abuse of magic ran your gate dry. Even if your physical wounds have healed, treating this affliction is a different matter. Surely you have noticed this yourself, have you nooot?"

"…Just 'cause you say I'm in bad shape because of some invisible thing doesn't mean—"

Emilia cut in. "Subaru. Mana circulating through the body is the lifeline of every living creature. When that flow stagnates, it retards the circulation of the very essence of life… Please, don't try to hide it."

As Wilhelm had pointed out, he was still experiencing the after-effects of his physical wounds, like his limbs feeling heavier than they should. Subaru scowled at having been found out so easily, but he couldn't just brush off Emilia's plea.

"I know my body's in rough shape. So how is healing it connected to the royal capital?"

Rem replied, "Because you need a top-quality healer to treat it. Subaru, did you meet the messenger?"

"You mean the cat-eared girl? To be honest, not the type I want to bump into again, really."

"That messenger is an especially accomplished user of water magic, even by the staaandards of the capital. With such skill, it is no doubt possible to restore your health. As the child has various quirks, Lady Emilia went through quite some trouble toooo negotiate for cooperation…"

"Roswaal, wait a…! That's…"

Roswaal, who'd apparently "slipped up" on purpose, feigned indifference to Emilia's indignation.

"…Emilia-tan, seriously? For my sake?"

Emilia blushed furiously as she raced down her list of excuses.

"I-I mean, it's partly my fault that you're not fully healed, Subaru. You wound up at the mansion because you shielded me… And I should really have done something about the demon beasts, but you did that in my place. So this is paying you back, or compensating you for your loss, however you want to look at…"

"Look, I know you're hiding your gratitude because you're embarrassed, but you don't have to put it like that!" Subaru wore a wry smile as he crossed his arms. "Sounds like you're all for me going to the royal capital. Why are you acting like you're against it?"

"Because if I just came out and asked, you'd get carried away and do something crazy. I know what kind of mischievous rascal you are…"

"No one says 'mischievous rascal' anymore…"

Subaru murmured his retort as he pressed his hand to his neck. Emilia stuck out her tongue at him and the meeting drew to a close.

"Weeeell then, the matter is settled. Subaru shall accompany you on your trip to the royal capital. Preparations will require about one day, so departure shall be the morning after tomorrow—is this acceeeptable?"

Roswaal's firm words were met by assorted replies from all assembled in the reception room.

"Haaah, I understand." "No objections!" "—As you command, Master Roswaal."

And so, the plan for the Roswaal household's visit to the royal capital was established.

6

—And two mornings later, Subaru's voice quivered with admiration at the gate of the mansion.

"Whoa, this is—!"

Subaru beamed at the huge carriage parked before him.

Of course, it was a land dragon that drew the carriage, but this one boasted a sheer size that put every other land dragon Subaru had seen to shame.

"He's so huge! And his scales are so hard! And his face is so scary!"

Emilia's lips softened into a slightly exasperated exhale at Subaru's exhilaration.

"He really is worked up like a little kid. Isn't he?"

She shifted her eyes to Rem, standing by her side, in search of agreement. But Rem gazed at the excited Subaru, enthralled.

"Subaru is cute when he gets like this. Do you not think so, Lady Emilia?"

"Well, I do think it's cute, but… Mm, Subaru's been a bad influence on you, hasn't he?"

Emilia exhaled once again.

Subaru, paying no heed to the girls' opinions, reached to touch the land dragon without a second thought and shouted in a strange voice.

"Hot damn! I'm so excited! I'm living the uber-fantasy dream right now, aren't I?!"

The land dragon's tolerance reached its limit around when Subaru lost himself in the moment and his touches turned into taps. A single sweep of its tail sent Subaru flying, spinning sideways.

Several seconds later, Subaru emerged from the foliage, spitting leaves out of his mouth.

"Wh-what happened there?"

"Subaru, land dragons are highly intelligent creatures. Even if they cannot speak, they can express themselves very well. That is why one must treat them with the utmost respect."

"Couldn't you have told me that a little sooner?!"

Brushing the leaves off his body, Subaru observed the shockingly huge land dragon. It narrowed its yellow eyes and let out a long breath, as if saying, *That's what you get for running your hands over me.*

During the exchange, he finally caught sight of the people he'd been waiting for. Roswaal and Ram were coming out of the mansion.

"Hey there, what's up? You're late, aren't you? You're the one who set up the schedule, Rozchi. The guy who sets the schedule oughta live by it, don't you think, Rem?"

"I agree! Although, I'm the one who woke you up today when you didn't wake up on time... You may praise me for it, if you like."

"Okay, all right, okay, that's enough, Rem."

Subaru stroked Rem while urging her silence after her unnecessary addition. That earned him a sharp stare from Emilia, but he bore it as best he could and dragged the subject back to Roswaal.

"So why were you late? Everything looked in order at breakfast time."

"Ah, so sooorry. You see, with Ram staying behind, I will not be seeing her for a little while, yes? Thaaaat is whyyyy, I siiimply wanted to have a sooomewhat thorough farewell before our departure."

Roswaal adjusted his collar, raising a finger as he excused himself.

Beside him, Ram hastened to ensure her hair and clothing were also in order, plainly in high spirits.

"Okay, let's pretend I didn't ask. She's really gonna stay behind, though?"

"It can't be helped. We can't leave the mansion unattended, and Miss Beatrice is here as well, so I must look after her. It's troublesome."

"You put what you really think at the end, huh. Oh well, Beako would have it rough if you weren't there to spoil her."

"I might point out that if Miss Beatrice heard that, she might smash you into little pieces this time."

This trip to the royal capital was for Emilia, a candidate for the royal selection, and Roswaal, her sponsor. Subaru was going along for medical reasons, with Rem serving and guarding the other three. The group totaled four people. That left Ram and Beatrice, who would presumably be holed up in the archive of forbidden books, remaining in the mansion.

"You gonna be okay here by yourself, Big Sis? It's not easy keeping a mansion running all by your lonesome."

"You do not understand, Barusu. People can survive three or four days without food, after all."

"No plans to eat your own food, huh?!"

After Ram's lively, defiant statement provoked Subaru, she abruptly grabbed his collar and pulled him aside. Subaru's breath caught as her immaculate face drew close.

"Understand, Barusu? Keep a firm grip on the reins so that Rem does nothing rash."

"...You're the one who always goes to the royal capital, right? Why is Rem coming this ti...?"

"It is infuriating you're forcing me to state the reason with my own lips."

Ram shoved him in the chest, letting out a *hmph* as she walked off. By the time she was gone and Subaru looked back at the dragon carriage, Rem was just about finished loading the luggage.

It seemed the time for friendly banter had passed; it was time to get the show on the road.

"Beako didn't come to see us off, though... What a cold-hearted loli."

Subaru glared at the distant entrance to the mansion, cursing the absent girl.

Of course, he had expected as much, leading him to mercilessly tease Beatrice the day before so he could leave without any regrets. Still, without her around to say good-bye, their departure was a bit lonely. But—

"—Oh."

His eyes met those of someone covertly watching them from the entrance to the foyer, open just a tiny crack. For a split second, the person in the dress recoiled at meeting Subaru's eyes, but she immediately reopened the door so he could see her more properly. It was as if she was trying to hide her sullen, forlorn expression.

Subaru waved at her with little smile thanks to her typical behavior. In response, the pale-faced girl waved at him like she was shooing him away. She returned inside a moment later, having fulfilled her duty to see him off with minimal effort.

When he turned back, Emilia was looking down at him as she leaned out of the dragon carriage's passenger cab.

"—Subaru? What is it?"

The others had begun to get aboard without him realizing it. Subaru hurried over and reached for the doorframe. But white fingers reached out to him right before he could take hold of it.

"Here."

Subaru hesitated for a moment before taking her hand. She pulled him up as he entered the cab.

Now that Subaru was aboard, Rem nodded from her perch on the box seat toward Ram, standing alone on the ground. She took hold of the reins. The land dragon began to gently tread forward and pulled the carriage along.

Subaru poked his head out of the window to give Ram one final wave.

"Well, we're off! Let's both take care now!"

"At least try to evade the blows if something happens, Barusu. I do acknowledge your talent...as a decoy."

"I'm good for a little more than that, right?!"

Such was their clumsy early morning farewell.

The land dragon accelerated, and their speed began to rise quite suddenly. The mansion grew distant in moments, and Ram's figure beside the front gate quickly shrank. A moment before Subaru lost sight of her, she held the edges of her skirt and slightly curtsied. It was an exceptionally maid-like way to see someone off.

"...I suppose that's picture-perfect for how a cute maid should do her job, huh...?"

When they entered a dip in the road, Subaru was no longer able to see Ram at all, and he finally sat down on his seat in the carriage and exhaled. He finally felt at ease enough to begin enjoying the comfort of riding the dragon carriage. The seat had a high-class feel appropriate to the expensive design of the vehicle, making for a surprisingly enjoyable ride given that the road was not an especially well-maintained one.

Judging from how fast the scenery was scrolling past the window and his experience with cars from his own world, he guessed he was traveling close to sixty miles per hour. And yet the vibrations felt far lighter than one would expect, on par with a typical sedan.

Roswaal laughed as Subaru turned this way and that, seat creaking under him.

"My myyy, are dragon carriages such a raaarity?"

"Hey, is Rem fine all exposed on the box seat with us going this fast? It's not like I'm worried about her falling off... But won't her hair and clothes be a huge mess by the time we get to the royal capital?"

Emilia cut in to reply.

"There's no need to worry, since the dragon carriage is protected by a blessing."

"Blessing?"

"Yes, blessing. Gospel granted by the world itself when a life is born. There are numerous kinds so there is no universal rule for them, but some species always receive one particular blessing. The 'wind repel' blessing land dragons receive is one example."

"Wind repel blessing, huh?"

"When a land dragon gallops, the wind doesn't affect it whatsoever. The blessing extends to the carriage connected to it, so it isn't affected by the wind, either."

"And that goes for Rem sitting outside, too?"

When Subaru indicated he understood, Emilia replied with a satisfied look, "Very good."

Then Subaru asked, "So, Emilia-tan, what about me? Do I have a blessing?"

Being summoned to another world was supposed to provide cheat abilities. Certainly, Return by Death was a special power without compare, but Subaru still hadn't lost his craving for something special that was a lot less…painful.

"Mm, I don't like to say this, but a majority of people are born without blessings. Also, everyone with a blessing is aware of it to my knowledge, so…"

"Damn it, no good, huh… Nah, I get it. Meeting Emilia-tan was the miracle granted to me by the world, huh?"

"Yes, yes. It'll be six hours until we get to the royal capital, so be a good boy and behave."

"Emilia-tan's so cooold!"

Emilia and Roswaal let Subaru sulk as they began to discuss what they would do upon arrival. It was serious business; naturally, Subaru couldn't get a word in edgewise.

Unable to get involved in the conversation, he soon began to get bored out of his skull. "Emilia-tan, Emilia-tan, let me sit by the window!"

"What's wrong? Ah, motion sickness, huh? It happens a lot to people who aren't used to riding. I understand. I'll lend you Puck, so…"

"I'm happy for the concern, but it's not that. And I'm not sure why you'd give me Puck for motion sickness. What, am I supposed to use him as my emergency barf bag?"

"If it goes that far, even Puck might get upset…"

Emilia sank into thought, murmuring to herself, when Subaru shook his head.

"No, I just meant, Emilia-tan's too busy for me, so maybe seeing the scenery would take the edge off my solitude?"

At that point, a new voice cut in. Rem peered in through the small front window to the box seat.

"—Well, if that's the case, you should come to the front here, Subaru. There's nothing to do inside the carriage if you're bored, right? Here, you can see the sights, and I'll be glad to talk with you."

"Th-that is a very tempting suggestion... Emilia-tan, you won't be lonely with me over there?"

"To put it plainly, I'll be completely, absolutely all right."

"Do you have to be *that* all right with it?!"

Though the lack of effort to stop him gnawed at Subaru, he did have Emilia's permission to go. Since Subaru didn't mind, Rem, holding the reins, checked with Roswaal to confirm.

"May I stop temporarily, then? The land dragon will not be able to run again for a short time, however."

"Why's it gonna take time?" wondered Subaru.

Roswaal replied, "Because blessings are not omnipotent eiiither. A land dragon's wind repel blessing, once suspended, cannot be reactivated for a brief period. Shall we stop for an early meal?"

"Well, I don't wanna ask you to do that... If I open the door while we're moving, it won't slow down, right?"

As Subaru rose and reached toward the door, Roswaal smiled as he inferred Subaru's intent.

"If you have a certain degree of athletic ability, there is no proooblem, but if you fall, you will die."

"Eh, a little detour's no big deal. Wait up, Rem, and don't make an acrobat out of me here."

"I am concerned, but I understand. I shall wait. Come soon, come *soon*!"

At first, Rem looked worried at Subaru's suggestion, but very quickly sounded like she couldn't wait.

Smiling thinly, Subaru rose to circle around the carriage to the box seat. But Emilia called out to stop him, handing over a belt attached to the wall of the carriage.

"Wait a moment, Subaru. —Here you go. It's not *that* dangerous, so I won't stop you, but keep a good hold on this."

"If this is connected to the wall of the carriage… It's kind of like a seatbelt?"

"The belts are for when the dragon carriage tilts to the side. Use it as a lifeline. I'll take it back when you get to the box seat."

Subaru gracefully acknowledged Emilia's concern and wrapped the belt around his right wrist. As a worried-looking Emilia saw him off, Subaru opened the carriage door and embarked on his short outing.

It was strange how the scenery passed so quickly, yet he didn't feel any wind whatsoever. Like he was traveling inside a glass bottle. Careful to not let the uncanny sensation get the best of him, Subaru gingerly grabbed hold of the carriage's rail and wound his way toward the box seat.

If nothing else, he had good spatial awareness. The footing felt precarious, but his movements themselves were smooth.

"This is really something. So this is what having a blessing is like."

Subaru took in the mysterious phenomenon of his current world as he suddenly regarded the whole situation objectively. The wind repel blessing affected the dragon carriage and everyone inside it. What would happen if something under the effect of the blessing touched something that wasn't?

Feeling the desire to test his largely meaningless hypothesis, Subaru stretched his fingers up. Then, Emilia remembered something.

"Ah, that's right. Subaru, I forgot to mention, please don't put any part of your body too far from the dragon carriage. You'll end up outside of the blessing."

"—No way."

The moment after his fingers grazed the air, wind slammed into Subaru's entire body so hard he thought his hand would be ripped off at the wrist. The unexpected impact loosened his grip on the railing, and thus his support, blowing him straight to the side.

—Off the dragon carriage, obviously.

"Ahbuhbuhbuh—?! This is bad, seriously bad, oh man!"

The wind buffeted him until he lost all sense of up and down. He would have smashed straight into the ground, but the belt around his right wrist snapped taut. Subaru's body floated parallel to the dragon carriage. Pain wracked his wrist until it seemed like it would tear off. His life was literally linked to Emilia's lifeline.

The fierce strain and the unlucky turn had already blanked out Subaru's mind, but head snapped up amid the ferocious wind when the high-pitched sound of a chain reached his ears. Right in front of him, he could see a silver-colored snake with large, round, spiked head.

"—I'm gonna have nightmares again."

A moment later, the snake wrapped around Subaru's body. He raised a pathetic cry at how much tighter it was than he expected. But his body was hoisted up just before he became roadkill. He floated up and over the dragon carriage with ease; at the apex of his arc, the chain released him and tossed him forward.

Subaru saw Rem at the bottom of his revolving world. She held the reins and her morning star with one hand, extending the other to Subaru to guide him down.

As he realized that his life had somehow been spared, Subaru reflected, "I'll live a slightly quieter life from now on..."

Subaru, saved from a messy landing, promptly blacked out.

CHAPTER 2
BLESSINGS, REUNIONS, AND PROMISES

1

—Subaru Natsuki's heart was beating at a fever pitch.

"Um, Emilia-tan… I'm a little conflicted saying so, but shouldn't we cut this out?"

Subaru wore an amicable smile, but cold sweat ran down his face as he made the suggestion. The point of concern was how they firmly held hands.

They were in the royal capital. Specifically, Market Street, an exceptionally congested thoroughfare. No doubt, two people holding hands amid the constant bustle would look like an intimate couple.

So long as no busybodies overheard scraps of their conversation, anyway.

"Absolutely not. This is you we're talking about, so you *will* do something strange as soon as you're out of my sight. I won't permit a single step unsupervised while we're in the royal capital. Understand?"

"I'm really sorry for my stupidity in the dragon carriage! But this is treating me too much like a little kid!!"

The gaze Emilia leveled at Subaru was sharp and cold. Her trust in him had plummeted to rock bottom levels. Even if he was reaping what he had sowed, the treatment was extreme from Subaru's perspective.

—Following his close call with an "unscheduled stop" from the dragon carriage, and the tragedy of waking up to a Roswaal lap pillow, the subsequent conversation created a plan to limit his activities in the royal capital. This situation was the result.

"I'm deeply aware that I was rash but… Could we at least not do the holding hands thing?"

"Hmm, so that's what you're complaining about. We did this plenty in the village when it was a 'date,' didn't we?"

"Back then I was fully prepared in mind and body, but I'm totally not right now. My hands are sweating!"

Even though his hands were sweating from the exceptional tension, Emilia looked completely at ease, which only made him more nervous.

And as for what the at-odds couple was actually doing in the royal capital—

A coarse, manly voice interrupted their cute little argument.

"—Hey, can you stop flirting in front of a man's shop like this?"

Emilia's face stiffened. *Well, that's sensible*, accepted Subaru. After all, the voice of the scar-faced man carried an irrefutable argument.

"You're driving my customers away. Buy something or get moving already."

"Well, that's rude and inconsiderate. Here I came all ready to keep my promise. The shock alone could've made me forget completely, you know? Makes me wanna cry."

As Subaru slumped his shoulders, the man, resting his elbow on the counter, indelicately snorted back at him.

Subaru thought the shopkeeper's foul demeanor toward his customers was a good indicator that he'd picked the wrong profession. The shop, with a sign reading CADMON in I-script with bright colors, was a fruit vendor with colorful produce on display. The shop had a deeper significance for Subaru.

"Here I am returning the favor to the first guy I met in a new world, and this is the thanks I get?"

"That's overstating it. It was almost a month ago, and we only spoke a few words, right? I mean, I vaguely recall it, but…"

The owner of the store, actually a very kind man, was striving to remember when Emilia pulled on Subaru's ear and bowed her head.

"Subaru, don't say crazy things. Sir, please don't force yourself on our account." Subaru pleaded with her, yelping "Ow, ow!" as she gave him a sharp glare and said, "I thought you said you wanted to say hello to someone who'd helped you…but I never expected this promise to be a one-sided deal. Unbelievable."

"Hey, Emilia-tan, you can't just throw a promise between men into the garbage like that!"

"Don't exaggerate! How many people do you think a shopkeeper meets in the course of one day?"

"Emilia-tan, you can hurt people when you overestimate them. I mean, there's no way a shopkeeper with a scary face like that is doing that much busin… Ow, ow, I'm sorry!"

The shopkeeper, watching their back-and-forth, clapped his hands as he watched tears well in Subaru's eyes.

"I remember that pathetic look now. You're the kid without a coin to his name. So the ingrate returns without buying a thing."

"I'm gonna ignore how you remembered me…and I told you, I'm back so I can repay you!"

"Ah, I see. Now that's a sense of responsibility. I like it."

Now that he recognized Subaru, the shopkeeper smiled generously, hauling a wooden box from inside his store and placing it on the counter with a heavy thud. The red, round, vibrant fruits inside glistened under the sun.

"Here y'go, abbles like you promised you'd buy. How many? They're two copper coins each now."

"I'll go big and get ten. That'll cover the promise and then some."

The shopkeeper clapped his hands at Subaru's magnanimity. In high spirits, Subaru put his hand into his pocket to get his wallet out when he noticed that Emilia, standing beside him, was doing the same thing.

"Er, Emilia-tan, why are you getting out your purse?"

"What do you mean, why? You can't pay for something without money, can you?"

"No, I mean, it's weird for you to pay instead of me, Emilia-ta… Old guy, what's with that look?"

"You said you'd buy them when you had the money, but I can't condone making a rich girl pay in your place…"

"Can't you see me arguing with my lovely lady here?! I'm trying to pay!"

The shopkeeper watched Subaru with suspicion as Subaru hastily thrust his wallet forward. The contents were his pay from his work at the mansion—and, since Roswaal was a generous employer, Subaru really did have money to spare.

"Lemme see, two coppers per abble… So two silver coins should cover ten?"

"Hey, don't you know the current exchange rate…? It's nine coppers for a silver coin right now."

"So two silvers and two coppers then? Here."

Subaru fished the appropriate coins out of his wallet and handed them to the shopkeeper. The man was stunned into silence, tilting his head as he sighed at length.

"Took my word for it, huh. Kiddo, you really need to not be so trusting. The changes in the exchange rates are posted on the sign at the entrance to the market. If you wander in without giving that a good look, some crooked merchant will have you for lunch."

The shopkeeper seemed to be warning him because his honesty made him a sucker here. True, paying based on only what he was told might be overly trusting, even if it was common sense back home.

Back at the village close to the mansion, everyone was so tightly related in an isolated community that deceit was inconceivable, but a huge city like the royal capital was fertile ground for mischief. In other words—

"Man, you really are a super-good person, old guy."

Subaru smiled playfully in a show of goodwill to the scar-faced shopkeeper.

"Only once in a while. I'd have nightmares if I swindled a customer who'd come back to fulfill a promise I'd nearly forgotten and who paid exactly what I asked for. That's it."

"So you're mean-looking guy with a heart of gold. Got it."

"Take it and go already! You've paid in full. Come again!"

The first half was intimidatingly gruff; the second half, a paragon of customer relations. Subaru, having a good laugh at the two extremes, picked up his bag of abbles with one hand, while Emilia led him away from the shop by the other.

"Thanks, old dude. Maybe I'll bump into you again someday."

"You're quite welcome as long as you buy something… And, miss, you really need better taste in men."

"Now, that's none of your business!"

As the shopkeeper watched them go, Subaru shot him the middle finger as he and Emilia entered the throng of people. As the distance between them widened, the human wave obstructed his vision, and the good-natured shopkeeper disappeared from view.

"I'm glad he actually remembered you… I'm a little surprised, though."

"Yeah, he definitely seems scary at first, but you get used to it pretty quick…"

"Not that. I mean, I'm flabbergasted you did the math that quickly."

"No one says 'flabbergasted' anymore…"

Even as Subaru teased Emilia for using outdated words, he didn't mind praise. He didn't look it, but he was actually pretty good at arithmetic. "I've got a knack for basic math. So you go for the intellectual, cerebral type, huh?"

"Cerebr…? I'm not sure what you mean, but that's not the only reason I'm surprised… Just a little coincidence. Tee-hee, it's funny, actually."

"Ah, that's a cute face. What, what, where's the coincidence?"

"That's a secret between me and the shopkeeper's daughter. So what's next?"

Subaru had some idea what Emilia meant by a secret, but he didn't probe deeper, opting to readjust his grip on the bag of abbles instead. The royal capital was far too big for casual strolling. His first objective of the day had been to visit the first person he'd met in this world. Now that he'd repaid his gratitude to the fruit merchant, his next objective was a no-brainer.

"My next goal…is to see Felt and Old Man Rom. Reinhard took care of them after I blacked out, right?"

"Mm, yes. At first, I thought he'd let them go without any problems, but…all of a sudden, Reinhard went pale and said he was taking the girl with him."

"That sounds like a criminal kidnapping her, but that doesn't exactly fit him… Crap, the good-looking ones get all the breaks."

Subaru clicked his tongue as he sullenly recalled the handsome, red-haired young man.

Emilia watched from beside him, putting a finger to her lips as she pondered the issue. "If you want to get in touch with Reinhard, we should go to the garrison on this side of the Nobles' District. There's a building there that's… Well, it's nothing but a pile of rubble now."

Subaru agreed with Emilia's suggestion. After all, the fact Reinhard had been walking the streets of the capital "off duty" made it clear he was a guard, most likely high-ranking—a knight.

"I guess that settles it. Let's head to the station and get ahold of Reinhard from there. Well, let's get a move o… Oh?"

"What? Something wrong?"

"Nah, I was just counting the abbles in the bag… There's eleven of 'em." He had counted a total of eleven big, round, ripe, vibrant red fruit. It was highly unlikely the merchant, proprietor of his own store, had miscounted. "That old guy's too generous."

As he recalled the prickly shopkeeper, he felt a warm, fuzzy feeling bubbling up inside and smiled to himself.

—Keeping his promise was the right choice.

2

"Come to think of it, what did you mean, get ahold of him from the garrison? There're no phones, right?"

As they walked toward the garrison, Subaru voiced a sudden doubt.

"'Phones'?"

Emilia's mystified expression suggested she'd never heard the word in her life.

"I mean, like, a device to talk directly to someone in a distant location..."

"You mean a metia? They should have magic mirrors..."

"Magic mirrors?"

"Metia that display one person to the other and let you talk between them. They're fairly common as magical artifacts go, so they're apparently used in a number of different places..."

"Gotcha. So there is a way to do it. Mirrors! That's so magical."

When Subaru thought about it, he realized he'd never laid eyes on a real metia. He'd heard the term *metia* from Old Man Rom at the loot cellar and pretended his cell phone was one, but that was it.

"Either way, it's a ray of hope. If we can get in touch with Reinhard we can clear everything up."

"I suppose so. Rem will be upset if we don't get back soon, so we'd better hurry..."

Rem had wanted to go with Subaru on his tour of the royal capital, too. However, she had too much work to do as the entire group's caretaker so, with great reluctance, she allowed Emilia to be his guide in the city.

No doubt she was tearing through her work out of spite at that very moment.

"Well, it's too bad for Rem, but for me, not having her here is a bit of a perk..."

"...? What did you say just now?"

"Ahh, nothin'. I'm just like, I don't have to be embarrassed if she sees us holding hands and stuff... Hey, Emilia-tan, about that royal selection thing tomorrow..."

Seeing the tense, guarded look on Emilia's face, Subaru abandoned his carefree tone. But then Emilia's expression vanished entirely, and the gloom filling her violet eyes only accentuated her demeanor.

The morning the envoy came, as well as during the time before their departure, Subaru had questioned Emilia several times, but she never lowered her guard. Their arrival at the royal capital had not changed that.

"I've told you several times, haven't I? I brought you here so you can keep your promises and get healed. You don't need to concern yourself with me."

"There's no way I can do that. I mean, here I am, holding your hand… How could I not concern myself like this?"

At some point during his reply, Emilia had stopped walking, holding Subaru back. Under her hood, a single lock of silver hair spilled down Emilia's face.

Subaru couldn't help but think about how it looked like a falling teardrop.

"I want to help you. If you're having a hard time, I want to do something. That's how it's been…and that's how it's gonna be."

"…"

Subaru admitted his feelings honestly. He intended to exhaust every effort on Emilia's behalf.

He knew exactly what motivated him, but—

"Why?"

"……uhh?"

"Why do you go to such lengths for me, Subaru? I don't understand."

The incredulity in Emilia's eyes thoroughly bewildered Subaru. When her hand squeezed his in search of an answer, Subaru's throat caught as he struggled for words.

"That's…"

"…"

"Th…that's…!"

Even if he knew what he ought to say, he needed the resolve and courage to speak the words. And suddenly put to the test, Subaru lacked both. In the end, Subaru said nothing as Emilia waited.

As the silence dragged on, he ran out of the time Emilia had given him.

"…Let's go. The sun will set if we don't do this soon."

Emilia started forward again, pulling him along by the hand. Subaru followed, clenching his teeth at his own lack of nerve.

As he watched her small, slender back, he hated himself for losing sight of what he needed to say.

He despised his weakness in the face of the girl who had saved his life and his spirit—the girl who lit the brightest fire in his chest.

As Subaru sank into a vortex of negativity and self-hatred, he started as he suddenly heard a genderless voice, like someone whispering straight into his skull.

"—*You'd best leave things at that, Subaru.*"

"...!"

"*It's me. I'm speaking directly into your mind, so Lia can't hear you.*"

The method of communication was odd, but the voice was certainly familiar. It was the spirit Emilia had formed a pact with, the supernatural cat always at her side—Puck.

Subaru was taken aback at the sudden telepathic communication.

"...! *So you can hear me, too, then?*"

"*You catch on fast. I wasn't sure at first, but...it was easy to make a connection, so you might have a high compatibility with spirits. Maybe that's why Betty likes you.*"

Puck's one-sided knowledge of the situation added irritation to Subaru's gloom. He felt left out.

"*Lia's all right. Don't lose hope from that conversation just now.*"

"*That's... How the hell do you know?*"

"*I just know. I know everything there is to know about Lia, after all.*"

Even if he didn't put it into words, Puck's fatherly love for her was evident in his tone.

The spirit's guarantee made Subaru feel worse about his own powerlessness. Puck had only reminded him that, when all was said and done, he didn't know a single thing about Emilia.

The Emilia he knew was a stunningly beautiful half-elf girl. She was a candidate to become the next monarch of Lugunica, under the care of her sponsor, Roswaal.

He knew she was honest, naive, willful, and soft-hearted; her personality drove her to help others even at the cost of herself, making her like an older sister, but also an easy mark.

But all these facts barely scratched the surface. He knew nothing of the girl inside, her emotions, or even how and why she came to pursue the monarchy.

"Putting your heart and soul into everything is pretty rough on you, huh?"

Even if closed lips could conceal his shallow thoughts, he could not silence his very mind. It was impossible to hide everything from Puck, who scooped up surface thoughts like so much soup broth.

"Hey, Subaru."

He didn't want to face his own wretchedness any longer. He weakly denied Puck, but these words, whispered to the mind and not the eardrum, never arrived. With Subaru expressing his will through silence, Puck instead continued, *"—Don't get my hopes up too much, or Lia's."*

"...Huh?"

"Hope is a gentle poison. Even if you know it will ruin you, you can't help but reach for the illusion that seems close enough to grasp. You are truly a poison."

To Subaru, who had viewed Puck as an unflappable, tranquil being, those words contained enough force to change his impressions completely.

"What do you mean by..."

But before he could finish his perplexed reply, Emilia, guiding his hand, stopped walking and said, "We're here."

Subaru pitched forward, in danger of bumping into Emilia's back, but he somehow managed to right himself.

When he raised his head, he belatedly understood why this was called the Nobles' District. The scenery was more refined than that of the slums or Market Street, with much more money invested in it. This was true for not only the buildings, but also the streets, the walls, and the trees had aesthetic appeal. As the name suggested, this was the ward where the upper crust resided.

Their destination was a building that served as the gateway, sealing off the single street connecting it to the outside world.

The solid stonework structure was far plainer than anything in the Nobles' District behind it. The back of the building contacted a section of the wall, allowing someone on the roof to survey the whole city in a single sweep. However, the purpose of this vantage point was obviously to keep watch over what was below, not to enjoy the sights.

"This is the garrison for the royal capital guards. They also check the identity of people entering the Nobles' District."

"So it's like a customs checkpoint, too. That's probably what they built it here for, huh?"

He could appreciate it on logical and practical grounds, but his aversion to it was no doubt an instinctive reaction to something so emblematic of bureaucracy.

Emilia said nothing to the reluctant Subaru as she headed for the garrison. Mindful of the time and place, she finally let go of his hand. He mourned the loss of her palm.

And just as Emilia was about to knock on the garrison's door, it opened toward the outside as a young man poked his face out.

"—My, it is not often I meet an acquaintance in a place like this. It has been some time, Lady Emilia. You have not changed at all since then."

The young man bowed formally to Emilia—whom he had recognized even though she was wearing the hood. That alone put Subaru on guard, but Emilia's expression was serene as she nodded toward the youth.

"…Yes, thank you. No changes in particular, no. I see you are also in good health, Julius."

"I am honored that you remember me. Your beauty has only increased, Lady Emilia."

The young man named Julius praised Emilia's good looks in a very polished manner. He had violet hair and an equal mix of snobbery and politeness. He was about half a foot taller than Subaru, putting him at around five foot nine, give or take. His body was slender, but he did not seem frail; rather, he had a handsome, supple frame. His amber eyes, no doubt bewitching to the opposite sex, suited him to a detestably fine degree.

"Is it not a rarer sight for you, a royal guardsman, to be here at the garrison?"

The man wore an extravagant uniform with a dragon emblem. A slender sword like a rapier hung from his hip. Julius's appearance and manner of speech suited such a title.

"I've come to express appreciation to the soldiers for their services and take the opportunity to observe the city…or something like that. A friend asked me to pay a visit, and I suppose it is good to put friends first once in a while. After all, I was able to lay my eyes upon a beautiful flower along my path through these streets."

With well-practiced motion, Julius intimately grasped Emilia's hand as he spoke, bending down on one knee. Without a single pause for breath, he brought his lips to the back of her pale hand.

Subaru watched this course of events in complete shock. After a few moments' delay, his emotions came to a boil as this man's conceited behavior rubbed him in every wrong way imaginable. His breath ragged, Subaru was about to rush over and give Julius a piece of his mind when Emilia held him in check with her other hand.

"Thank you, Julius. I regret that this is very sudden, but…I would like to get in touch with the castle about a certain matter."

As Julius listened to Emilia's request, his voice lowered as he looked at Subaru.

"Ah, so that is why you came to the garrison… This matter, does it concern him over there?"

Not enjoying Julius's condescending gaze, Subaru locked eyes with him and glared back.

"—His character and demeanor form a poor match for those clothes. Such an appearance does not make a good first impression."

"Thank you for the kind advice. I have some advice for you, too. If you eat curry udon in an outfit like that, the broth stains will really stand out, so you definitely should pass."

"Thank you for going out of your way to say so. I shall pay it heed if I should ever have such an opportunity."

The smiles they exchanged were most certainly not friendly. Subaru did not like him. Julius no doubt thought the same. In that spirit, he promptly ignored Subaru and turned his attention back to Emilia.

"I shall guide you to the magic mirror, then, though it pains my heart to bring you into a humble place such as this, Lady Emilia."

"You needn't be concerned. I'm quite all right, so please."

"Very well. Come in."

With that, Julius went back inside first. Subaru snorted a bit and stepped forward. But Emilia turned to him in front of the doorway, obstructing his path.

"Subaru, you wait here."

"...Huh?"

Subaru was taken aback. Emilia's long eyelashes trembled a bit as she lowered her eyes.

"I'd like to have you come, but I don't think Julius will take it well, so wait here."

"The heck? You care about that annoying jerk's feelings more than mine?"

"It's not that. It's not about upsetting him, it's that I don't want to put you through something you'll probably hate, so please, Subaru, wait here."

"I hate it enough as it is already. The way that bastard licked Emilia-tan's hand all over like it was nothing...!"

Subaru had pegged that particular action as a sign of perversion, adding one more item to his list of negative impressions. It only compounded how he didn't want Emilia to have any contact with that man. Subaru's masculine instincts wanted desperately to warn her to watch out for Julius.

"This won't take long, so please, be good and wait."

Her words were very gentle, yet heavily tinged with rejection. Emilia was fundamentally distancing Subaru from her own affairs. But afraid of incurring her displeasure for intruding, he was unable to speak a word in protest.

She vanished behind the door as it closed, separating them physically and metaphorically with a dull thud. Subaru murmured, "...I'm super-uncool."

Kicking around a rock some distance from the entrance as he waited for Emilia, Subaru distracted himself from his seething self-hatred as he recalled the annoying man.

"She said he was a royal guard, didn't she?"

If Subaru's hunch was correct, that meant he was a Knight of the Royal Guard. If knightly orders existed in this world, surely Knights of the Royal Guard served the royal family directly. But where did they stand in a country with no sitting monarch?

"The whole royal family died from plague, huh. They might make the elites in the Knights of the Royal Guard take responsibility for not seeing that coming and disband them, tossing them and their families out onto the street... Well, that sucks for the rest of 'em, but I wouldn't mind that annoying bastard going through a little hell..."

The somber thought gave him some small measure of satisfaction. He wondered who he'd picked up that pettiness from.

In the past, Subaru would have never directed his ire about the inconveniences that befell him toward another person. He wouldn't have given a single thought to speaking ill of heaven or venting his frustrations.

In a good sense, he was now concerned with appearances in a way he had not before arriving here. He wanted to live a life that he could show the honest and forthright girl close to him without shame.

It was a vague thought... But he wondered if he had really changed a little? He couldn't tell.

"—Mm?"

As Subaru ruminated, he felt a disturbance and frowned at a glimpse of something at the edge of his vision. For a brief moment, his gaze had wandered toward the city for no particular reason and caught sight of a colorful dress disappearing into a back alley. The color was such a vivid red that it seemed to sear itself into his eyes, even with only a glance. And had the dress been merely traveling down the street, no doubt it would not have registered in Subaru's mind whatsoever.

Even entering a back alley, the garment would not have caught his attention, save for the fact that the girl wearing it was being led there by seedy-looking men.

"Just now... There's no way it could be a *that*, right...?"

A major crime in broad daylight in front of the guards' garrison—or so he thought, but perhaps this was a case of hiding in plain sight. Upon closer inspection, the location was in the garrison's blind spot. Subaru had seen them by dumb luck the instant he'd entered an alleyway while he moped.

"Setting aside that I just feel calmer in narrow spaces, I'd better go get the gua—"

Subaru hesitated. He hadn't witnessed an actual crime taking place. It was very possible he'd misinterpreted what he'd seen.

At any rate, Subaru bore a powerful, arbitrary grudge against the garrison at that moment.

"Plus, if I'm wrong, it might make trouble for Emilia… It won't be too late to call for help after I confirm things first."

Voicing this excuse to himself, Subaru shot a glance at the garrison as he ran toward the alley. He felt guilty about going back on his promise to wait patiently for Emilia, but a higher duty called. Plus, Subaru's resentment toward Julius.

And hearing an angry shout the instant he entered the alley, Subaru was firmly convinced he'd made the right decision and picked up his pace.

"—Why, you little bitch! I'm not messin' around here!"

3

"Don't mess with me, woman! You want a punch to that pretty little face?!"

"Do not get ahead of yourself, peasant. Those of low character enjoy appropriately lowly fates."

Several voices argued, and three men surrounded a lone woman in the narrow alley, cutting off her avenues of escape.

This was a stereotypical street punk encounter, but what left a burning impression on Subaru was the striking appearance of the girl who repulsed the atmosphere hanging over the cramped alley.

Her hair was a radiant orange like the sun itself, flowing through a single barrette before spilling down her back. Her dress was blood crimson, and above all, the overwhelming beauty of the girl herself shone in her sordid surroundings. Even untrained eyes could tell at a glance that the jewelry on her neck, ears, and fingers were of the highest quality. Her full outfit, coordinated from top to bottom, had to be worth at least a hundred times the money Subaru had on him. And yet, all that extravagant jewelry was incomparable to her face.

She had red, defiant eyes. Her faintly pink lips emphasized the hue of her skin, white as the purest snow. One might spend an entire lifetime and fortune in search of such beauty and never find it. Subaru realized all over again how often this world defied his idea of common sense.

The girl crossed her arms in a calm posture that only accentuated her bountiful breasts. He couldn't just stand back and watch while her attitude raised the men's hackles ever higher.

"—H-heya! Sorry to keep you waiting, honey!"

Subaru immediately raised a hand and wedged himself into the middle of the action. Laughing by himself as he interrupted the surprised trio, Subaru put his hands together in supplication. "It seems that she's caused you a little trouble, but could you do me favor and let it slide? I'm sure you can tell just by looking at her, but the girl is a little…y'know…in the head. You get me?"

Her celebrity-like style practically screamed "Rob me, please!" and she was hanging around the alleyways in a city with questionable levels of law enforcement. What sane person would be so reckless?

Subaru asserted to the stunned men, "So that's how it is!" and grasped the girl's hand.

"Mm…!"

"Hey, let's move on before you cause the good boys here any more trouble. Let's do like we promised today and feed each other sweets, just the two of…"

Subaru quickly laid things out, casting her in the role he'd assigned Emilia in his fantasies, aiming to get her out of there as fast as possible. However…

"Uhh?"

"Do not…touch me so freely!"

She put her other hand on top of Subaru's, twisting her body to yank the boy forward. A moment after he realized he'd lost his hold on her wrist, his face slammed right into the wall.

"*Wht th hll?!*"

"Goodness, I take a step outside and this happens? Commoners drooling all over me..."

As he stood back up, Subaru glowered at her, as if finding her words beyond comprehension.

"Play along, damn it! That's the time-honored method of saving a girl from street punks! You're supposed to catch on to these things!"

"I do not know what you mean. I simply do as I please."

"A woman who slams your face into the wall is the worst kind of first meeting, you know?!"

Not only had she not picked up on his attempt to extricate her, but she treated him as a pervert. The pain and humiliation made him regret exercising his limited courage. Thinking that the men must find it hilarious, Subaru turned toward their pitying gazes again.

"Hey, wait a minute, I remember you guys."

Subaru tilted his head with the bad feeling that he was reliving a prior crisis. Subaru compared the faces of the men before him against the ones in his memory, clapping his hands together when a light suddenly came on.

"Ah, Dumb, Dumber, and Dumbest. Eh, wait, no way. Does this city have any other punks besides the three of you?!"

Of course he remembered them. These were the Three Stooges he'd encountered on the first day of his summoning. Having experienced death at their hands once already, Subaru regarded them with caution. But...

"I'm more depressed than anything else. Don't you guys have any other way to make a living?"

The three men looked at one another and began to talk, oddly relaxed about Subaru's presence.

"First he sticks his nose in, gets his face smashed on a wall, and now he says he remembers. He bonkers?"

"Hey, I don't wanna mess with him. You deal with him."

"I don't wanna, either. Why don't we just shiv him somewhere?"

With the supposed thieves having finally lost all vestiges of belligerence, the silent girl broke the atmosphere.

"Oh my, so irresolute. Are you a bunch of little girls? If so, adorn yourselves in a manner suitable for my eyes. Yes, some fine jewelry on your burly, hairy bodies would make for quite a sight."

The girl put a hand over her mouth, ripping into them with a look of complete contempt. For an instant, the men did not understand what she had said to them. A moment later, they seethed as one.

"Don't mess with me, bitch!"

"Who do you think you are, girl?!"

"What's with the high and mighty talk, huh?!"

Subaru chimed in. "You're seriously off your rocker! We oughta spank into your girly butt the fact that we're guys—wait, why am I jumping in with these idiots?!"

Subaru was surprised at himself for impulsively taking part in a four-man gang. He was acutely aware that blame for the incident lay on the girl's side, too.

"So I get where you guys are coming from, but I'm not turning back now. Besides, I'm carrying my own grudge from the first day we met."

"I dunno what's with that little bitch, but what's the deal with you, shit face?"

Apparently they didn't remember Subaru at all, a pretty meager reaction considering Emilia had sent them packing with magic, they'd suffered a crushing three on one defeat at Subaru's hands, and they'd knifed Subaru to death sometime after that.

"Well, none of those events happened in *this* world, so all they'd remember here is… Oh yeah, the good-looking guy showing up?"

"—! Hey, I remember him! From an alley off Market Street a little while back…"

"Oh, *that* one! The brat with a screw loose! He hasn't changed one bit, huh?"

"It's really him. The clothes are different, so I didn't recognize 'im!"

When realization came over Dumb's face, Dumber and Dumbest followed in short order. Though Subaru was no fan of how they'd characterized him, he clapped to applaud their effort.

"Good, good, I'm glad you remember me. So since you know me, how about you let this slide?"

"Are you nuts? We like you way less than someone we don't know. Just 'cause it's three-on-two instead of three-on-one doesn't change a thing."

Even though Subaru hoped to bluff his way through the scene, the willful girl paid no heed to his plans whatsoever.

"Correction. It is not three-versus-two, it is three-versus-one-versus-one."

"Can you shut up for a bit?!"

He wished he could have gone back in time five minutes and told himself not to bother, but the die had been cast. Besides, Dumb, Dumber, and Dumbest weren't patient types. Watching the temperature in their eyes dropping, Subaru knew it was only a matter of time before there'd be blood.

"...No choice, then. I really didn't want to resort to this, but..."

"Ahh? Would you stop messin' around already? What the hell can you—"

"I'll have you know, I know Mr. Reinhard, guys. Reinhard and I are best buds. If I yell, he's gonna come running right over!"

"—Wha?!"

This was his trump card, "The Fox Invoking the Lion," and it worked wonders. The mention of Reinhard's name scared the trio witless.

The effect was immediate, and Subaru forced himself to act like a big shot to cow them further.

"So what'll it be, guys? One shout and he'll make mincemeat out of you with his bare hands."

It was a desperate bluff, but the men gritted their teeth resentfully.

"W-we'll let you. This time."

"Remember this, it's not like you beat us or anything!"

"And it's not like we're scared of Reinhard's name or anything!"

The men immediately fled the alley, their weak, stereotypical parting shots only enhancing their petty crook image. Only when they had completely gone did Subaru exhale deeply.

Somehow he'd ridden the crisis out.

Now if he could only get the girl to soften just a little—

"What? Are those the eyes of a beggar? You shall receive nothing from me, commoner."

"They are not. Well, would it kill you to thank me for saving you at least?"

"Save?"

The girl inclined her head slightly with a mystified expression.

She closed her eyes, sinking into thought, and let out a small sigh when she arrived at an answer.

"So that prattling of yours earlier was meant to save me. Mm, I had not noticed."

"You didn't notice?! This sets new standards for dense, you know?!"

"Do not misunderstand. No difficulty would have befallen me even without your help. I can only marvel at your taking pride in resolving something that was not a problem to begin with."

"I don't know what you mean, so what *do* you mean? I mean what, like, okay, you're super-strong, so you'd have been fine even if I hadn't saved you?"

"Not at all. It is far simpler. —This world is composed solely for my convenience. Nothing occurs that is not to my benefit. It is thanks to me that I was saved, yet you attempt to claim this as your own exploit. Have you no shame at stealing credit from another?"

With one blatant forward thrust of her bountiful breasts, the girl was asserting, as if it was natural, as if it was obvious, as if it was common sense—that she was absolute.

The way her eyes radiated like an arrogant sun made Subaru keenly aware that this was someone he absolutely should not associate himself with whatsoever.

"Th-that so. My bad for being too big for my britches. Sorry to interrupt. Bye now."

He determined it was best to agree with such a person as much as possible—not provoke her, just nod enthusiastically, avoid any defiance, and do a quick about-face away from her.

But an unexpected call came from behind, and Subaru cursed his feet for stopping.

"—Wait."

"Wh-what?"

"What is in that bag there? Show me."

The girl strolled around him, nodding to indicate that Subaru should put down the bag. He didn't want to oblige, but defying her would only prolong things, so Subaru reluctantly opened the bag and showed its contents—a mountain of ripe, red fruit.

"I do not recognize them. These fruits… What are they?"

"They're, um, abbles. The fruit of knowledge. Never seen one before?"

Blinking at his reply, the girl snorted as she looked at Subaru like he was an imbecile.

"You lie. Do not make me laugh. Abbles are white, understand? I have absolutely never seen fruits such as these."

Astonished, Subaru replied, "Well, they're white when you peel them…"

It was the girl's turn to stare blankly.

He remarked, "Wait, don't tell me you've never seen an abble that hasn't been peeled…?"

"Mm, I have indeed never seen one that was not at the dinner table. —Very well. Hand them over."

Nodding in satisfaction, the girl audaciously demanded he give up his the abbles.

He'd saved the girl from a robbery only for the girl to attempt robbery on him.

Subaru wanted to see Emilia again. He wished Rem were healing him that moment.

"Hand them over. I shall split one open and see for myself. Or is it only lies that dribble from your lips?"

"…Handle with care, okay?"

Judging resistance to be the fool's choice, Subaru took an abble out of the bag and placed it in her hand. The girl took the abble, turning it around as if studying the sensation upon her palm.

Then, her left hand flashed toward the abble—neatly severing it vertically and horizontally into four equal pieces.

The girl licked the fruit juice off her fingers, satisfied at the cross section.

"Sweet and sour… Certainly, this is the taste of an abble. I will spare your life."

"Spare my... No, never mind. Anyway, you're satisfied now, I take it?"

"*Ab-so-lute-ly not!!*"

Her statement, crossing the line from arrogant behavior to tyrannical, made even Subaru erupt in indignation.

"You don't even care that you sliced one up out of the blue. Why do I have to give you all of them? These abbles aren't just abbles. They're the bonds between two men!"

"Enough prattle. How about this?"

The girl pointed at the bag, her lips cracking into a wry smile.

"We shall wager for them."

"—Wager?"

"Yes, a simple wager. Something easy, flipping a coin and guessing whether it is heads or tails. A single abble shall rest upon each attempt. How about it?"

She was proposing a contest, but all Subaru could do was laugh at her suggestion.

"You just say the darndest things. Why would I agree to that in the first place? There's nothing in that gamble for me. I can just run like heck out of here!"

"Of course, I shall have something worth winning at the ready. Let's see..."

The girl touched her tongue to her lips as she sank into thought. She shifted her bewitching eyes toward Subaru, lifting up her ample bosom with her crossed arms.

"Should you win the wager, you may touch my breasts. How about it?"

Subaru sighed at length and shook his head at her offering up her own body as a gambling chip. The way she offered herself in a wager without a single reflection on the consequences of losing indicated the kind of personality that ruined gamblers' lives.

No doubt she thought that her beauty allowed her to seduce any man setting eyes on her. He thought her worldview was regrettable and rather sad.

The girl gave Subaru a slightly suspicious glance, perhaps wondering what was taking him so long.

With that gaze bearing down on him, Subaru told her exactly what he thought.

"You need to take better care of yourself. That's crazy talk… And you can't seduce me with that look!"

—And so, Subaru found himself still in the alley, having lost seven straight bets.

"That makes seven wins for me. There are only three abbles left, you know?"

"No way! You're robbing me blind!"

4

"Now, then."

The girl picked up one of the abbles lying before her and deposited it into the bag at her side. Subaru was down to his last two chips, so to speak. When their game had begun, he had ten—he never imagined he'd go on an eight-in-a-row losing streak, leaving him in danger of losing the shirt on his back.

"Now you know what happens to those who challenge me. I am the pinnacle, and you are suited only to wriggling around at the bottom."

"Hey, isn't it a little extreme to treat me as the bottom of the pyramid just because I'm losing? Pride comes before the fall, you know… a fall to rock bottom!"

"You may rest easy. All is rock bottom except for me. The world has me, and all else is beneath."

Subaru wanted to refute her irrational logic, but that would only make him sound like a sore loser.

"Now then, what shall we do next? If you do not trust your luck at coin flips, a different wager is fine."

"Oh, now you've done it… I'm down in the bottom of the ninth, but I propose we do rock-paper-scissors!"

"Rock, paper, scissors…?"

When the girl raised an eyebrow at the unfamiliar term, it gave Subaru a tiny ray of hope.

"Rock-paper-scissors is a way to settle things. At the signal, you make a shape with your hand, and the stronger shape wins. There're three shapes: rock, paper, and scissors. Paper beats rock, scissors beats paper, rock beats scissors. Understand?"

"Oh, yes, I understand. A rather amusing game, it would seem. What is this signal?"

"Well, when you finish saying rock-paper-scissors, you show your hand when you get to the 'scissors' part. Oh, and if you both show the same hand, you say rock-paper-scissors again as the signal and do it over on the spot."

"That is all there is to it? Very well. I shall go with paper."

"You're already showing your hand?!"

Subaru shuddered at the breathtaking speed with which she strategized. He'd just finished explaining the rules, and here she was, picking it all up like a pro, poised greedily with victory in her grasp. He supposed he should praise her.

She said to him, "Let us begin, then. Rock…paper…"

Subaru felt nervous about falling behind.

"Ah, wait, time-out. I haven't decided what I'm gonna go with ye—"

With his thoughts still in a jumble, the girl reached the signal and raised her hand high.

"—scissors!"

The girl's hand indicated paper, just as she had proclaimed. Subaru's hand was rock. She commented, "It would seem that you owe me another abble, complaints about the method notwithstanding."

"It's not that! Statistically, people subconsciously keep their hand closed when they're tossed into rock-paper-scissors without warning! Ugh, I'm such an idiot!"

The strategist had been defeated by his own scheme. Subaru certainly looked defeated as he handed the girl her abble.

—With this, Subaru was down to his very last abble.

"Now, let us gamble for the last abble and bring this to a conclusion, shall we?"

"You wouldn't show mercy on me and let me keep the last one, would you?"

"All the abbles you carried belong to me. Leaving one in your hands is the same as leaving you all. It is all or nothing. That being the case, we may as well gamble for all the abbles on the final round. That goes for both of us," the girl added, meaning it would be her ten abbles against Subaru's one. It was truly emblematic of the girl's ruinous, high-stakes way of thinking.

He asked, "—How about rock-paper-scissors for the last one, too?"

"I have already made my decision. All that remains is for you to choose the method and present me with my abble."

The girl showed no doubt about her victory, nor any intention of letting Subaru go. In other words, he had no choice but to harden his resolve—to trap a Rakshasa by the vilest of means.

The two called out simultaneously, "Rock...paper...scissors!"

When both showed their hands, sound vanished from the world.

With her fist clenched in a rock, the trembling in the girl's red eyes only grew.

"Th-this is..."

"Listen and be amazed, look and be astounded! Behold, the ultimate combat technique—RoSciPer!!"

"What is that...thing?! You did not inform me such a hand was possible!"

"Shut up! I didn't mention it, but it's your fault you didn't ask! That part is rock, this here's scissors, and over there is paper! In other words, my hand's beaten your rock!"

"If such logic holds, a different part loses to my rock."

"Ahh! Ahh! Ahh! I can't hear you! My rock is borrowing power from the scissors and paper, forming the holy trinity of friendship, effort, and victory! It's all here, baby!"

Raising the hand of RoSciPer to the heavens, Subaru boldly proclaimed victory with his flagrant cheating.

He was well aware his logic was absurd, a desperately underhanded attempt to throw the wager itself into doubt. But the girl defied Subaru's expectations, sighing deeply as she said, "I see. Certainly, it is I who was in error. At the same time, I am amused at how my expectations have been surpassed... Very well, you have won. You may do as you please. Here you go." After her minimal warning, she abruptly stepped forward. Without thinking, Subaru, floored at how quickly she jumped to the next step, stepped back a distance equal to the one she had advanced.

"...Do not tell me that now it is time to feel my breasts, you have lost your nerve?"

"Huh?! I-I seriously don't know what you're talking about! Who's s-s-s-scared here?!"

"...Truly, you are a vexing man. I suppose such bashfulness is adorable in its own way, but..."

And there they stood, Subaru getting cold feet at the last moment versus the girl whose pride did not permit her to take back what she had offered. One advanced and the other retreated—a standoff that continued until outside forces intervened.

Abruptly, the girl's gaze left Subaru and focused on the entrance to the alley.

"—Mm, it seems this will become troublesome."

"Er? It looks like some pretty rough-looking dudes are coming this way."

"And the one at the vanguard is a commoner, I recall. Goodness, these fools do not interest me even slightly."

"What are they thinking, coming back after hearing Reinhard's name like that?!"

"It would seem they have called your bluff about being acquainted with the knight among knights. It is rather easy to understand. Even they have reputations to protect, so they have returned in greater numbers for retribution."

"Damn it, this day is just nothing but trouble!"

First, he had a close call back on the dragon carriage, then he had gotten on Emilia's bad side, and now this. *Today's really not my day.*

Since the girl was just standing there, Subaru grabbed her hand and dragged her along, carrying the bag of abbles as he rushed deeper down the alley.

She protested, "Hey, what are you doing? Do not touch me so carelessly."

"Now is really not the time! If you don't wanna get all beat up before marriage, run!!"

The girl wasn't very motivated to run as Subaru pulled her down the beat-up alley and plunged into the darkness. The men behind them pursued with a great shout and a flurry of footsteps.

Subaru, cursing the heavens for his truly unlucky day, kept running with a desperate expression on his face.

5

"If we do not hurry they will gain on us. Is this time to play around?"

"I d-don't wanna hear that from y... Time out, seriously, wait a...!"

They'd been racing through run-down streets for the last five minutes, but the girl was running well ahead of him, showing no sign of losing her breath. On the other hand, Subaru, never one to hold up for long sprints, was about to collapse from exhaustion. At first, he had been in front, but his endurance issues soon switched their positions.

"I'm convalescing, so this is really pushing it... But we're in a pretty bad spot. Doesn't look like many people live here... You have any ideas?"

The other group was a fair distance behind them. However, they were in one long alley, so slowing down meant it was only a matter of time until they were caught. He'd have liked to get on a thoroughfare, but all he could see was a maze of other back streets.

"It is not my problem! Everything I set out to do turns out well for me. I do not think deeply about things, for I do not need to. I need only trust in this fact."

"Yeah, well you lost at rock-paper-scissors to me earlier..."

At least they hadn't bumped into a dead end, but that didn't improve their predicament.

Right in front of the winded Subaru, the girl suddenly came to a halt.

"—Mm, this is indeed rather vexing."

Subaru, still holding her hand, also stopped. He looked at her, wondering what the deal was.

"Hey, we don't have time to stop here. If we don't put in as much distance as we can, they'll catch up with..."

"—I have lost interest."

"I see, you've lost intere... Wha—?!"

Subaru was in utter shock at the girl's unbelievable statement. She returned his gaze, apparently bored.

"I said, I have lost interest. In the first place, why must I run? I shall decide what I do myself. I absolutely shall not be forced to do anything because of what lowlifes say or do."

"Th-that's easier said than done, you know?! That ain't gonna fly in a situation like th—"

"Mm, I have decided. You shall have the honor of carrying me."

"No thanks!!"

As Subaru crossed his arms in a clear sign of refusal, the girl scowled as if he was putting a damper on her mood.

"The honor of carrying me is not for just anyone to receive. Only a man who does not know fear would reject such a thing."

"Do I look like a macho man that can carry someone and run?! Even when I was at full strength, it took everything I had to carry a girl with way fewer style points than you! And I'm about worn out now!"

As Subaru used the remains of his energy in protest, the girl shot him a look of scorn, but he couldn't use what he didn't have.

Her games led them to a stalemate costing them precious time. That was the thought in his head when, out of the blue, he heard an aged voice.

"It's been some time since I've seen you. What are you doing here?"

The speaker's large frame emerged from the darkness. Subaru lifted his gaze to a typical height for making eye contact, but found himself staring at this man's chest. He raised his gaze even farther to his ugly, balding head.

—A familiar and very muscular old man gazed down at Subaru and the girl.

"Gramps is here to save the day! We can win this—!"

"You're quick to annoy someone who hasn't seen you in a while. I'm leaving you here."

"Wait, I really need your help! It's, like, the tenth crisis I've had in the last month!"

"That's too many!!"

As they exchanged banter in lieu of greetings, the giant—Old Man Rom—peered at Subaru and the girl.

"What, in more trouble, are you? Causing a ruckus with a woman? Quite the adventurer you are."

"Do not look at me so rudely, you filthy gnarled tree."

"Hey, I'm ribbing him, too, but that's really harsh!! Don't say that to the old man giving us a get-out-of-hell-free card! Don't take it personally, Old Man Rom. We've just got a little case of excessive honesty here!"

"You certainly are good at wearing a man down. Hurry and hide!"

Subaru covered the girl's mouth before she could spew insults again and rushed toward the place Rom had silently indicated. There was a pile of scrap wood there that seemed able to comfortably conceal two people.

Subaru pushed the girl down first before squatting himself. She looked like she wanted to complain about the dust, but his hand over her mouth managed to keep her silent.

"We're okay on this end, Gramps!"

"No, you're not… I'll hide you with my body. If they see you it'll be trouble for me, too, so don't move."

Grumbling all the way, Old Man Rom hid them completely behind his huge body. A mere ten seconds or so later, a commotion of footsteps came from a nearby alley—

The leader of the men shouted, "The hell, I thought it was the brats, but it's the old man! Shit!"

Old Man Rom fielded the foul language with a serene expression.

"What? You shouldn't surprise your elders like this."

Old Man Rom hadn't put any special invective into his sentence, but the displeasure of a giant like him carried a force all its own. The entire group shuddered, the leader included. But one of the members of the group pointed at Old Man Rom and mocked, "Hey, wait, it's Grandpa Cromwell. Hey, should you really be talkin' smack to us here?"

The furrows of Old Man Rom's wrinkled face deepened further in a bitter response.

"I do not like being called that name."

"Get outta here, old man, or we'll bust up your loot cellar and make you the laughingstock of the slums."

"That place has gotten incredibly dirty over the years. If you destroyed it entirely you'd be doing me a favor. So how about I do as I please?"

"Yeah, fine. Now, Cromwell... Did you see two brats runnin' this way?"

"I didn't see them. Do *you* know where my blond daughter is?"

"Beats me. You picked her up off the street, so what's the big deal? Man, goin' senile must suck."

The men waved farewell, laughing derisively as they noisily left the area. Old Man Rom watched their retreating backs, biting his lip as he held back his anger.

As Subaru watched his face through a small gap, he couldn't help but feel bad for him. He was glad that Old Man Rom was friendly for their belated reunion, but he seemed a little different from the Rom Subaru knew.

"Hww wong rre..."

"Mm?"

A whisper-like voice interrupted Subaru's thoughts, prompting him to look to the side. Right beside him was the beautiful girl, so close they were practically breathing the same air, her mouth still covered by Subaru's palm.

"...you gonng to cvrr my...MOUTH?!"

Chomp.

"*—Yipe!!*"

At the merciless bite, Subaru let out a high-pitched, puppy-like yelp that quietly echoed through the nook in the back of the alley.

6

"Thanks for hiding us, Old Man Rom. The last time I saw you, I thought you'd had the sense knocked right out of you, but I guess you made it through fine."

"...Do you want me to change my mind and call those youngins back?"

"You sure are petty for a big guy! With me here, there's more than enough petty for everyone!"

Subaru grinned and shot him a thumbs-up. Old Man Rom sighed with a worn-out look.

They'd moved from the previous narrow alley to a more open city street. Old Man Rom conversed with Subaru while guiding the pair to a place where they could blend in.

The girl, having kept her silence until that moment, finally tugged Subaru's sleeve in irritation.

"Hey, you. I see you having an intimate conversation. Who is this old man? Explain it to me."

"This old man is the face of the royal capital's slums. The giant's Old Man Rom—trader for the bosses of the sticky-fingered types and all-around stingy bastard. He's got bad eyes, loves his cute granddaughter, and he's not nearly as tough as he looks."

"That is his worth after having lived a long life? I see. I pity your pathetic existence, gnarled tree."

"Your lady friend is an annoying little girl, isn't she?"

Old Man Rom was indignant at the harsh appraisal. Though Subaru's explanation was the truth, he set that aside and gave Old Man Rom a warm smile.

"I'm so glad I ran into you, really. Even I was getting desperate back there. I didn't have a clue what I was gonna do."

Old Man Rom made a strained laugh and casually looked Subaru over.

"...The way you switch gears so quickly really throws an old man off. Seems you managed to escape with your life back then, too..."

His face twisted painfully as he saw the scars on Subaru's body.

"I may not be one to talk, but it seems that knife wielder got you pretty badly."

"Nah, that babe only got me in the stomach. All the other wounds are from a thing that happened after."

"Goodness! Something else happened to you, not even a month later?!"

Subaru thought Old Man Rom's loud reaction was quite sensible as he reviewed the last month—though in truth, the boy had experienced nearly twice that time. Those turbulent weeks had included the maid sisters, the demon-beast incident, and the Liliana issue.

With Subaru keeping his mouth shut, Old Man Rom seemed to accept things all on his own, shaking his head as he brought up a separate issue.

"—Hey, brat. Do you know where Felt went off to?"

"...Haven't you heard? Reinhard took her with him, or so I'm told..."

"Reinhard...the Sword Saint? Why would the knight among knights take her with him?"

Apparently, this news was a bolt from out of the blue.

Subaru thought back to how things had gone down at the loot cellar, finally noticing the inconsistency. Old Man Rom was out cold before Reinhard had entered the fray. Rom and Reinhard hadn't interacted while Subaru was conscious.

"So, what, you just woke up in a wrecked shop without any explanation, and all you could do was wonder?"

"It wasn't nearly that bleak. I woke up in the guards' garrison. I appreciated their healing me, but I let myself out right after."

"Ah, yeah. Not exactly a comfortable place for you, huh."

A criminal wouldn't feel at ease waking up in a police hospital. Subaru couldn't blame him for getting out of there ASAP without hearing all the fine details.

"So that's why you didn't hear, huh? Okay. Anyway, let me fill you in on what happened before I blacked out, plus the little bit that apparently happened after."

After that preamble, Subaru acted out a dramatic retelling of the events at the loot cellar. Old Man Rom watched Subaru's meaningless theatrics with admiration, and even the bored-looking girl leaned forward, gripped by the performance from start to finish. Subaru concluded, "She was so surprised! And then I said, '—I want you to… tell me your name.'"

The girl replied, "Ho-ho, a rather fine choice of words, if I do say so myself. I must grudgingly approve."

Rom followed up, "Keh, you really told her… Bah, this is no time to admire! The bottom line is that you don't know any more about Felt other than the fact the Sword Saint took her with him, do you, brat?"

"Part of why I came here today was to do some footwork to find out exactly what happened…"

But he'd hit a roadblock right at the heart of it, the attempt to make contact with Reinhard.

Rom murmured to himself so faintly that Subaru did not hear.

"But… The House of Astrea, of all things…"

Old Man Rom had a serious expression as he lifted his face. Subaru helplessly shrugged.

"Well, I'm gonna see if I can get ahold of Reinhard, so I'll let you know if I hear anything. I mean, I wanted to find out if Felt was safe and sound to begin with."

"That'll be a big help… You seem oddly trustworthy. Is this girl involved with this somehow?"

"No, not a bit. I don't even know her name."

"Just how many scrapes do you get into for girls whose names you don't know?!"

"Hey, back when I didn't know Emilia-tan's name, I was pretty desperate, so I don't think anything I did was that weird."

Subaru's indifferent reply made Old Man Rom rub his eyebrows in exhaustion.

"No point thinking about it. All right, fine. I'll rely on you, so let me know if you find out anything about Felt. If I can repay you, I will."

"You're really gushing. It's because it's your adorable granddaughter, huh?"

"—That's right. She's…like a granddaughter to me, so please."

Subaru's jaw dropped at Rom's straight-up, unashamed agreement with him. He wondered if the blond thief girl really knew how deeply he felt for her. Knowing her, he figured she'd go red in the face and try to blow it all off.

As Subaru's discussion with Old Man Rom wrapped up, the girl haltingly murmured, "Reinhard... To hear the name of Reinhard here, of all places..."

She suppressed a laugh. Subaru's relaxed expression tightened again as he turned toward her.

"Hey, it's not polite to eavesdrop. Don't go listening in on other people's business like that."

"I did not listen in. You two oafs simply began speaking right in front of me. —You. From the way you speak of him, it seems your claim to know the Sword Saint was not a bluff. Are you close?"

"It'd be a bit much to say we met once and became best friends forever, but we're on good terms, yeah."

Subaru owed a debt to Reinhard. He had enough of a sense of reciprocity to pay it back...even if he couldn't exactly imagine Reinhard in a crisis that Subaru could bail him out of.

Subaru asked his new companion, "Well, what do you know about Reinhard? You don't seem like a fan of his."

"From what I have heard, he is a rather twisted person. Beyond that, I have only seen him slightly from afar."

The way she declared someone to be twisted without having even spoken to him suggested it was her own thinking that was twisted. But with the girl's silence indicating she had no intention to elaborate, Subaru turned his attention back to Old Man Rom.

"Leaving her aside, how should I get in touch with you?"

"There's a store called Cadmon on Market Street. Give my name to the grumpy-looking man there and he'll get in touch with me."

"All right, all right. Cadmon... Cadmon?"

As Rom explained how to get in touch, Subaru tilted his head at the familiar-sounding word.

Either way, he'd fulfilled his promise to pay Old Man Rom a visit. That was one thing off his to-do list. To take care of the rest, first, he needed something else...

"Incidentally, the girl and I are actually completely lost. I don't want my adventure to end here before I can fulfill my promise, so ah, could you lead us back to the main street?"

"Mm, all right. Leave it to me. Which street is it?"

"Back to the garrison. Please and thank you."

"Didn't you hear me tell you I escaped from that garrison?!"

Old Man Rom's exasperated shout filled the sky above the alleyway.

According to that sky, he'd been separated from Emilia for nearly an hour.

7

The orange-haired girl gazed at the back alley indifferently and muttered, "At first, I thought the disorder of such a grimy place held promise, but now that I am accustomed to it, it has nothing to draw my eye. It is quite useless for assuaging my boredom."

She raised the hem of her dress and shook it, a blunt expression of her insufferable displeasure.

"I don't think the royal capital's designer drew up these streets to be exciting," Subaru remarked.

"The world exists for my sake, so should not everything in it serve to amuse me? I have no idea what the man who approved such boring streets was thinking. Royalty should have a keenly discerning eye. Lack thereof seems to have been decidedly fatal of late."

Just hearing her statement set Subaru's heart racing. His head whipped back and forth to see if anyone had overheard.

"Th-that's a pretty arrogant thing to say right at the king's door, you know..."

The girl snorted at Subaru's caution, or rather, cowardice.

"A dull reaction and a futile concern. It would seem that you, too, are part of the common rabble."

"I'm well aware I'm a one-hundred-percent common, ordinary, straight-down-the-middle guy, and I'm fine with it. I don't want to waste any more time hanging around you, anyway. The girl who's waiting for me will hate me."

"What absurdity. It is an insult for you to think about anyone besides me during the time we are together. I may be accompanied now, but I think nothing at all of walking alone."

"Well, you *should* think about it. Being with you is miserable."

He was the chaperone for a girl who seemed to be arrogance incarnate. Subaru's self-pity flared up again at how he'd once again thrown himself under a bus in no time flat for the sake of someone he'd never even seen before. But he remarked to himself, "Ah, whatever…"

They were strangers to begin with. Neither knew the other's name. Once they reached the main street, they'd never see each other again. He wasn't magnanimous enough to shut off his own feelings of discomfort to try to make friends with just anyone. In Subaru's book, forcing yourself to like something you hate was among the most distasteful things around.

That Subaru had decided this, yet had no intention of leaving the girl on her own until they'd exited to the main street, was evidence as to what kind of person he was.

Coincidentally, Old Man Rom was not accompanying them. He abhorred going out onto the main street, so he led them to an adjacent alley before heading off. Subaru somewhat regretted the loss of his company, but…

"—While I was thinking about all that, here we are."

Just ahead of a bend, he could finally see the bright, western sun over the road. Subaru beheld the uninterrupted flow of people passing to and fro, relieved that his suffering was finally at an end.

"Now that we're out of there, we're total strangers again. I have to look for my cutie-pie companion, so I don't wanna get into any more trouble, like hanging around you. I'm sure your escort has been desperate to find you, so if you stay put I'm sure you'll meet up with him soon."

With the moment of their parting so close, Subaru vented out all the resentment that had built up during that time. Naturally, the girl was poised to respond, but instead, she halted and crossed her arms in silence.

"What, nothing to say? Okay, maybe I went a little too far, but I can't change how I feel. Things haven't exactly gone smoothly, but if you try a little prudence now and again, I'm sure…"

Subaru was simultaneously excusing his resentful words and lecturing her when she sneered back.

"Mmm, I think I pity you just a little. Whether you are aware of it or not, you so thoroughly play the fool. It is no virtue. It is merely a thin shell within which you conceal your weakness. It is as repellant to the eye as your face."

"The first part sounded serious, but that last part was definitely making fun of my looks, wasn't it?"

"If you intend to maintain the game to the very end, it is no concern of mine..."

Whatever the girl wanted to say wasn't registering with Subaru. Consistent with her bearing and actions, she made statements without any consideration for the comprehension of others. No doubt he wouldn't get a straight answer even if he pursued the matter further. With that in mind, Subaru gave up on speaking to the girl further.

Or, perhaps telling himself the girl was incomprehensible was his way of avoiding the truth. But he wouldn't receive any more answers here to begin with. After all, the instant the two exited the alley, they were greeted by a voice—Emilia's voice.

"—I've finally found you."

Unlike the back alley, the bright rays of the sun illuminated everything on the main street. The sunshine dazzled and burned his eyes. That radiance haloed her white robe as she looked at Subaru.

Her elegant brows were furrowed. Her fingertips restlessly toyed with her sparkling hair. Her gloomy, violet eyes quivered as her lips loosened in slight relief. It was plain as day how much she'd worried about Subaru.

Subaru both deeply regretted making her worry and was happy she had worried. His expression brightened at their reunion, unexpected but eagerly awaited.

"Ah, Emili—"

But as Emilia let out a soft sigh, he felt that something was wrong. He began to call her name but stopped when he saw someone beside her—a male someone with a burly chest.

"Wait, wait, wait! Don't go flirting with Emilia-tan when I'm not around!"

Subaru dashed forward to put himself between the man and Emilia. But his glare at the silhouetted man froze in the face of a torrent of sharp words.

"Hey, hey, lil' missy. I think your guy here has a screw loose. Is he all right?"

The chummy voice addressing Emilia was a bit hard to make out. That was only natural, since the speaker's head was covered in a full-face helmet.

The jet-black helm, meant to conceal his entire face, looked highly refined, but the headpiece alone wasn't what made him stand out—though that description is misleading. He stood out because the helmet actually was alone.

"More worried about an interloper than excited for your reunion? What a fascinatingly complicated sense of masculinity."

"Well, you've got pretty horrible fashion sense, don't you?!"

"And you've got quite some lip toward your seniors. I'm an easy-going old man, so I'll let it slide, but someone else might chop your head off."

Subaru gaped as the man tapped a finger against the nape of his neck in obvious amusement. Yes, the bare nape of his neck, for while the man wore a pitch-black helm over his head, beneath he wore only a shabby mantle and an open linen vest-and-shorts combo that made him look like some bandit. His "shoes" were sandals with split-toe socks. Behind his waist, he carried a handsome sword with a fat blade resembling a Chinese crescent sword. Everything clashed with everything else.

Subaru's tracksuit was no less out of place, but the man's attire was surely the greater offense to common sense. Subaru tentatively asked Emilia his burning question.

"Emilia-tan, don't tell me this guy's outfit passes for normal here in the capital?"

"Don't worry, Subaru. I'm as shocked by what he's wearing as you are."

The man erupted into laugher and promptly divulged what he was doing with Emilia in the first place.

"Oh yeah, she was really shocked. It was so cute. I said I was look-ing for someone, and I was pretty surprised when she said she'd come along, though."

Subaru put a hand on Emilia's shoulder and stared at where the man's eyes probably were.

"Emilia-tan's kind-heartedness is a real virtue, but you still have to pick who you help. Why do you think a poisonous mushroom looks so bad? It's saying, 'I'm poisonous. Danger. Eat me and you'll die.' That's to stop damage before it happens."

The man replied, "You're making it sound like I'm a dangerous guy. That's horrible."

"Back where I come from, one look at you and they'd bring all the local school kids together and tell them about kidnappers."

Subaru blew off the man's flippant comment and returned to Emilia.

"Anyway, Emilia-tan, like I'm always telling you—watch out for men and cars. Men are wolves, so you can't show them that defense-less, adorable, smiling face... Are you upset?"

"No, I'm just thinking that sounds more like something I've said to you than something you've said to me, Subaru. No offense."

Subaru was tempted to cover his face, regretting that his slip of the tongue had only heaped more trouble onto him. But the com-ing lecture was mercifully interrupted by an outside party. The orange-haired girl stepped forward and pompously declared, "Mmm. How perceptive of you to wait for me at my destination. Your loyalty is admirable, Al."

Her words made the man—Al—laugh out loud.

"...To be honest, I want to say it was dumb luck I happened to be here, but that'll just put you in a bad mood. I agree with you, Prin-cess. Yep, it's just like you said!" He stood beside the girl and ruffled her orange hair with the palm of his hand. "Apparently, by sheer coincidence, the person the lady here was looking for and the person I was looking for were together. Maybe you could call it fate?"

"So it's like the saying, even chance meetings are the result of karma? No thanks, I don't want any threads of fate except red ones with Emilia-tan."

There was a momentary pause before Al's reply.

"—This guy's got quite a mouth on him."

But Al's laughter and the light wave of his hand wiped Subaru's doubts away. All his actions had been with his right hand the entire time—for the man didn't *have* a left hand.

So the man had one arm, a pitch-black helmet, and a haphazard threadbare outfit. Judging from his tone of voice and his appearance below the neck, he was probably a bit more than twice Subaru's age. In spite of that, he didn't come off much like Subaru's senior, sporting an attitude as light as his clothes.

To put it kindly, he was easy to get along with. To put it rudely, he was an adult that needed to pull himself together.

Subaru commented, "With Puck there as your guardian, I'm wondering why he let you go around with this guy…"

Puck replied to Subaru's question telepathically.

"Lia spotted him looking in garbage bins on the side of the street as soon as she stepped out of the garrison. Her meddling happens at lightning speed, so I didn't have any time to stop it."

"Oh, come on…"

Subaru's reply couldn't hide his exhaustion. True, Emilia's softhearted nature was nothing new, but Al looking for his traveling companion in trash bins was completely off the rails.

He wondered if the man had put any funny ideas in her head while they'd been alone. Subaru gave Emilia a look of concern when he realized that…

"—?"

…without a word, Emilia had slipped behind Subaru's back as if to avoid the eyes of other people. She pulled down her hood to hide her face again, keeping her voice quiet as if that would erase her presence.

Subaru dubiously raised his eyebrows and looked toward the orange-haired girl who seemed the cause of Emilia's misgivings.

"What, staring at me?" the girl said. "Drinking in the beauty you will dearly miss once I depart? Certainly, it is cruel that my beauty is so divine, but it is rude to stare in silence."

"Sorry, my eyes are in perfect shape... Everyone found who they were looking for, so how about we break this up?"

Subaru gave the girl—the one Emilia seemed to be hiding from—a dismissive reply as he directed the spotlight away from her and toward Al. He didn't know why, but Emilia seemed averse to the attention.

So Subaru did what he felt would serve her best.

Al replied, "Well, that's all fine... The decision to shift the talk to me instead of Princess included."

"...I sympathize with you more than a bit... No, a lot."

Al shrugged at Subaru's rather earnest words and looked down at the girl.

"An adult with a broad mind can put up with a lot without gettin' sick of it. Even a proud cat that's never been housebroken. Maybe I've just gotten old enough to find it adorable."

Subaru couldn't see his eyes through the helmet, but he sounded like a father figure protecting his beloved daughter.

They get along pretty decently, huh, thought Subaru vaguely in his mind. He added out loud, "Well, we're gonna head this way... How about you?"

The girl replied, "Then I shall go that way as well."

"...Then, we're gonna head the other way."

"Then I shall go the other way as..."

"Oh, good grief. Are you stalking me?! What, did you fall in love with me or something?!"

"I imagine that is a joke, and a petty one at that. Lackluster men die in lackluster ways, you know."

With great pomp and ceremony, the girl, dispassionate to the bitter end, departed with her companion. Her hesitant steps proclaimed that even though she wanted them to part ways, she found it unamusing to do so.

So with all the invective remaining in him, Subaru said to the departing girl, "Hey, arrogant chick, take this."

"What an insolent tongue to direct at me. With one command, Al could take that head off your—"

As the girl turned around with some very menacing words on her lips, her red eyes widened. Her hands stretched and caught the pair of abbles lazily arcing toward her.

"Take 'em. These are bonding abbles. In the end I may have won the bet, but the winner has the right to show mercy like a noble warrior. Take care not to wander into bad guys like that from now on, okay?"

"I will have you know I did not become involved with those men by acting like some foolish child."

"...Incidentally, why did you get involved with them?"

"When I asked them if it was not inexcusable that they should live with such impoverished faces and attire, they became agitated."

"You're the one in the wrong there!!"

Subaru sympathized with Dumb, Dumber, and Dumbest all over again and turned his back to the girl, pulling Emilia along by her arm. The small measure of payback gave him some satisfaction.

Emilia kept her head down as she went along with him. As they quickly departed, they heard one final muffled shout from the street behind them, filled with apparently genuine gratitude.

"—Lil' missy, thanks for comin' with me on my search!"

8

"Hey, Emilia-tan, they're gone now, so why don't we talk finally?" Subaru asked.

Parting ways with the arrogant girl and her guardian, Subaru and Emilia walked together for a while before stopping.

He was worried that something he'd said had brought about Emilia's sudden change in behavior. After a brief silence, Emilia lifted up her face and, just as Subaru expected, the subject was the girl she'd attempted to hide from.

"Subaru. —About that girl from earlier... She... Where did... Why were you...?"

"Ehh, Emilia-tan! What, are you jealous? We're at the point where you're just burning with envy?"

"—Subaru."

With one word, Emilia cut off Subaru's typically glib reply. She had a solemn expression, and the tension in her cheeks told even Subaru that bad jokes weren't going to cut it.

"Err? Emilia-tan, what's with the really serious look…?"

"Please, Subaru, don't make light of this. Why were you with that girl…?"

Emilia seemed to want to hear something from Subaru. It threw him off, but he sank into thought to try to give her the earnest reply she sought. But just as Subaru focused properly about things for once…his efforts were for naught as an angry, rough, and coarse shout interrupted their conversation.

"Finally found ya! You're a lot of trouble, damn it!!"

At the voice, Subaru scanned the area, aghast. Roughnecks were on both sides, blocking the street to prevent their escape. Dumb of Dumb, Dumber, and Dumbest stood at the vanguard of the men, glaring at Subaru.

"I've been lookin' for you and the woman to pay you back for makin' fun of me before."

Subaru replied, "…So you brought all your friends for payback over a war of words? No matter how much you resent an insult, a man with a spine wipes his own butt… That's what I…always believed in…!"

"Hey, don't try to make me feel bad! What do you know about me, anyway?!"

Subaru listened to Dumb's abuse, complete with spittle flying, as he quietly looked around. There were fifteen or sixteen men blocking the street. He couldn't exactly expect Reinhard to bail him out of this one.

"Meaning, it's pathetic, but the best thing I can do is rely on Emilia-tan and Puck, so…!"

Puck telepathically praised Subaru's quick turn to the aid of others.

"It really is pathetic, but I think it's commendable you accept your helplessness so quickly."

Subaru felt sorry for Dumb and company, but Puck the Great Spirit could take on street thugs regardless of their numbers. It'd be WinterFest in Lugunica's summer.

But before Subaru could shout, "Take it from here, maestro!" and yield the path like a villain in a historical play, a telepathic thought rich in meaning arrived from Puck.

"You have quite a disturbing image in your mind there... But apparently I'm not needed."

Faster than Subaru could ask what he meant, a rather scary statement came from overhead, heralding the descent of a certain blue-haired maid.

"—I came here tracking Subaru's scent. What kind of disturbance is this?"

Tumbling end over end as she descended, Rem held down the hem of her skirt and landed with a boom. She brushed the dust from her sleeves as everyone gawked at her.

Rem made an adorable little tilt of her head.

"So, Subaru. Do you have something you wish to say to me?"

Subaru pointed at her feet and voiced his question.

"Let me start with, err... He's ah, not dead, is he?"

Rem lowered her gaze. Underneath lay Dumb, smashed to the ground the moment she landed.

Head buried in the city street, the hoodlum said one last thing before he ceased to move altogether.

"Not another...maid..."

Rem slowly nodded.

"He is breathing."

"It's all good, then!! That's Rem for you, the all-purpose maid everyone wants in their time of need!"

"Oh no... Saying how you can do nothing without me, you are making me blush."

Subaru and Rem engaged in their daily routine, even as Rem's violence had the thugs reeling. Subaru's praised made Rem's cheeks go red as she demurred. In the meantime, the men gradually regained their bearings.

"D-don't toy with us here! You really think you're gettin' out of this alive...?"

Rem's voice lowered as she switched to her emotionless Work Mode.

"I judge that these men are threatening Subaru and Lady Emilia's safety."

The hooligans faltered at the change. Subaru felt a pang of pity for them while raising a finger to Rem.

"Rem."

"Yes?"

"Don't kill them, okay?"

"You are as kind as ever, Subaru—I shall half-kill them, then."

In a miraculous combination of equal parts violence and loveliness, Rem leaped into the mob.

Some lunged at her only to be thrashed. Others turned tail and ran. Others still squatted down and cowered, unable to grasp what was going on—Rem heaped punishment upon them all impartially.

Subaru gawked at the sight of people flying through the air like they weighed nothing.

"Whoa, that's amazing."

The impending end of the strife before his eyes filled Subaru's head with tranquility, as if he were removed from the uproar. He never even noticed the violet eyes staring at him, nor the pleading murmur that accompanied them.

"—Subaru."

9

"So that's why we're gonna rough you up a little. Just a little, wee bit," said a thug to the girl.

The men blocking off the road and laughing lewdly included Dumber and Dumbest. Their group, separate from Dumb's, had surrounded the girl and her companion. They didn't need to put into words exactly what kind of payback they had in mind after capturing her. The vulgar lust in their eyes said it all.

But the girl paid the men around her no heed as she brought the slice of abble to her lips.

"…Mm, bittersweet. It is indeed an abble on the inside. I am forced to conclude that the clown from earlier did not simply dye them red as some kind of joke. So abbles are indeed this color? I am shocked."

Al replied, "Hey, ah, Princess, you seeing what's happening here?"

"Whatever you wish to say, speak it clearly. I dislike all this indirectness."

"Fine, I'll come right out and say it. —There's two abbles, so ain't one of 'em mine?"

"Ha! How absurd. Now hear this, I caught both abbles that the clown tossed. Consequently, both are mine."

"It's common sense that if you have two of something and two people, each of 'em takes one."

The disregard of both master and servant drove the ruffians' anger to its limit. With clear malice, each one drew his blade as they began to tighten the circle.

Al asked her, "So, Princess. What about what the world around you wants?"

"My choice *is* the world's choice. You should bear that in mind, Al."

"I try."

The girl nodded with satisfaction at Al's words and resumed nibbling on her abble. Her cheeks relaxed at the bittersweet taste, bringing an angelic smile over her beautiful face. And as if ripping off an insect's wings with cherubic innocence, she stated matter-of-factly, "I am now in a very good mood. —Consequently, you may spare their lives."

Hearing those words, Al put his hand on the handle of the large sword sheathed horizontally behind his hip. There was a slow *shing*—the sound of a blade being drawn from its sheath. With that as background music, he stated, "—Aye-aye, ma'am."

The smile under the pitch-black helmet was vivid and fierce.

CHAPTER 3

ON THE VERY WORST OF TERMS

1

"—Ehh?! You're leaving me behind?!"

Early in the morning at the inn, Subaru raised his voice in shock as he learned the day's schedule.

Subaru was stunned while Emilia and Rem sat before his eyes at the table. Roswaal had left the inn earlier, stating that he had a prior engagement; the other three were just finishing the breakfast Rem had prepared.

Emilia answered him, "Of course I am. Subaru, the reasons you're here in the royal capital were to see if your acquaintances are all right and to get you treated. That was the deal."

"Er, but, since I'm feeling pretty well, you could loosen up the interpretation a little…"

"Absolutely not. Today really isn't fun and games, and outsiders are forbidden to enter. I can't even bring Rem with me."

Emilia's atypically strict instructions were hard for Subaru to argue with given how he'd wandered off just the day before. He looked to Rem for salvation, but the blue-haired maid shook her head.

"This time, Lady Emilia is absolutely correct. Please listen to her."

"Crap, isn't anyone on my side here?! And I can't say anything because of what happened yesterday, either. Ugh!"

Even if Rem was fundamentally biased toward Subaru, priorities were priorities. As a result of his failing to uphold Emilia's instructions and wandering off on his own the day before, he was totally grounded.

With Subaru directing his lament skyward, Emilia put her hands on her hips and exhaled.

"It won't be that long... Or I'd like to say that, but I don't really know when I'll be back. So go ahead and eat supper together with Rem. Otherwise I think it might be a rather long wait."

"Pfft. If you're going to be that mean about it, I've got my own ideas, Emilia-tan. Hey, Rem. Let's have a feast all by ourselves!"

"No, today's menu is abble chips with abble salad, abble pie filled with abble jam, and I have freshly squeezed abble juice ready for dessert."

"Abbles all the way down?! Damn you, Scarface!"

Apparently, since he'd returned with nine abbles in his bag, it meant the evening's menu would be a veritable abble festival. Subaru laughed desperately as the image of the scar-faced shopkeeper smiling and giving him a thumbs-up came to mind.

"Well, that's fine, abbles are my favorite fruit, anyway! Being surrounded by abbles is heaven itself! Okay, Rem!! Let's eat the whole thing up between the two of us!!"

"Oh, I couldn't. If you like it so much, I'll let you have all of it."

"You act like you're cozying up to me, but sometimes you just chuck me over the cliff, you know?!"

Subaru was aghast at how Rem acted less out of concern for his position and more out of how to use his position to her advantage. Emilia slumped her shoulders at the interaction between the two before focusing on the maid.

"Anyway, I'm trusting you with this, Rem. I think Roswaal has told you this, too, but... Be strict... Really, be strict, okay?"

"The way you repeated yourself after that pause—Emilia-tan's super trusting of me, huh?"

Subaru gave a thumbs-up at Emilia's earnest reminder. Emilia, already accustomed to the sight, gently rested a hand on his fact.

Subaru's breath caught at the sudden contact.

"Subaru, I'm not asking much of you..."

"R-right...?"

"Please, let me trust you, okay?"

For a moment, the sound of Emilia's plea froze Subaru's thoughts solid.

Then, he caught her meaning, chewed it over, and swallowed with a nod.

"Y-yeah! I'll do just that! I practically live to meet Emilia-tan's expectations!"

He still didn't understand the cause of the lingering unease in her eyes when he reflexively agreed to all her conditions. He'd just accept them for now and take them into account when he shifted to action.

In contrast, Emilia's violet eyes darkened. Then, she quietly added...

"Yes—I trust you."

2

It was probably less than an hour after Emilia had left for the royal palace.

Subaru was spending his time studying the world's writing system under Rem's tutelage at the inn. He was mechanically copying characters, his thoughts consumed by just one thing.

—Namely, how he could be at Emilia's side as she competed in the royal selection.

Emilia was right to worry about how he would take her entreaties for him to wait. Subaru hadn't considered patiently waiting at the inn for her return in the slightest.

He felt a little guilty about disregarding his promise to her. Even so...

"There's definitely people here in the royal capital who have it out for Emilia..."

The last time she had been to the royal capital was the first day Subaru had met her.

Apparently she had snuck her way in to visit. In spite of this, enemies had targeted the emblem she carried, attempting to rob her of her qualification for the royal selection, and even her very life.

—Thinking back upon their fateful encounter, Subaru could not endure the burning in his chest.

Having been suddenly summoned into another world, he'd lived until that day without a single word from anyone. He still had no idea who had summoned him or why. He didn't have any leads. That was why Subaru was thinking about how to blow the current situation wide open.

If no one was going to grant him a purpose, he'd decide his purpose for himself.

"—I'm gonna…help Emilia."

Subaru had probably been summoned to that world for that very reason. And if not, he'd do it anyway.

That was the thought that animated Subaru Natsuki and gave him strength.

"And that's why…"

"—?"

Rem just happened to catch a glimpse of Subaru's eyes as he hardened his inner resolve. With a slight blush of her cheeks, the maid stood firmly in his way, forming an impassable barrier in front of the door.

He'd tried various methods to get her to leave her post already, but she'd even brought a chamber pot in with her.

"*Stare…*"

"What is it, Subaru? Those intense eyes are making this a little awkward…"

"*Stare…*"

"Y-you may not. Even if you look at me like an abandoned puppy, you may not."

"*Stare…*"

"I-I promised Sister that I would fulfill my duties. So you may not."

The power of Subaru's silent stare was backing Rem into a corner.

She seemed increasingly agitated as she endured Subaru's gaze, glancing back at him with reproach.

"Are you...worried about Lady Emilia that much? The royal palace is filled with numerous privileged guests besides Lady Emilia, so I imagine security is very tight."

"It's not how good the security is... I hate being left behind when Emilia has something really important happening."

"Subaru..."

What Rem was saying made complete sense. He was acutely aware of his own deficiencies. The power Subaru possessed was meager and useless, and could only lead to pain and sorrow.

But he didn't care if he was useless.

"If something happens, then I probably won't be any use. And if it isn't likely to happen, it's great if it doesn't. I get that."

"—"

"But if something does happen, maybe it won't get resolved if I'm not there. I don't know when that something might come, so I want to be there with Emilia when it counts."

If some events could not be undone save through Return by Death, a tactic that only Subaru Natsuki could use, then that was a stage he ought to be fighting on.

—Subaru did not realize that his thought process, taking his own "death" into the calculation, was warped to begin with.

"...My goodness, Subaru, you really are incorrigible."

Rem's halting murmur sounded like surrender, making Subaru lift up his face in the hope that his wish had been granted.

"Then you'll..."

"No, you may not. Even so, I cannot permit you to pass, Subaru."

"Wait, what's with the way you were talking just now?! It totally sounded like..."

As Subaru chewed her out, Rem dodged his question and raised a finger.

"However... I will be working on a new abble dish that I suddenly thought of. As this requires great concentration, I will be extremely busy in the kitchen. It is highly probable that someone could slip out of this room without me realizing."

"..."

"But you must not do anything untoward. Please continue your studies until I return. When everything is settled…I will treat you to the finest abble cuisine anyone has ever made."

Subaru was cowed into silence as Rem gave him a motherly smile before standing. Just as she'd announced, she tied on an apron and left the room. Subaru listened to her light footsteps go down the stairs before he slumped back heavily in his chair.

"Ahh, Rem's so adorable… I'm the worst for taking advantage of her."

Closing his eyes, he thanked Rem for her clumsy idea and rose from his chair. Before leaving the room, Subaru reconsidered for a moment, took a pen, and tore out a page from the workbook.

3

Rem returned to the empty room, touching the table as she murmured offhandedly, "…I am slightly disappointed that he did not say, 'Come with me.'"

He'd left behind a note on the table with *"Sorry, and thanks"* written in crude I-script.

"Subaru, you truly are incorrigible…"

As Rem gazed at the note, her expression betrayed the true meaning of her words.

Rem picked up the note, pressing it against her chest and closing her eyes as she treated it as a precious gift from Subaru.

"—But I wonder what Master Roswaal is thinking?"

She inclined her head slightly as she voiced her doubts about the instructions her master had left that morning.

"He said, 'Do not stand in Subaru's way no matter what Lady Emilia may say to you.'"

It was as if he'd anticipated Subaru's actions and had instructed her accordingly. She also wondered why he was valuing Subaru's opinion above Emilia's. But at any rate…

"—Please come back to me safely, Subaru."

She did not think he had run off without any plan, but she knew he was a boy who would do such a thing for the sake of another, putting the safety of others before his own. All Rem could do was fulfill his request and pray he would be unharmed.

For a time, Rem closed her eyes, picturing Subaru in her mind as she offered up a prayer. She then finished the tidying up of the half-completed study materials Subaru had abandoned before she retreated to the kitchen.

And so, Subaru Natsuki was let loose in the capital a second time, perhaps dancing in the palm of someone's hand—though none could tell.

4

Subaru, having skipped out of the inn thanks to Rem's kindness, ran downtown in the royal capital, his feet taking him to the Cadmon fruit store so he could contact Old Man Rom.

"Sneaking into a castle…is not very realistic, is it? Well, nothing's gonna happen unless I make it to the entrance of the royal palace…"

It might have been possible to gain entry by explaining that he was connected to Emilia and Roswaal. But Subaru had few cards to play to even get that far.

"Even if I got to the garrison and explained, Emilia would probably turn down a magic mirror message…"

If he could make it to the foot of the castle, he was confident he could verbally wear Emilia down. Emilia was weak under pressure. He didn't think she'd chase Subaru off after he'd undergone a dangerous adventure to reach her.

Subaru went to Market Street in the hopes of improving his chances of success. He wanted to get in touch with Old Man Rom and relay his plan to infiltrate the Nobles' District as soon as possible.

The day before, Emilia had attempted to contact the royal palace from the garrison, but her efforts had apparently failed. But as it was clear that Reinhard was assigned to the Knights of the Royal Guard, he would surely be attending the royal selection meeting that day.

Before Emilia had left the inn, she'd said that she would ask him about Felt afterward. Subaru wanted to tell Old Man Rom, a worrier in spite of his large frame, as soon as he could.

Weaving his way into the crowd with quick feet, Subaru found the shop sign that was still fresh in his memory. The eccentric colors of the Cadmon sign were easy to mentally associate with the unmistakable scarred face of the shopkeeper.

It's a small world, thought Subaru as he leaped out in front of the shop, when...

"Hey, old guy. Long time no—"

As Subaru tried to call out to the storekeeper, a congenial voice interrupted from right beside him.

"You're late, bro! Just in the nick of time. Lucky you, I was gonna wait just a bit longer before heading off."

A heavy metallic rattle accompanied a muffled laugh. Subaru shrugged off the arm openly wrapped around his shoulders, putting some distance between himself and the very close voice.

"Who are... Wait, you're the guy from yesterday?"

"Yeah, I'm the guy from yesterday. I'm glad you showed up. Now I won't get an earful over it."

Not minding that his arm had been brushed off, the man in the black helmet—Al—patted his chest with his one arm. The appearance of the eccentric swordsman was just as unbalanced as it had been the day before.

Al chuckled again, seeing Subaru's obvious shock at the unexpected reunion.

"Hey, don't get bent out of shape. It's your fault for talking about meeting up here right in front of Princess. She's a sharp cookie to begin with."

"Right in front of...she was eavesdropping! So why are you at the place I'm supposed to meet Old Man Rom, anyway? I get that the girl ordered you to, but not the reason why."

"Hey, don't ask me why. Princess does things on a whim so much, a lot of the time there's no point asking why. —So let's get goin' then!"

"'Goin''?"

Apparently, both master and servant expected him to charge off into a new affair without his misgivings being answered. With Al ready to move out without a sufficient explanation, Subaru furrowed his brows and objected, "Hold on a minute. Go where? You haven't explained one thing to me... I mean, I've got a place I have to get to!"

"Why're you dragging your feet? Hey, it's a big world out there and people get carried away by the currents, so just forget your doubts and go with the flow. It's fun!"

Subaru pointed at Al's helmet, unable to see the expression behind it as he soundly declared, "I don't wanna hear philosophy from a grown-up slacker like you. I've got things to do. I don't have time to mess with you or your princess!"

Subaru had no idea how Al had wound up associated with said princess, but that didn't mean he had to shut up and play along. He continued, "You should really reconsider spoiling her before it gets both of you in really hot wa—"

"—You're looking for a way to get into the royal palace, right?"

"_____!"

Al's murmur stopped the stern lecture on Subaru's lips.

"Whoa, that sure worked. That's Princess for you. It's just like she said."

"Wh...what do you know...?!"

"Nah, I don't know nothin'. I'm just saying it 'cause Princess told me to. And it worked, huh?"

Al's shoulders rocked in delight as Subaru bit his lip and held his breath. If what the man said was true, Subaru was dancing on the palm of a girl who wasn't even there. Suspecting he was completely boxed in, Subaru licked his parched lips.

"...I can...get into the castle, if I...go with you?"

The way Al avoided the heart of the matter was unsettling.

"Well... You'll find out if you come along, won't ya?"

Subaru averted his eyes and resisted the urge to click his tongue. Al had tossed the ball into his court and now calmly awaited his reply.

In spite of that, he seemed to know exactly what reply Subaru would give, which burned Subaru to no end.

After a brief, silent pause, the boy scowled in defeat as he raised a white flag.

"—Understood. I'll go with you."

"Don't look so sad. I knew how this was gonna go down the moment you arrived in front of this shop with me waiting for you, just like Princess wanted."

"...You seriously believe in her like that?"

Al didn't reply to Subaru's feeble question, using his one arm to fend off the issue as he moved the conversation forward.

"—Well, out of time. If we don't get a move on, she's gonna leave us behind. She's really strict about that stuff."

Subaru was about to fall into step behind Al, but first he looked back and said, "So there you have it. There's stuff I wanted to talk about, but I'll save it for next time, old guy."

He was speaking to the shopkeeper, who'd been grimacing as Subaru and Al conversed inside the store. The shopkeeper traced his facial scar with a finger and let out a brief snort.

"I don't really mind. Can't be helped... Having a weirdo like that in front of my store was driving my customers away. Get going already."

"I'm not sure Al's the cause of your customers staying away, but... I've got one favor to ask you. You can get in touch with this crazy-huge geezer named Old Man Rom, right?"

Subaru, feeling confidence in the unusual connection, chose his words with great care as he added, "I want you to tell Old Man Rom this: —Subaru Natsuki says, I'm heading to the castle to check on Felt. Wait up for good news."

5

—When Subaru reached Al's destination, he looked up, completely and utterly overwhelmed.

"This is… How to put this…"

Standing beside him, Al nodded to display his sympathy with Subaru's halting words.

"I know, bro. I get it, looking at this and wondering what you should say."

Then, the two met each other's eyes, pointing at what stood in front of them, and said simultaneously, "—Rich people."

The dragon carriage was the very definition of needless extravagance.

The passenger cab was subtly engraved and adorned with numerous flamboyant ornaments. Glittering, radiant gold leaf had been applied to the exterior, and even the wheels had been jewel-encrusted. The land dragon in front also had an ostentatious appearance. The crimson-skinned, two-headed land dragon had extravagant feathers all down its back, with the intricate designs on the reins and bit completing the image of quintessential opulence.

"…People ride this? This isn't some kind of mistake?"

"Unfortunately, even in a vast kingdom such as this, only Princess would ride such an embarrassing thing."

Subaru did a double take as Al patted him on the back and walked ahead of him toward the occupied vehicle.

It was parked on the side of the street, but nonetheless, an unnecessarily huge dragon carriage just sitting there made a large impact on passersby. It received many stares, more out of raw shock than indignation at the interference.

Deeply conscious of their stares, Subaru finally resigned himself to climbing into the dragon carriage. He could almost hear the unvoiced whispers behind him: *He's getting into that…*

Sitting by herself in a custom seat, a girl greeted them with a crafty smile.

"—You have made me wait some time. Such rudeness can cost you dearly."

The girl's attire for that day polished and amplified her beauty more than ever. The dress was wide open at the chest, presenting her ample bosom with such assertiveness that her sensuality tempted eyes to wander.

"...I'm extremely humbled and delighted by your invitation."

"'Tis no trouble. You are riding for my entertainment, nothing more. A minor amusement I am slipping in at the last minute."

"So I'm a super-outstanding servant here to serve as your entertainment for the evening? You're gonna make me cry."

As Subaru scoffed at the door, the seated master and servant traded glances with each other. The awkwardness had Subaru grinding his teeth by the time Al said to him, "Sit. We can't get this dragon carriage moving if you just keep standing there. Even if the blessing makes it not rock on the inside, it's a hell of a lot more comfortable sitting down. Besides, Princess hates being looked down upon."

"Indeed, you understand me rather well, Al. So, commoner, that is how it is. Sit down at once. If you continue to tower over me like this, I shall have your height reduced...by about half."

Since it really didn't sound like a joke, Subaru plopped down immediately. That instant, the dragon carriage started. The scenery outside the window moved gently. Very gently.

Al guessed what was on Subaru's mind, trying not to laugh as he said, "Appearances were prioritized at the cost of speed. Form over function. Easy to understand, yes?"

Subaru scratched his head at the way of thinking so different from the world he had come from, but the girl in the carriage prodded him, speaking in a fairly playful tone.

"So, peasant. What is the purpose of your riding in this dragon carriage?"

"Err... Uh? Purpose or not... It's because you told the guy there to invite me aboard, right?"

"No. That was the trigger, but not the reason. I am not asking you why you came here. I am asking you, what is your reason for *being* here?"

For a moment, Subaru refrained from a comeback as he searched for better words.

It burned him, but it clearly was not the time to get on the girl's bad side. She might just threw him out of the dragon carriage, but worst case, he'd be finding out what it was like to be on the business end of the sword on Al's hip.

Besides, she had chosen her question deliberately—not why he had come, but why he was there at all.

"...Because I need to go to the royal palace. That's why I'm in this carriage."

"Correct. That is your reason for being here. Put another way, so long as you carry that reason with you, you would be hunting for another way to get into the palace, even if you were not on this carriage, yes?"

Subaru lowered his head, unable to refute the girl's words.

"That's...right... Maybe I'd end up sneaking in on one of the rich folks' carriages."

So long as he could not accept "giving up" as an option, Subaru would have groped for a way to get into the royal palace by any means necessary, even if it meant sneaking in aboard a nobleman's vehicle. But as Al pointed out, "That's reckless talk. Even if you could normally, this is a real special day. The checks are gonna be a lot stricter. There's pretty much no way that'd work without help from guards at the garrison and people taking care of the carriages."

Naturally, Subaru had no connections with which to make such arrangements. No doubt he'd have completely failed if he had attempted such a plan without being prepared.

"If that's the case, getting invited here is a huge lifesaver, huh...?"

"So you boarded this dragon carriage because you aim to enter the royal palace. In other words, you believe this carriage is heading to the royal palace... There is no meaning in hiding it. Surely you are well aware of this."

"...Yeah, that's right... And if this isn't going there, let me off now because I'm on the wrong ride."

Al interrupted with a low chuckle.

"Sorry, this is a special express that won't stop until the fourth station down the line."

Subaru raised his eyebrows at the expression, but the girl continued before he could follow up. She glanced over at Subaru as she said, "Luckily for you, this dragon carriage is in fact heading to the royal palace... And do you understand why this dragon carriage is heading to the royal palace?"

"........."

"I pray you do not disappoint me by being a foolish commoner manipulated by the information before your eyes and fail to miss the obvious. If you are, that makes you a fool whose life bears no value. —Answer with care."

As Subaru swallowed his breath, the girl uncrossed her legs and sat up. She sat with her legs off to the side, her back straight and deep in her seat as she gazed at Subaru and asked, "Why is this dragon carriage heading toward the royal palace?"

"This dragon carriage's...heading toward the royal palace, because..."

Held captive by those two red eyes, Subaru felt his stomach squeezing. The extreme pressure rolling off the girl no doubt would make the weak of spirit buckle then and there.

She was a proud girl who spoke and acted like she viewed the entire world from a position above it. She had an obedient servant and a luxuriant dragon carriage. These formed the outline, and when Subaru added the final piece, the puzzle was complete.

There was only one possible answer.

"...Because you're participating in the royal selection. This carriage is carrying a candidate."

"—My. In other words, you do understand."

"...You're one of the candidates fighting for the throne of the Kingdom of Lugunica, aren't you?"

At Subaru's reply, the girl narrowed her blood-colored eyes and let loose a bloodcurdling, sadistic laugh.

"—Al."

"Right, right, understood. It's what you figured, bro. This young

lady is a candidate for the royal succession of the Kingdom of Lugunica. —This is Lady Priscilla Bariel."

Al called the leisurely posing girl Priscilla—a name he spoke with
reverence.

Priscilla nodded in satisfaction at her servant's words before looking at Subaru.

"One might argue that even a fool would have answered thusly
after being provided with so many hints. Regardless, you may rest at
ease. At the very least, you have avoided an immediate shedding of
your blood."

"Well, I'm relieved, too. This thing may be huge, but I don't think
we'd ever get the smell of blood and guts out of it."

"I would simply arrange a new carriage in that case. Worry less
about such trivial things and more about my mood."

"A petty bourgeois like me just can't understand a princess's sense
of money."

Priscilla and Al engaged in casual master-servant banter. As
Subaru watched, he subtly let out a long sigh.

He'd hazarded a guess when they'd parted ways the day before.
Without doubt, Priscilla's haughtiness marked her as someone from
society's upper class, telling him she had a strong pedigree. But what
had really settled it was Emilia's reaction.

Emilia had been fearful of coming into contact with Priscilla in
spite of the robe she wore meant to conceal her identity. If Priscilla
was Emilia's political rival, it all fell into place.

In that light, the fact she'd invited Subaru aboard the dragon carriage meant…

"You knew who I was with yesterday, then?"

"It would seem she attempted to conceal herself with some
pathetic rags. The way she hid in a nook along the street suited her
public image very nicely."

"Why, you. There's things you say and things you don't…"

Subaru was unable to conceal his indignation at Priscilla's mockery of Emilia.

"Hey, lay off, bro. I only just got her to chill out on the spilling blood stuff."

It took only an instant. As Subaru stood up, Al drew his crescent sword and touched the thick of the blade against the bottom of Subaru's chin. One step farther and Subaru's head would roll from his shoulders.

Al continued, "You get how Princess is by now, right? That's her default mode, so just be the bigger man and accept it. If you don't… Well, you chose wrong."

"For a one-armed guy, you're pretty handy with that thing."

"I've lived longer with one than with two. People adapt."

Unable to see Al's face to judge whether he was joking, Subaru clicked his tongue and backed off a step. Accepting this, Al twirled his razor-sharp weapon and returned it to its sheath. Subaru sat back down in his seat and calmed himself.

He scowled as Al's helmet made a satisfied shake, rubbing salt into his wounds. Subaru gazed at him and broached the subject that had been nagging him all this time.

"Is it too rude for me to ask where you lost that arm of yours?"

He was pointing at Al's left arm, the most distinctive thing about him. *If he has trouble answering for once, I wouldn't mind*, he thought.

—But that spurred a turn of events far different than he had expected.

"Sure, I can see why it'd bug you. It was my baptism to a whole different world. You know what I mean, don't you, bro?"

"—Ah?"

Subaru had meant to gain some measure of revenge upon him, but the unexpected truth washed that thought away. He stared in abject shock while Al toyed with the gap of his helm with his left hand and tilted his head a bit.

"Wha, don't tell me you didn't notice by now? I'm the only one who knows what you're going through, bro."

"—Huh?"

Subaru let out a breath as his eyes opened as wide as plates. Al's

words had frozen his thoughts stiff. With his brain blanking out, he was at a complete loss for words.

The boy raised a hand, his head feeling dizzy as he chewed over the implications.

"Wait... Wait. Understand what I'm going... You're, ah, really?"

"Can't really blame you for doubting me. I couldn't believe my ears yesterday. That stuff about how even chance meetings are the results of karma, the red threads... Haven't heard those quotes in eighteen years."

"Eighteen...?!"

That outrageous length of time caused Subaru's voice to catch in his throat. In real time, he had only been summoned one month prior. But if what Al said was true...

"That's right, bro. It's been eighteen years since I got summoned here. I lost my arm around the same time... Right around the age you are right now."

Just like that, Al confessed to Subaru that he'd experienced the same situation. However, Subaru was far from overjoyed at having so easily found someone like him. Al had spent eighteen entire years in that place knocked the wind right out of him.

"Did you ever find out...how, or anything...?"

"What, how I lost my arm, or the summoning? If it's the arm, it was when I didn't know right from left here. It was a plain, ordinary mistake. If you mean the summoning... I still don't know."

"—"

"It's not like I've looked under every rock for the reason I got called to this world... I've been working my ass off to survive."

So Al truly had lived eighteen years in another world. Being blessed with a relationship like Subaru's with Emilia wasn't common. It really did hit close to home: He could very easily have lost an arm or spent his days desperately trying to live, forgetting all about the time. It was by good fortune that Subaru Natsuki was not walking a path quite that bleak.

Priscilla's haughty behavior shattered the gloomy silence that fell over the carriage.

"You two men and your glum faces are dulling the luster of my dragon carriage. From what I have heard, 'tis all trifling issues of the past. Even those clownish tall tales about your homeland beyond the Great Waterfalls make for a more amusing conversation for me."

"Beyond the Great Waterfalls…?"

"Do you not know? At the ends of the maps of the continent, the land ceases at the four corners of the world, with all washed away by great cascades of water—in other words, the Great Waterfalls. From time to time, there are rumors of people who have come from beyond them, such as you and Al. Most are simple nonsense… But Al is different."

"—! Why do you think that? Do you have some kind of concrete reason to think…?"

"—Intuition."

It wasn't what Subaru expected, but the response fit Priscilla perfectly.

"Understand? Nothing happens in this world that is not convenient for me. In other words, my intuition is not a reason, for I require none. It is an answer all by itself. Al is a buffoon of a different breed than the other vulgar peasants and their nonsense. And…it would seem that you are, as well."

"You're unbelievable… Does it really benefit you for me, someone related to your political rival, to ride on the same dragon carriage as you?"

Even if her words were consistent, her actions were not. That was what Subaru was trying to get at. However, Priscilla smiled at him like a carnivore surveying her prey.

"…How about this? I take you, someone related to my political rival, hostage and use you to blackmail her into abandoning the royal selection. Or, I deliver her your head and threaten her by telling her that she is next. Either way, 'tis a simple matter, is it not?"

"—"

Priscilla rolled her tongue around in delight at how Subaru's eyes widened in distress.

It was a possibility he had not even imagined until that very moment. The reason for this was simple: Subconsciously, he didn't think he was valuable enough to capture as a hostage to bait Emilia.

"Your face says that is beyond what you anticipated. That makes you an even greater buffoon, yes?"

Subaru hadn't even considered the risk he could become a liability to Emilia. Priscilla clapped her hands as if she were making sport of her own, hand-raised pet.

"Judging from your eyes, you have taken the girl's side for reasons of passion. Your mad emotions have clouded your vision, making you neglect what lies at your feet... No words exist to describe your foolishness."

Subaru was unable to even let out an *ugh* as he wilted before Priscilla. He'd meant to rush to Emilia's side because he wanted to help her, to be there for her, but that had turned into a tragicomic farce.

Al interjected, "Hey, Princess, he's from my homeland. Don't tease him too much, okay?"

Priscilla shrugged her shoulders as a look of tedium came over her.

"I am not berating him, whatsoever. This peasant has realized his oversights and fallen into despair and gloom all by himself. —It bores me. You need not overthink things, commoner. Had I intended to use you in that manner, I would have had you dismembered in the street yesterday. That I have not done so, and invited you to ride within my dragon carriage, makes my intentions crystal clear, does it not?"

"...Whether you're taking me hostage or not isn't where my self-loathing's coming from... I'm pathetic for not having thought of it. —And why *did* you get me to ride this thing, anyway?"

Subaru couldn't help but think that many of his actions had rebounded on Emilia. Priscilla's declarations might have been hard to listen to, but they'd merely brought the facts to his attention. However harsh the lesson, it was the truth.

When Subaru turned a questioning gaze toward Priscilla, she altered her position again, resting her chin on a hand.

"I have told you already. You are here for my entertainment. I think it will be more amusing to bring you to the royal selection assembly than to use you as a hostage or for threats. That is my decision."

Subaru was taken aback by her completely unexpected thought process. To this, Priscilla yawned.

"Everything in this world exists to convenience me. Furthermore, I shall decide the course of whatever I please. Whatever I decide, it shall be. Therefore, all I need to do is decide what will entertain me, and what will not. There is no inconvenience to me."

"—"

With Subaru still dazed, the girl closed her eyes, declining to discuss the matter further. Judging from her posture and demeanor, she intended to nap until the time of their arrival.

Given there was a meeting crucial to the royal selection in under an hour, it was truly bold.

When Subaru looked Al's way, the guardian raised one hand to indicate subservience to his carefree master again, sinking soundlessly into his seat. Subaru was unsure whether he should do similarly and settle in for the long haul when Priscilla added, "If there is one reason beyond my amusement…"

"Eh—?"

"The abbles."

After those two words to a thoroughly dumbfounded Subaru, Priscilla went silent entirely. Since her conduct made clear she would not permit him any questions or doubts, Subaru wracked his confused mind, finally coming up with a single possible answer. In other words, "The old guy at the fruit store saved my life, then…?"

He recalled that, for whatever reason, the shopkeeper had been involved in a large percentage of his exploits in the royal capital. The thought of having survived thanks to something so banal and trivial provided Subaru a brief respite from his self-loathing.

6

—The carriage arrived at the palace and entered through the main gates.

As Subaru walked straight up the front stairs, he felt painfully aware of just what a little fish he was in that ocean.

"Hey, um, am I all right here? To be honest, I'm so out of place it's kinda scary..."

Subaru looked down at his own outfit before glancing at Al, walking beside him.

"Well, yeah. We're basically party crashers. No question they aren't rolling out the red carpet for the two of us."

Al's ever-aloof attitude suggested he had no qualms about looking far more out of place than Subaru.

Apparently, his eighteen years in another world had washed away all concerns about dress codes.

Not only that, all eyes were on the girl walking before them—Priscilla—as she continued toward the central chamber. The corridor was decorated with paintings and other works of art, and guards in full armor lined it on the left and right, swords raised in salute.

Subaru had difficulty breathing under the pressure even though he wasn't the object of attention. In the meantime, they arrived at the end of the corridor. He raised his eyes to see an enormous pair of double doors before them.

"Soldiers lining the corridor, huge doors..."

The sight of the closed doors overwhelmed him with its grandeur. He felt himself standing straighter just from being in its presence, his discomfort reaching a fever pitch.

As Priscilla led the party onward, a fully armored soldier in front of the door took a step forward, saluting her with his sword. He removed his great helm and looked over Priscilla and the others with an intellectual air.

"We have been expecting you, Lady Priscilla."

The man was around forty years old, give or take, with an expression that was not so much tough as stern. His face was as austere as an image carved into a boulder, giving off the air of a man who'd seen plenty of combat.

Priscilla replied to his salute with a haughty nod and turned her head slightly toward Subaru and Al.

"They are with me. One is my knight, and the other...my abble boy."

"Hey...!"

Subaru immediately started to refute Priscilla, but stopped very quickly when he realized that such a thing was impermissible in that place. The knight's face didn't even twitch.

"—Abble boy, is it?"

"Yes, abble boy. He is a type of clown, bearing the exalted duty of providing me with red, bittersweet abbles. He is harmless. Surely you do not mind?"

Without replying to the imperious Priscilla, the knight appraised Subaru and Al as his blue eyes faintly twinkled.

"I cannot detect any dangerous magic. That sword is the only one you carry, sir knight?"

".........Oh, by 'knight' you mean me. Yes, yes, that's right. If I see any dark-haired, mustache-twirling villains around, I'll chop 'em in half with one hand."

"Should an incident occur, please concentrate on protecting your master, Lady Priscilla, and leave the rest to us guards."

With his casual banter brushed off, Al halfheartedly replied, "Sure thing." The man dipped his head and shifted his gaze toward the huge doors, which slowly began to open.

"Everyone is already waiting inside, so with all haste..."

"I am superior, so it is fitting that the masses wait for me. The reverse is impermissible, however."

Entirely self-absorbed, Priscilla stepped through the door, all eyes still on her. Seeing Al follow her without hesitation, Subaru firmed up his resolve and entered as well.

—As his view expanded, he found himself in an enormous room with a red carpet covering it.

The glittering adornments on the walls were illuminated by extravagant lighting hanging from the high ceiling. The room had few places to sit considering its size, though a small set of steps led to chairs on the far side of the chamber. There were five seats from left to right, and what stood out most was the one seat in the center.

Resting against a wall, the innermost chair was fashioned into the form of a dragon, as if to show that he who rested in that chair shouldered the dragon upon his own back, while being protected by it in turn.

It was a classical throne room of a royal palace. Meaning that chair had to be the throne of the King of Lugunica.

After the throne caught his attention, Subaru timidly looked around the rest of the chamber.

Unlike the exterior, he couldn't see a single sword-carrying guard. Instead, he saw rows of elite troops dressed in white-themed uniforms with knights' swords at their hips—the Knights of the Royal Guard.

Farther within was a group of apparent civil officials in ceremonial dress, all men of high rank based on their appearance. Their dignified faces suited a throne room.

And at the center of the room, removed from the cluster of knights and nobles, a small group of people stood in a line. And among them was—

A silver-haired girl. When she saw the three people entering through the large doors, she called out with obvious surprise.

"—Subaru?"

Her wide-open violet eyes wavered with bewilderment, like she was unable to believe that Subaru was there. Inundated with Emilia's shock and surprise, Subaru's heart beat so loudly it hurt.

Now that he knew Emilia was there, he felt joy, but also guilt at having betrayed her to get there. In spite of all the thoughts and feelings that had spurred him into action, he was at a complete loss for words in front of her quivering eyes.

"Er, Emilia, I..."

"—"

Even though this was what he had sought, words just wouldn't come out. Emilia's gaze wandered over Subaru as she, too, searched for words, but her lips were drawn tight. Neither of them broke the silence, but rather a voice and bump from behind...

"What are you doing staring at my servant, you imbecile?"

"—Err."

The touch against his back was frighteningly soft. The arms that wrapped around his chest and neck were outright bewitching. Priscilla, pressing against him from behind, rested her chin upon

Subaru's shoulder so that they gazed at Emilia together, their faces side by side.

"What are...! G-get off! Emilia-tan's gonna get the wrong idea!"

"The wrong idea? Do the bonds between you and I not form a deep and intimate relationship? I permit it. Come close."

"I didn't give you those bonding abbles to have you use them for nefarious purposes!"

As Priscilla teased, Subaru extricated himself from her and put distance between them. The apparent rejection prompted Priscilla to stomp a heel, narrowing her eyes in displeasure.

But before any unrest could break out, the familiar voice of a man with delicate features intervened.

"My, oh myyy. Lady Priscilla, I am dreadfully sorry for the trouble my house's servant has caused you. And you even cared for him after he became lost in the castle... Please forgive this terrible rudeness."

Before Subaru knew it, Roswaal, the character with long, violet hair, was standing beside him with a dubious smile, wearing a formal uniform with a maple emblem unrelated to his status as Court Magician.

"And so the swindler steps forward. I have no recollection of such a thing. I picked up that peasant myself... And do you have proof that he is any servant of yours?"

Priscilla had a crafty comeback. However, Roswaal greeted her question with a shrug.

"Fortuuunately, I do. I have looong been in the practice of marking that which is mine. My family crest should be sewed into the liiining of his uniform."

"——"

Priscilla's face went blank. She looked at Subaru as if seeking confirmation of the tale. Under her gaze, Subaru turned up the sleeve of his coat and saw that there was indeed something resembling an embroidered hawk in the lining. He showed Priscilla the embroidery as well, to which she responded with a short snort.

"A cheap trick. Well, fine. Toying with the clown and the imbecile has driven away much of my tedium along the way—And besides, my vassal asked it of me."

"Princess, you promised not to mention that p..."

"Do not be concerned about little things. You'll never grow taller otherwise."

"You shouldn't expect a guy pushin' forty to be growing anyway..."

Priscilla silenced Al with a glance before striding forward, not paying Subaru the slightest heed. She was heading toward the gathering at the center of the room near Emilia.

Emilia stiffened when Priscilla walked close, but the orange-haired girl passed by without paying her the slightest heed. Emilia slumped her shoulders at being ignored before turning back toward Subaru.

"But I must saaay, that you were found by Lady Priscilla along the way... Your jinx is truly quiiite something. I wonder what might have haaappened to you if she had not been the one to find you."

"The hell? You're not trying to tell me that peacock is famous for her vast benevolence and compassion, are you?"

"Oh, nooo. I simply thought that the others might have haaad you imprisoned or cut down then and theeere. In that sense, Lady Priscilla gave you equal odds of survival, depending upon her mood."

"Yeah, I get that I'm walking quite a tightrope here... You're...not upset?"

With Roswaal speaking to him like it was nothing, Subaru timidly posed the question.

"Why would I be? After all, I was thiiinking that you might show up. And in truth, you have arrived. It would seem that the family creeest upon your uniform was of some value midway."

"Midway...? Er, not really, I thought I was ninety percent likely to kick the bucket just now, but..."

Subaru inclined his head at the odd choice of words, but it was Roswaal's face that registered surprise.

"You were not stopped when entering the castle? Then just hooow did you get in to begin with?"

"That selfish princess picked me up outside the castle. Er, it's a pretty long story…"

They spoke past each other, each with a different understanding of the situation. But before Subaru could bridge the gap, he realized that Emilia was walking resolutely over to him.

"Why…?"

"—"

With a single earnest word, Emilia conveyed the full gamut of conflicting emotions swirling inside her. Her *why*, with the many doubts within it, made Subaru's breath catch.

"How did you…? No, why. Why are you here, Subaru?"

"That's…going to be a long story… I suppose I could sum it up in one word, but…"

"Don't make light of this. Subaru, I told you. I told you, didn't I? Don't you remember…?"

The way Emilia repeated her words for emphasis made Subaru shut his mouth and avert his eyes. She was, of course, referring to the promise he'd made with her at the inn—the promise to wait for her that he had broken.

On the one hand, he had indeed broken that promise. But on the other, it was no lie he had gone out of concern for Emilia. And so, relying on a series of coincidences, he had arrived for her sake.

He wanted her to at least trust his motivation. But before Subaru could clarify how he felt inside, a clear voice echoed from in front of the throne.

"—All have been assembled. The Council of Elders may enter."

The great doors opened once more. The armored knight stationed at the door led a group of old men filing into the chamber. All the men wore robes identifying their station. Each solemn stride made plain that these were men of great dignity and experience.

The one who stood out the most was a white-haired man with a beard so long it nearly touched the ground. Though his back was not stooped, he stood almost a head shorter than Subaru. Even among the others, the deep wrinkles of his face made him seem especially old, but his eyes were sharp enough to cut steel.

As Subaru observed the silent procession, he remarked to Roswaal with a whisper, "The Council of Elders, that's the people running the kingdom in place of a king, right?"

Roswaal shrugged and stated with extreme disrespect, "Formally they are an adviiisory body, but yes. Matters of state currently rest in the Council of Elders's hands... But having said that, it is not reaaally much different from when the royal family still existed."

It sounded like the Council had been holding the reins since the rule of the previous monarch, apparently a man of little talent in public affairs.

Al, silent until that point, motioned with his chin toward a section with Knights of the Royal Guard neatly lined up.

"It's time, bro. We need to line up over there, not over here."

Those assembled had naturally sorted themselves out, with knights and officers on the left, and civil officials and nobility on the right.

"Seems like it, but is it all right for me to line up over there?"

Roswaal replied, "The proper thing to do would be to immeee-diately throw you out of the castle, but as this will be amusing, you may go with him."

Emilia's eyebrows shot up at Roswaal's attitude. She approached to object.

"Roswaal, wait a...!"

"Unfortunately, Lady Emilia, this is not the time or place for you to argue. If all the facts become clear, Subaru will be staying here... for a very, veeery long time."

"But if we let Subaru stand over there, he'll—"

"The time for argument is at an end, Lady Emilia. The conference is beginning. To the center..."

Roswaal's face tensed as he gazed at the seats around the throne, being filled by the Council of Elders that very moment. The only vacant seat left was the throne of the king at the heart of the chamber.

And in front of the old men of the Council was a tidy line of people who had given off a special aura since the moment of their birth.

The girl with orange hair was at the top of the list of three girls with magnificent posture, conspicuous and vibrant. Standing in the center, Priscilla put a hand on her hip and pushed her shoulders back, causing her skirt to sway slightly. Even before the elders that governed the nation, she still had that belittling look on her face.

To Priscilla's right stood a girl dressed in clothes resembling an army uniform. The color of her hair was such a deep green it nearly seemed black, but upon closer inspection, the glossy luster definitely reflected green. Her long hair was tied at the end by a white ribbon. Her beautiful, dignified face was trained straight ahead. She was tall for a girl, about the same height as Subaru, but their legs were very different lengths. On her hip, she wore a sword bearing a family crest with a lion baring its fangs. She looked like a beautiful girl disguised as a handsome man.

And in contrast to the green-haired girl's serious ambiance, the girl to Priscilla's left with light violet hair exuded a serene image. Her wavy hair fell down to the middle of her back, looking cottony soft. She was short compared to the other two girls and wore a white dress made with generous amount of fur. Particularly eye-catching were the white fox muffler and the ridiculously large purse at her hip.

All were beautiful, projecting a particular unique aura. They were clearly cut from a different cloth.

Emilia bit her lip in regret, delivering Subaru a reminder before trotting back to the line of girls.

"—We will discuss this later."

When Emilia lined up with the others, her silver hair dancing about, her attire definitely seemed a step behind everyone else's. However, the loveliness within excelled above all the others, at least according to Subaru.

"In other words, they're the future royal candidates for the selection… Huh?"

All the participants were girls, Emilia included. As he realized this with surprise, the people around him began moving one after another. Subaru followed Al's lead and headed toward the lined-up

Knights of the Royal Guard. As he did so, a certain red-haired, handsome young man standing at the head of the knights, greeted Subaru with a bright, friendly smile.

"—So you did come, Subaru."

It was Reinhard. The agreeable young man apparently hadn't forgotten him in the last month. He still had flaming red hair and eyes as blue as if very sky had been trapped in them. The only change was that he was wearing a formal royal guard uniform. He added, "When I heard that Lady Emilia would be attending, I wondered if you might show up."

"That's a crazy-high appraisal of me on your part, isn't it...? I thought the main image you had of me was pathetically crying for help and getting sliced open..."

Reinhard replied to Subaru without the faintest trace of sarcasm.

"I think you underestimate your own virtues. You, of course, protected Lady Emilia from a wicked blade, but you also made virtuous choices in other areas as well."

He shrugged good-naturedly. Even that gesture was perfectly polished, and Subaru couldn't help but be a jealous.

And so Subaru stood to Reinhard's side, and Al to his. Just as he realized that they were in the front row among the knights in a very prominent position, he heard the overly friendly call of a cat-eared girl, accompanied by a playful smile and a wave...

"Subawu, it is you!"

It was the messenger girl who'd triggered their trip to the royal capital. Subaru was a little surprised to see her standing with the knights, dressed in a female uniform for the Royal Guard, complete with a skirt.

And standing by the cat-eared girl's side, giving him a silent nod, was none other than Julius.

"Subaru, what's with that scowl all of a sudden?" Reinhard asked.

"In my homeland, they teach you to make this face when you look at an insect called *archnemesis*."

Reinhard attempted to smile as Subaru tried to hide the disgust making itself plain on his face.

"I hope you don't take this personally, Julius. It would seem Subaru does this to make a more humble first impression on people."

"No, there's no deeper meaning here. Can you not make me out to be sneakier than I am?"

Reinhard ascribed uncomfortably great praise to Subaru's words and deeds, so Subaru shot him down immediately. Julius, in response stroked his hair back as he said, "I do not mind, Reinhard. It is the duty of a knight to behave in a manner befitting his station. —I am Julius Juukulius of the Knights of the Royal Guard. It is a pleasure to make your acquaintance…and that of the good knight beside you."

After his pompous introduction, Julius tried to draw Al into the conversation. Without much energy, Al replied, "Aw, don't get stuck on formalities, okay? Stop calling me good knight or sir knight or whatever. I'm, whatchamacallit—a common cutthroat. I'm not one of the high and mighty like you."

Subaru reflexively raised an eyebrow at his behavior. He'd thought Al was the type to get along with anybody, so his attitude toward Julius was unexpected.

But unfortunately, there was no time left for a follow-up.

"—The gentlemen of the Council of Elders and the candidates have been assembled. If I may be so bold, I, captain of the Knights of the Royal Guard, Marcus, shall oversee these proceedings."

"Mmmm… Very well, please do."

Still at his seat, the one who crossed his arms and made a faint nod was named Miklotov. Marcus, captain of the knights, nodded and presented a solemn expression to all assembled.

"I have an important announcement to make to this assembly for the election of the next ruler…for the royal selection. It is for this purpose I have gathered the Council of Elders and called you all the way to the palace."

Marcus's voice was not especially loud, yet it reverberated so that everyone in the throne room could hear. The captain of the knights had a voice fitting his title, one that marked him as a man destined from birth to lead others.

"Half a year ago...beginning with the late king, the members of the royal family passed away in rapid succession. Any kingdom lacking a king is in crisis, but it is an especially grave matter for the Dragonfriend Kingdom of Lugunica, deeply related to the Covenant."

The Covenant—apparently this indicated the pact between the kingdom and the Dragon.

He'd heard the term in fairy tales and in conversations at Roswaal Manor several times. However, just like the royal selection itself, there were numerous details that remained unclear to him. In that sense, Subaru was grateful for how the conference was unfolding.

"The kingdom's relationship with the Dragon began several centuries prior. The king of that time, His Highness, Falseil Lugunica, and Holy Dragon Volcanica formed a covenant between them. Since that time, the kingdom has been rescued from crisis by the Dragon several times over, preserving it and its prosperity."

"Holy Dragon Volcanica is extremely faithful, with a deep sense of duty. Even many generations later, he has continued to protect us from beyond the Great Waterfalls far away."

As Marcus delivered his solemn speech, Miklotov stroked his beard and nodded.

"Mmmm. Furthermore, the continuance of the royal family is deeply related to maintaining the Covenant. This makes the loss of all members of the royal bloodline to plague an especially regretful matter. A Dragon Maiden is required to begin the next era without a moment to spare."

"Renewal of the Covenant through the Dragonfriend Ceremony, a meeting of the minds with the Dragon, requires a maiden that meets select criteria. This duty was shouldered by succeeding generations of the royal family, but now we seek another to carry it."

Keeping the emotions in his voice as restrained as possible, Marcus faced the Council of Elders sitting on the dais and touched a hand against his chest.

"For this purpose, we, the Knights of the Royal Guard, upon the command of the Council of Elders, have undertaken the duty of locating maidens selected by the light of the Dragon Jewels."

Marcus slid his hand into a pocket. Upon his palm, he raised up a gemstone with a tiny emblem upon it. It was one Subaru had seen many times, for it marked those qualified to participate in the royal selection.

"Everyone, present your Dragon Jewels—"

The girls responded, presenting their own emblems.

Instantly, the throne room was bathed in a vivid glow from the jewels bearing the insignia. The one in Emilia's hand was red, and each other emblem dazzled the room with a different color.

The knights sighed in wonder. Even the wrinkled faces of the Council of Elders showed a faint sign of relief.

"As you can see, each of these candidates is qualified to become a Dragon Maiden. Having beheld this fact, we shall do as commanded by the Dragon Tablet and…"

The solemn proceedings came to a halt at a soft voice.

"…Excuse me?"

As Marcus's breath caught, a girl in front of him bearing a twinkling blue Dragon Jewel inclined her head. She had violet-hair and wore a white dress.

"I understand the captain wants to tell his story, but as folks say in Kararagi, time is money."

In contrast to her gentle tone and docile face, her request was as straight and to the point as a fastball. She put her Dragon Jewel away and smiled softly.

"If you're repeatin' what we already know anyway, I'd rather hear more about why we're here."

The demand by the girl with a peculiar accent seemed to rock Marcus back on his heels. But Subaru was rocked to a far greater degree.

"Hey, wait a… No way, that's Kansai dialect?"

Al, standing next to Subaru, could only whisper back in sympathy to Subaru's murmur.

"Oh, first time you've heard it, bro? Apparently they all talk like that in the Kararagi area to the west. I mean, I've never seen the place myself, but the way they talk sure stands out."

To him, hailing from the same homeland as Subaru, Kansai dialect should have been familiar to him. The way he phrased things put Subaru off a little, but he suddenly became very curious about what this Kararagi land to the west was like.

The next girl over said, with a clear voice that echoed across the surprised occupants of the throne room, "She has a point."

As the violet-haired girl crossed her arms and tucked in her chin, the green-haired girl offered her agreement. Marcus appealed to her, "Lady Crusch, the head of the House of Karsten should not be..."

"Formalities may be important, but we don't have all the time in the world. We should touch upon the reason for our being gathered as quickly as possible. In fact, I have largely guessed already."

The girl Marcus addressed as Crusch closed one eye, surveying the Council of Elders with the others. Miklotov let out a sigh of admiration.

"As expected of the Duchess of Karsten. So you already understand the meaning of this gathering?"

"Yes, Lord Miklotov. —A banquet, yes? We shall eventually be rivals, but there is still much we do not know about each other. By sitting us at the same table to exchange toasts, we may gain some understanding of the character of our competitors..."

Crusch had decided the occasion was a particularly formal banquet when Miklotov interrupted.

"No, that is not the case."

The girl raised her eyebrows at his reply and slowly turned toward Subaru and the others.

"Ferris, this is not what you told me."

"Oh no. All Ferri said was that they're bringing lots of food and wine into the castle so *maybe* they're going to have a banquet. Oopsie."

"I see, I assumed too much. I'm sorry for doubting you."

It was an odd kind of master-servant banter, without much affection.

Crusch faced the front again, letting out a small sigh as she put that brief conversation behind her.

"And so, with some embarrassment, I take back my previous statement."

"Oh my, Lady Crusch, you're being way too manly...!"

The girl named Ferris put a hand to her cheek with an air of concern. Apparently, she wasn't particularly bothered that she'd leaked false information to her master. Given her current reaction, Subaru felt she'd done it on purpose.

The girl speaking in Kansai dialect clapped her hands in search of agreement from the other candidates.

"Hey now. Just because Crusch backed off doesn't mean my opinion's changed. Everyone knows the gist of this royal selection thing by now, right?"

Crusch nodded in reply to the question, but Priscilla rudely blew it off with a small snort. Then, Emilia raised her hand a little.

"I think th-that we should listen to the full story."

But the girl's treatment of Emilia was altogether too cruel.

"Sorry, but I'm not asking your opinion here."

As if she had been struck by the hostility, pain ran across Emilia's profile. Subaru couldn't bear to watch.

"Why, you, what's with that attit—"

As Subaru bellowed angrily, Al stepped in front of him from the side, raising his arm up high.

"Yeah! I don't know about this royal selection business, so I want to hear the rest and stuff!"

As all eyes gathered on Al's buffoonish behavior, he comically waved his hand to further establish his harmlessness.

"Hey, don't look at me like that, I'm gonna blush. I know I'm really out of place, so don't treat me like some suspicious intruder or something. You're gonna drive a middle-aged man to tears."

Marcus seemed to be the only one keeping his complete cool.

"Lady Priscilla, your knight has requested it, but...would you like to hear the explanation about the royal selection?"

Priscilla fanned the flames in a grandiose tone.

"Whether I desire it or not, you love your long-winded stories all on your own. It is a waste of time to me. Repeated words are no different than nonsense. I do not even speak nonsense in my sleep."

In contrast to the selfish bearings of the others assembled, Emilia's good character stood out. But it was clear from the earlier exchange she was not being treated fairly.

Al said to him, "—That's one you owe me. No, two now?"

With Al holding up two fingers and tilting his head toward the younger boy, Subaru was grateful on the inside. It was scary to even think about what would've happened if he'd continued and blown a gasket. Al had taken all the blame on himself in Subaru's place.

Priscilla continued, "By my grace, we shall follow the commoner's view. Rejoice and dance upon my palm. Continue, Marcus. Tell my knight how I shall become monarch."

The violet-haired girl slumped her shoulders and threw in the towel at Priscilla's demeanor.

"It's really somethin' how you pass the buck onto everyone else. I'm just gonna keep my mouth shut."

With a consensus seemingly forming, Marcus looked at Emilia and Crusch, with both nodding as well.

"Very well, with that brief digression finished, I shall return to the topic. —You who are qualified to become Dragon Maidens are assembled here because of the prophecy carved into the Dragon Tablet. This prophecy states, 'Should the Covenant of Lugunica lapse, the nation shall be guided by she who forms a bond with the Dragon anew.'"

Miklotov replied, "Mmmm. The words on the tablet are providence itself. The Dragon Tablet, with a history at least as long as that of the Covenant, contains the words by which the fate of the kingdom shall be decided. Considering the impact of these details upon subsequent history, surely it is our duty to obey them."

The other members of the Council of Elders solemnly nodded in response to Miklotov's words. Marcus continued, "The Dragon Tablet, handed down by Holy Dragon Volcanica, has guided our kingdom's path since the days of yore. They have provided the land with advance warning of various crises, from the Great Cuedegra Famine and the Nightmare of Blight Dragon Balgren, to the onslaught of the Black Serpent in recent years, enabling us to minimize the damage incurred."

"Mmmm. There is no need to continue listing these achievements. They are known to all present."

The aforementioned achievements were likely major affairs in the kingdom's history, but they didn't ring a bell with Subaru, ignorant as he was. He thought that a prophecy letting you plan for upcoming events was a pretty nice thing to have.

Either way, apparently Emilia and the other candidates, or rather, maidens able to communicate with the Dragon, had been gathered in accordance with this prophecy.

In a quiet voice, Subaru raised a doubt he'd been harboring with Reinhard beside him.

"I just thought of this, but if the problem's just the Covenant with the Dragon, the Dragon Maiden doesn't actually have to become queen, right? Can't you have the ruler and the maiden be separate?"

The corners of Reinhard's lips rose in a strained smile.

"I think you have a valid point, Subaru. But it can't be done."

"Mind if I ask why not?"

"Because the Covenant for the prosperity of the kingdom is formed between the Dragon and the king. The Dragon isn't simply choosing someone able to communicate with. The pact is formed because that person is carrying a kingdom on his shoulders. In other words, the Dragon is very particular about his partners."

"But if that's the case, won't rushing a maiden into a monarch just annoy the Dragon more? It's, like, I close my eyes for one moment and poof, the king is gone, and here's a maiden to take the place of the king. Would the Dragon go for that?"

"That's a fairly strong argument. But in the end, the Dragon Tablet upon which the fate of the kingdom is engraved takes precedence. That is what the Council of Elders has decided, and they have commanded us knights accordingly. I want to think that it was the right thing to do."

Even if he had doubts, the higher-ups had settled the issue. The only one who knew how the Dragon would judge was the Dragon himself. It was truly as Ram had said: Only the Dragon knows.

With one issue having been settled, Marcus's voice echoed across the quieted gathering.

"The prophecy continues thus: 'There shall be five able to lead a new nation. Of these, one shall be selected as the maiden to form a new Covenant with the Dragon.'"

Hearing that sentence from the prophecy, something tugged at Subaru's mind and made him frown.

"Five…?"

"Yes, five. Currently there are only four candidates—so the royal selection has not even begun yet. It is our shame that we have been unable to find a fifth."

"Your population's, like, fifty million people, right? Finding four in half a year sounds downright speedy."

They had to search for people on a world without any national transportation networks. Those were pretty harsh conditions. Subaru thought finding four candidates in such a short time was worthy of serious praise.

Marcus finished his explanation, apologizing to the girl who'd raised the initial objection to his carrying on.

"That summarizes the present circumstances. Lady Anastasia, please forgive my great rudeness."

"Don't, don't. This mess isn't my fault. Happy now, Princess?"

"I wonder. Al, has your little head gained any new insights?"

"Yeah, I've got it. Sorry for makin' ya go through the trouble. Sorry to the lil' lady from Kararagi, too."

As Al flippantly waved with his one arm, Priscilla replied, "There you have it." The girl—Anastasia—rubbed her forehead at the irresponsible master and servant and looked back up to the Council of Elders.

"Anyway, if there's still more, can we get on with it? I don't have forever, and I got a lot to do later. You old men with the purse strings get what I'm sayin', right?"

The rudeness of Anastasia's statement stirred the room up, and Subaru stiffened. But Anastasia seemed to have a very good read on her position, and the Council of Elders showed no sign of irritation.

Abruptly, Miklotov lowered his voice.

"It pains me to take so much of your busy time, Lady Anastasia, but I must ask you to remain with the conference a little longer. After all…this day shall be marked in the history of the kingdom."

Though the room had gradually lost its original tension, the statement triggered an ambiance that compelled everyone to stand a little straighter.

And moving the proceedings forward was Priscilla, pushing out her chest without a single ounce of shame.

"So history shall move, you say, old fossils? In other words, you mean *that*, yes?"

Miklotov replied to Priscilla's quiet question with a small nod from his perch. Then, the eyes under his thick eyebrows sought Marcus. The look was some kind of signal, as Marcus saluted and suddenly bellowed across the chamber.

"—Knight Reinhard Astrea! Come!"

Subaru's shoulders trembled out of the blue as Reinhard, seemingly having waited for the call, replied, "Yes, sir!"

He advanced straight forward, saluting the four candidates before standing to attention before Marcus and the Council of Elders.

"Very well, Reinhard. Report!"

"Sir!"

Marcus took a step back and yielded the center of the platform. With all eyes upon him, Reinhard stepped forward and faced the Council of Elders without a single trace of timidity.

"Esteemed members of the Council of Elders, I am Reinhard van Astrea of the Knights of the Royal Guard, here to report that my mission is complete."

Miklotov instructed, "Mmmm. Say it so that all may hear."

Reinhard turned around, looking over everyone in the room.

"—We have finally found the fifth candidate to become Dragon Maiden, and monarch."

The ranks of knights stirred and formed a space between them. The expressions of the candidates changed, registering strong emotions: determination, delight, tedium, and bewilderment.

"Bring her in," Reinhard curtly called.

Receiving his command, two guards before the entrance saluted and slowly opened the doors. Beyond them a girl, accompanied by ladies-in-waiting, was led into the throne room.

When Subaru laid eyes upon her, his jaw instinctively dropped in absolute shock.

The hem of her light yellow dress fluttered as her high-heeled shoes stepped upon the carpet. Her scrupulously arranged blond hair practically sparkled. The girl was remarkable for the strong determination in her red eyes and the impish appearance of her snaggletooth smile.

She looked so different that he almost doubted what he was seeing. He couldn't help but be lost for words.

With Subaru paralyzed by surprise, the announcement seemed to echo against his eardrums several times over.

"This young lady who seeks the crown is called…Lady Felt."

—And so, the royal selection that would determine the fate of the Kingdom of Lugunica began.

CHAPTER 4

THE CANDIDATES FOR THE THRONE AND THEIR KNIGHTS

1

The wild-eyed girl with scruffy blond hair had worn, grimy old rags. She was a tempestuous girl of the slums, more grubby than hardy. That was the image of the girl named Felt in Subaru's mind.

As Reinhard made his declaration, the ladies-in-waiting quietly accompanied Felt as she walked into the throne room. Gracefully walking atop the red carpet, she looked like a nobleman's daughter.

Subaru had thought long before, *She might sparkle if someone polished her up.* But this unhewn stone, polished via the power of Reinhard's family, was not only sparkling. —Indeed, the only term to do her justice was *radiant.*

Felt slowly passed by Subaru's dumbfounded gaze and stood before Reinhard. He nodded with a charming smile at her appearance and addressed her with the utmost respect.

"Lady Felt, thank you for gracing us with your presence."

Felt raised her eyes and called out to him.

"—Reinhard."

Reinhard responded to her clear-as-a-bell voice.

"Yes?"

Knight and lady, their eyes met. And then…

"—Why you. What's the big idea, dragging me in here with no explanation?!"

...she raised the hem of her dress, her long, slender leg tracing an arc—an arc that was about to slam right into the tip of Reinhard's chin when the knight raised a hand, stopping it short.

"I am quite surprised. What brought this on so suddenly?"

Remaining balanced on one leg, Felt violently slapped at her dress in anger.

"Don't block me and then play dumb! It's this place! These clothes! Them! You! What the hell is going on here?! I can't take any more of this!"

It was an expensive dress, no doubt custom-ordered for her. Seeing it treated so roughly sent the ladies attending her wilting to the floor as if their eyes were spinning.

"You did not like the dress? I believe it looks very good on you."

"This isn't about the dress, and it's not that it's embarrassing! I'm saying that I hate it! And not just the dress! I hate you too! Don't you think abducting and holding a girl against her will is embarrassing for a knight of honor?!"

Reinhard declared without hesitation, "If it is for the prosperity of the kingdom, it must be done."

Felt put a hand to her forehead as if he was giving her a headache.

Subaru remarked to himself, "I'm so glad. I thought she'd completely changed, but it's only how she looks. I guess leopards really don't change their spots, and it isn't just me!"

It would've made a sorry story for Old Man Rom if he'd had to report back that she'd become a whole different person.

He was relieved at being able to confirm she was safe and sound in a place he never expected. On the other hand, he couldn't help but think Felt being dragged into becoming a royal candidate was prearranged rather than mere coincidence. After all, Reinhard had met her in the first place because she'd been the one to steal Emilia's badge...

Emilia, realizing who Felt was, had apparently reached the same conclusion as Subaru.

"That girl...from back then...?! That's why Reinhard was so surprised..."

From Emilia's point of view, Felt had gone from the thief of her badge to her rival for the very throne.

The other candidates, the knights, and the nobles all displayed appropriate reactions to the newcomer's crude behavior, none friendly. Under the austere stares, Felt clicked her tongue rudely.

In the short time Subaru had known her she'd never been this much of a brat. He guessed that it was a product of various things during the last month. Subaru had been through a lot, but her transformation from a street urchin to a royal candidate was a Cinderella story to rival his.

Felt was scanning the chamber to size up her surroundings when she suddenly noticed Subaru among the knights in the front row and brightened.

"Oh, hey! What are you doing here, mister?"

Felt shoved Reinhard away with a hand on his chest and walked over without a care.

Where did all that ladylike behavior go? Subaru wondered as he raised a hand, delighted to greet a friendly face.

"Hi, it's been a while. Looks like you're in good health!" said Felt.

The instant the sunny greeting escaped her lips, she kicked Subaru straight in the stomach, sending him crumbling to his knees.

Violence out of the blue. Subaru groaned, forcing himself up with one leg as Felt crossed her arms and nodded, remarking, "Looks like your belly's all healed up, but you've got a whole bunch of new scars in other places. You okay there?"

"If you're worried, take it easy on me, damn it...! What's with the hard smack instead of a hi? Geez, what if you'd broken something... It's not like it's been that long, either."

Even though the wound was now fully closed, Subaru had a big, white horizontal scar right across his belly. He had scars from demon beast bites all over his body, too.

He couldn't talk about scars on the back being the shame of a knight any longer.

Though calm and reserved on the surface, Marcus motioned toward the dais, wanting to continue the meeting's proceedings.

"Lady Felt, if you are finished greeting your old friend, could you please come this way?"

Felt scowled at the solemn look on his face, glowering as she stepped forward.

"So what do you want me to do here?"

Reinhard replied, "'Act more like a lady,' I would like to say, but instead, I would have you hold this."

Felt scowled at Reinhard's joke. Reinhard took a dragon emblem out of his pocket and deposited it in her palm. The gemstone immediately emitted a white light.

"I thought this back when I stole one of these, too, but these are strange rocks. Why do they glow?"

Felt had blithely said something very dangerous. Marcus seemed to notice her careless statement.

"Stealing?"

But Reinhard immediately followed up, "As you can see, the Dragon Jewel acknowledges Lady Felt as a maiden. Now that her participation has been confirmed, I believe that this royal selection now begins in a true sense."

Marcus put a hand to his chest and knelt down on one knee. Reinhard followed suit, then all the Knights of the Royal Guard.

The knights reported their mission was a success. Thanks to their efforts, five Dragon Maidens had been found—in other words, the candidates for the next queen of Lugunica had been assembled.

Priscilla remarked, "I see. Thus, this day will go down in history."

This was the very definition of a huge, must-see event. *Surely, everyone present had to be deeply moved by the occasion*, or so Subaru thought as he watched—and noticed that, for their part, the government officials appeared troubled, with bewilderment and astonishment plain in their expressions.

And one man from among them stepped forward.

"Pardon me, if I may?"

He was a middle-aged man with a stoop and unhealthy-looking

bags under his eyes. He stroked his thick beard as an apparent nervous tic.

"I have no words sufficient to thank the knights of the kingdom, and the Knights of the Royal Guard in particular, for everything related to this royal selection ceremony. Without their assistance, it surely would not have been possible to arrange this in such a short time."

Marcus replied, "You are too kind."

"However, and it brings me no joy to say this, even though we are following the Dragon Tablet, are there not various...issues, with those selected?"

"You are saying what, exactly?"

"I am wondering if we have been too focused on those qualified to be Dragon Maidens, and not enough on those qualified to wear the very crown of the kingdom without becoming an object of ridicule?"

The declaration of the hunchbacked man was clearly tinged with anger.

"Hear, hear!" said a few other civil officials in a display of support.

He continued, "The Covenant with the Dragon is the gravest matter. Lugunica has come this far as the Dragonfriend Kingdom and cannot survive as a nation without the Covenant. But valuing the Covenant so much more than the people will sow the seeds of future discord."

"In other words, the Dragon Maidens that we knights spilled our blood to search for would not make kings worthy of our fealty?"

"Th-that is not how I would put it, but essentially, yes."

The man broke out in a cold sweat at Marcus' frank summation, and after a moment he acknowledged the true meaning of his oblique comments. The knights had desperately toiled to solve a nearly unsolvable problem. This ridicule of their efforts did not exactly instill pleasant emotions in them.

Subaru, standing with the knights, felt the hot anger all around him on his skin. He remarked, "Smells like something's burning in here..."

Hearing Subaru's murmur, Al cheerfully spoke to two other people in the same row.

"Well, it sure sounded like he was insulting the knights. I don't mind, but what do you two think?"

The two he'd addressed, Julius and Ferris, turned their heads toward Al and Subaru. Ferris spoke first.

"Your dear Ferri doesn't really mind, *meow*? I mean, whatever Beardy says, Ferri's fealty is already to one person alone, you see."

Julius followed up. "I will not go quite as far as Ferris, but I feel the same. I have already pledged my blade. One day, they will offer their fealty to another. I do not intend to be so narrow-minded that my heart should be disturbed prior to that day."

Not one to be outdone, Al said, "Ha, that's mighty fine of you. Of course, it's the same with me where Princess is concerned."

The two others could only make wry smiles at that.

Subaru wasn't exactly enjoying being the odd man out.

Ferris had Crusch. Al had Priscilla. That would have to make Julius a supporter of Anastasia. They were three knights, bearing the full trust of their masters. Comparing their position to his own sent a keen sense of inferiority through Subaru, even though he no doubt wanted to fulfill Emilia's wishes at least as much as any of the rest…

Subaru felt a strange feeling of unease as the back and forth in the throne room intensified. The earlier opinion was only the beginning as the civil officials aired their discontent one by one.

"One must be both maiden and king. Perhaps they are not sufficiently aware that they must wear the crown?"

"No matter how dressed up they are, their demeanor exposes their true natures."

"They are not refined enough. Their education is lacking. How can they be monarchs like this?"

A familiar voice interrupted the civil officials.

"Surely it is not a proooblem. I would think such a bounty of personaaality will make for a highly amuuusing royal selection."

"You be quiet!"

Subaru looked at Emilia and the others. No doubt Felt's crude, in-your-face attitude earlier was what had really set the civil officials off. But he couldn't say the other candidates hadn't sparked any unease themselves.

In truth, Emilia's expression, as if trying to endure the pain, hurt him acutely. He wanted from the bottom of his heart to rush over that moment and give her a shoulder to lean on.

Miklotov's single word quieted the throne room.

"—Silence."

As the man of highest stature there, Miklotov narrowed his eyes as he regarded Felt. After keeping his silence for a time, the old man let out his breath.

"Mmmm. That was somewhat irreverent behavior, so I do understand Mr. Rickert's view. In that light, I believe everyone should hear a brief summation of the candidate's personal history."

A bald, stern-faced old man seconded Miklotov's opinion.

"...Indeed. We can decide whether she is suitable or not from that."

Seeing the rest of the Council of Elders nod, the civil official apparently named Rickert took a step back. Miklotov continued, "Sir Reinhard. We would first hear the highlights of what you know."

After he was called, Reinhard bent down on one knee in a show of the utmost respect. Subaru wasn't even involved, but a cold sweat broke out over him nonetheless. After all, a blunt telling of the truth would naturally expose Felt's life of crime and stir up more problems.

"Until approximately one month ago, Lady Felt was living in a corner of the Lower Quarter of the royal capital—also known as 'the slums.' An occasion arose where she had an opportunity to touch a Dragon Jewel. Having judged that she was qualified to be a Dragon Maiden, I brought her with me as a matter of course."

Assuaging Subaru's concerns, Reinhard made his report while deftly dancing around the problematic parts. The explanation had huge, glaring gaps, but the assembly did not focus on those, but rather, certain other things.

"A waif from the slums... Sir Reinhard, are you insane?!" Rickert exploded. "You bring a vagrant from the streets to a ceremony to select the monarch who must shoulder the future of Lugunica?! Just what do you think the royal throne is?!"

"..."

Reinhard had done as asked, expressing utmost courtesy to those on the platform. His gallant profile did not reveal the slightest hint of negativity. Rickert directed his words at Miklotov next.

"Someone should be selected who is suitable for the crown. We cannot simply lay our hands on whoever happens to walk be—"

As Rickert eloquently attempted to sway Miklotov, a familiar voice dashed cold water over his efforts.

"Mr. Rickert, you are sliiightly too heated over this matter, are you nooot?"

"Nonsense, Roswaal. Nor do I approve of your conduct. Not only I, but all of the officials. Until now we have overlooked this because we are in a time of crisis, but I shall still my tongue no longer. Not about the House of Astrea hauling a waif into these halls, nor you, the fool nominating a half-demon to be monarch...!"

"—Mr. Rickert. I would suggest you amend your comments."

The frigid words reverberated throughout the chamber. Rickert's face, red from indignation, paled. Roswaal continued, "It is poor manners to address a half-elf as a 'half-demon.' Furthermore, Lady Emilia remains a royal candidate... Do you understand which of us should remember his place?"

Roswaal's tone of voice was unchanged from the norm, but the power behind it made Rickert avert his gaze. He shook his head, as if to conceal his intimidation, and dramatically motioned to the dais.

"A-and what of it? I do not believe my claim to be in error. Qualified as Dragon Maiden does not mean qualified to be king. Lord Miklotov! Please reconsider! The future prosperity of the kingdom cannot be built upon the election of an obscene royal candidate such as—"

"—Sir Reinhard."

The sage addressed not Rickert, attempting to sway his view, but the red-haired knight.

"Is this girl...?"

"I cannot be absolutely certain, for the means to prove with certainty no longer exist. —However, I must resist the urge to call this coincidence happenstance."

"What would you call it, then?"

"—I would call it fate."

At Reinhard's reply, Miklotov closed his eyes as if that statement held some special meaning.

Neither Subaru nor those around him had any idea what the two were talking about. It seemed only the pair knew to what they referred. Surrounded by such confusion, Miklotov put a hand to his forehead, as if lamenting the situation, and looked across the other old men.

"Have you not noticed? Take another good look at Lady Felt. —If you cannot tell even then, I must question your fidelity to your own kingdom."

In response to Miklotov's challenge, the occupants of the chamber held their breaths and gazed at Felt. Felt, at the eye of a storm of unrestrained stares, scowled openly.

Rickert bluntly pointed out Felt's shortcomings.

"Looking at her, of course one can tell…she is still very young, and there are far too many things she would have to learn before setting foot near a thro—!"

Suddenly, his face stiffened as if he'd realized something, his eyes opening wide in shock.

"B-blond hair and crimson eyes—?!"

Once Rickert said it, the other officials were struck with similar force like a row of dominos. The only one not affected was Subaru, ignorant of common knowledge in that world.

When Subaru glanced to the side, Ferris and Julius appeared to understand. He couldn't tell what in the world Al was thinking, per usual, but Al showed no special sign of surprise.

"Blond hair and crimson eyes—these are peculiar to the bloodline of the Lugunica Royal Family. But! It cannot be! The entire royal bloodline passed away in that incident half a year ago! It is simply impossible that this girl could—"

Reinhard calmly interrupted Rickert's forceful denial.

"—Mr. Rickert, are you aware of a certain incident in the palace some fourteen years ago?"

The words from Reinhard's lips struck Rickert with even greater force.

"Sir Reinhard… Surely, you are not saying that…"

"Fourteen years ago, thieves infiltrated the castle and abducted the daughter of the late second prince, Lord Fold. The thieves were permitted to escape, and the daughter was never found."

This was the kind of national failure that was never leaked to outsiders.

"As the matter was not written upon the Dragon Tablet, the thieves were easily permitted to infiltrate the royal palace at the time. Since there were a number of other urgent matters, an all-out search for the daughter was not conducted."

"Mmmm. That incident was the trigger for the dissolution and reconstitution of the Knights of the Royal Guard. Your kinsmen were not uninvolved in this matter, I believe?"

"Thus, I have information that would otherwise be unknown to me. And based upon this..."

Miklotov replied to Reinhard's minimalist reply with a nod of his own. However, Rickert's frenzy showed no sign of diminishing.

"That is an extreme—no, an irrational position! Are we to believe a daughter of the royal household vanished without a trace fourteen years ago, came to live in the slums, and now you incidentally discovered her with the royal selection nearing?! And furthermore, you just so happened to find out that she is qualified as a Dragon Maiden?!"

Even after the barrage of information Rickert was still standing.

"This is absurd!" he laughed. "This is all too contrived. You could easily have found a girl with maiden qualifications and dyed her hair and used magic to alter the color of her eyes. —Surely you have not engaged in such shameful behavior?"

"I swear it upon my sword."

Reinhard laid the sword at his hip upon the floor, offering it in a show of the highest respect. Rickert, seeing the knight among knights displaying such deference, sank into a heavy slouch.

"...With all of the royal family already lost, no means exist to confirm whether she has royal blood or not. I do not think anyone will bow their heads based on mere supposition about her identity."

"That is natural. However, I am certain that Lady Felt is worthy of throne...even without a claim by blood."

Reinhard's unshaken reply drew a resigned sigh from Rickert.

"It seems that the Sword Saint of our age is rather invested in her."

Once more, he turned his gaze to Felt, the subject of the matter at hand.

"Setting aside your maiden qualifications, you hail from the slums. —And it is possible you possess the royal bloodline, presumed lost. I cannot even begin to fathom the distress this must bring you. Are you determined to see this through?"

The statement sounded like a test, a ritual so that Rickert could use her reply to let go of his misgivings. Only when he received Felt's reply could he allow the discussion to end.

But Felt flatly denied her qualification, completely ignoring the flow of the conversation to that point.

"Huh? What are you talking about, old guy? I never said one word about being king."

The unexpected reply caught everyone in the chamber off guard.

"I got dragged here out from the slums against my will," she continued. "I told him to take me back and he wouldn't, and he hid my old clothes so I had to wear this stupid thing. I am way past ticked! I'm annoyed a million times over! No, I don't accept this!"

Felt's rage-filled rant brought another awkward silence over the hall. Even Subaru, famously unable to read the mood, could tell that things were going south.

Among the silent remaining candidates, Priscilla, her arms crossed with a bored expression, spat out, "—How long are you going to entertain this boring, pointless discussion?"

As all eyes fell upon the girl, her full bosom shook above her folded arms.

"Even if it is in name only, five have been assembled so the process can commence. All we need do is begin, and the unworthy will be culled in due course. After all, I shall be the last one standing. Whether the excess baggage is qualified to be king or not is completely beside the point."

Priscilla's brash, irrational argument drew a heated reaction from Felt.

"Ahh...?"

She leaped down from the dais and glared at Priscilla head-on.

"I was thinking earlier you were a good-looking chick, but I guess it's a flower bed inside your head, too, huh? If you wanna pick a fight, I'm game. Everyone knows with me you get more than you bargained for."

"Such arrogance. Do you know who I am...?"

"Ha, like I'd know...!"

Felt brushed off Priscilla's statement with a loud laugh. Priscilla's eyes cruelly narrowed.

With Subaru's breath catching from the decisive change in the atmosphere, Al shouted from beside him, "Princess, this is—"

He must have known exactly what Priscilla was about to do.

Then, at Al's shout, a gust wind cut across the chamber. Reinhard moved directly in front of her in a split second and spoke in a quiet voice.

"—Pardon me, Lady Priscilla."

In the literal blink of an eye, the knight, on one knee on the dais a moment before, had come between the two royal candidates. The red-haired knight was facing the orange-haired girl—and behind him, Emilia held Felt close to protect her.

Emilia's violet eyes filled with anger as she chewed Priscilla out.

"Such hostility in an important place like this... What are you thinking?!"

However, Priscilla waved off the nuisance with a hand, numb to any pangs of guilt.

"I am merely teaching an untrained bitch her proper place. After all, impoliteness toward me can only be repaid with one's life."

Emilia pressed the point against the unrepentant Priscilla.

"Won't you say you're sorry? Or do you actually not realize you've done something wrong?"

For an instant, the words made Priscilla's face go blank. Then, she glanced at Emilia with barely constrained laughter.

"Ahh, this is most amusing. I have rarely been so entertained. You may take that as a compliment."

"What a disagreeable child you are. What are you talking a—"

"One should apologize for doing something wrong, you say? If that is the case, why do you not apologize, silver-haired half-elf? In your case, 'I'm sorry I was ever born.'"

Even Subaru could tell that the shock had shot right through Emilia's entire body. Her shoulders shuddered, and her fearlessness faded from her eyes, replaced by acute pain.

"I-I have…no relationship to the Witch…"

"Does such an excuse mean anything to anyone? You are the spitting image of the being that is taboo to the world. The very sight of you fills people with fear and makes their hearts tremble. Is that not why you cover yourself and obscure your appearance?"

Assaulted on all sides by Priscilla's acrimonious words, Emilia silently bowed her pale face.

Even Subaru understood Priscilla's meaning. He understood it, but he could not accept it, for it unjustly brought pain to Emilia for reasons that had nothing to do with her whatsoever.

He couldn't take it anymore. Yet, once again, Subaru had to wait to act as Al, his face unreadable under his helm, offered a frank critique of Priscilla's despotism.

"Princess, can we leave it at that? Adding more enemies here seriously puts us in a bind, especially if one of 'em's the Sword Saint. How 'bout you just apologize?"

"My vassal should not make such a pathetic display. And what of the Sword Saint? Merely the supposed mightiest in the land. Do something."

"I wouldn't last one minute…"

Al had calmly assessed the tale of the tape, raising the white flag in short order. His demeanor brought exasperation to Priscilla's face, and all the malice and enmity to that point seemed to dissipate.

No one in the room, Subaru included, could conceal their shock at Al's skillful handling of such a ferocious beast. But at the very least, the immediate threat of an explosive situation had been defused.

With that matter settled, the chamber settled into silence once more. Abruptly, a high-pitched ring echoed throughout—the sound of a coin being tossed into a bowl. Miklotov thus gathered the group's attention.

"—Is everyone satisfied? It would seem that both Lady Felt and Lady Emilia have calmed sufficiently..."

Emilia replied first.

"Y-yes... I'm all right. It would seem she is also..."

"Let me go, already! It's not like I even did anything!"

In response to Felt's outburst, Emilia hastily nodded and let her go.

"I was fine, so you didn't need to do nothin'!" she fumed. "Do I look like some weak little kid to you?!"

"...Yes, it was unnecessary. I am sorry."

"—I'm not thanking you."

Felt scowled. Noticing her attitude, Reinhard politely nodded to Emilia before returning to the knights, leaving Emilia and Felt to uncomfortably line up with the other candidates. Only Priscilla seemed unchanged, wearing the same bored look she had begun with. She didn't look like she was reflecting on the error of her ways in the slightest.

Either way, Miklotov, seeing that the dispute had been settled, announced anew, "Then, let us proceed with our agenda—the dispute over the royal succession. The Council of Elders hereby proposes a meeting between all the candidates for the royal selection."

2

Miklotov's most solemn announcement brought tension to the chamber again. Spontaneously, even the candidates stood a little straighter; the faces of the spectators no longer looked relaxed.

Miklotov scanned the expressions of the other members of the Council of Elders, seeking confirmation with his announcement of the formal start of the meeting. In answer, the old men dipped their heads in assent one by one.

"I thank you for your approval. Let us begin the debate. Though the subject under discussion is who shall be king...the issue is the method of selection. We have assembled candidates via the Dragon Jewels, but the method of selection is not set in stone. To determine this, I thought it best to first ask how far the candidates are willing to go."

The members of the Council of Elders nodded alongside Miklotov's words. Seeing that there were no objections, Miklotov looked toward Marcus, standing at the ready on a corner of the dais. The knight stepped forward once more, bowing deeply as a proxy for everyone in the hall.

"Then, if I may be so bold, I shall continue. I believe each candidate present has a case to make. I would have all in the chamber hear these arguments. First, let us please begin with Lady Crusch. —Sir Felix Argyle!"

Crusch calmly nodded at Marcus's words.

"Mm."

Ferris casually raised a hand.

"Yes, sir!"

As Ferris jogged ahead to join Crusch's side, she looked up at Marcus along the way, pushing up her cheeks with her index fingers.

"Captain, Ferri keeps telling mew, it's *Ferris*, not *Felix*. It hurts Ferri's feewings."

Marcus's chin shot up immediately.

"I have no intention of granting special treatment to any subordinates, including you. Present yourself."

Ferris stuck her tongue out in dissatisfaction as she stood by her master's—Crusch's—side.

"Crusch Karsten, royal candidate and head of the House of Karsten."

"Ferris of the House of Karsten, Lady Crusch's knight."

Crusch announced herself without the slightest display of timidity, and Ferris remained as casual as ever. Marcus amended her self-introduction.

"Sir Felix Argyle."

The scowl on Ferris's face was quite blatant.

Subaru remarked, "Huh, so her real name is Felix? That's a very guy-ish name there."

In Japan, the eldest children of old samurai families were known to inherit a certain name regardless of gender. There was also a well-established fad where dating games would gender-swap generals out of the history books and turn them into very pretty girls.

"Subaru, haven't you heard?" Reinhard replied.

"Heard what?"

"Ferris doesn't just have a man's name. He is very much a male."

"—"

Reinhard's statement brought Subaru's thoughts to a halt. He folded his arms, inclined his head, closed his eyes, and earnestly mulled over the meaning of those words.

"What…did you say…just now?"

"Ferris doesn't just have a man's name. He is very much a male."

Word for word, syllable for syllable, Reinhard repeated the very important statement.

The instant his mind processed the information, Subaru's yell echoed throughout the hall.

"Whaaaaaaaa—?!"

"That's a guy?! Or is the knight among knights just really bad at jokes? This isn't funny!"

He wailed as he looked Ferris over from top to bottom.

Certainly, Ferris was tall for a girl. But those facial features and body contours struck him as completely feminine. Some parts were understated for a woman's body, but there were plenty of women in the world with flat chests, even as adults. That wasn't proof of anything.

However, Crusch, having maintained her silence on the matter until then, affirmed that the cause of his shock was the truth.

"Ah, it is your first time seeing him? I can firmly declare that my knight, Ferris, is a man."

"A-anyone can say anything… I need proof. Yeah, I won't believe without proof!"

"When I was young, Ferris and I bathed together, and he certainly had a male organ between his…"

"I'm very sorry!! I don't want to make a pretty girl speak of male organs! My mistake!!"

And thus, Subaru surrendered in spectacular fashion. He glared at Ferris, now standing at Crusch's side.

"This is your fault, too, damn it! You led me on! A guy under those cat ears, ugh! Just remembering that nibble is making me shudder!"

"Hey *meow*, you got it wrong all on your own, Subawu. Ferri never said one word about being a girl."

"Don't mess with me, you bitch—correction, you bastard!"

Ferris giggled, sticking his tongue out with a wink. Crusch seemed satisfied as she commented, "Everyone makes that face when they find meowt. It's so amusing and never gets old. —Not many have such a big reaction, though."

This brought an uncharacteristic scowl to Miklotov's face.

"Mmmm. It is in poor taste to continue this, knowing what shall result, Lady Crusch."

For her part, Crusch's face firmed up again slightly as she shook her head.

"It seems that you misunderstood, Lord Miklotov. I do not instruct Ferris to dress like this. All of it is of his free will."

Rickert lodged an objection to Crusch's words.

"Though I believe it is a master's duty to see that a vassal is appropriately dressed..."

Crusch's eyes narrowed in response.

"It is a master's duty to see that a vassal is appropriately dressed, you say? In that case, I indeed desire that Ferris be dressed as he is now. Do you understand why?"

"Why, I wonder?"

"It is very simple. —One should be attired in the manner that makes one's soul shine the brightest. Ferris's current attire suits him far better than knightly armor, just as I wear my own outfit because it suits me better than any dress."

Crusch pushed out her chest in a display of personal pride as she spoke. As Ferris stood beside her, she—or rather, he—smiled at the sight of his gallant master.

The sight of Crusch so poised made Rickert lose all stomach for an argument. As he kept his silence, Subaru too could not help but feel his chest stir in the face of Crusch's composure.

Reinhard remarked, in a voice that seemed rather loud considering the circumstances, "That is Lady Crusch for you... Among the candidates, she is the first to voice her opinion but also the one with the strongest support. Whatever she says, she speaks with a different sense of confidence than the others."

"What do you mean?" Subaru asked Reinhard from the side.

"The House of Karsten that Lady Crusch heads is a family of dukes and duchesses that have supported the Kingdom of Lugunica since early in its history. The house has proven its loyalty to the nation through many deeds. And the wisdom with which Lady Crusch herself leads as such a young duchess makes her the favorite of the royal selection."

"So she's… I see, the favorite based on early scoring."

Even Subaru, lacking detailed knowledge of ranks and titles, knew that she was only a few steps removed from the top of the pyramid. With the royal family wiped out, public opinion probably favored someone close to the late king.

The faint murmur spread through the hall as people all around nodded to each other about Crusch's superiority. Apparently, her being the favorite in the royal selection was something to accept as fact.

However, it was Crusch herself who interrupted the murmurs.

"It would seem many here harbor a minor misconception."

As calm returned to the hall, she nodded with a composed look.

"I strive to be fully aware of what everyone expects by having me take the throne. The House of Karsten is a house that has carried great authority and political influence for many years. Should I succeed as monarch, politics and national policy are guaranteed to continue without so much as a ripple… Correct?"

Several people in the chamber nodded as they listened to Crusch's eloquent speech.

"I regret to dash your expectations, but I can guarantee no such thing."

At Crusch's statement, the throne room briefly fell silent, only to erupt in an earthquake several seconds later.

"What's the meaning of this?!" several of those assembled exclaimed as Crusch looked up at the dais, her expression unchanged. She shook her deep green hair as her gallant gaze looked past them to a mural etched on the wall behind the royal throne.

"The Dragonfriend Kingdom of Lugunica... This nation has remained prosperous by honoring the Covenant made with the Dragon long ago. Thanks to the Dragon, various crises have been averted, from war, to plague, to famine. The word *Dragon* has never vanished from the kingdom at any point through its long history."

All of this was according to Marcus's tale of "The Covenant with the Dragon" at the start of the meeting.

Upholding the Covenant between the Kingdom of Lugunica and the Dragon had brought fame and prosperity throughout history. As everyone mulled over the meaning of her words, Crusch folded her arms and scanned the gathering.

"For the most part, prosperity brought by reaching the Covenant with the Dragon has been a good thing. If war arises, the Dragon breathes and burns our enemies away. If there is plague, it employs its mana to heal people. If there is famine, soaking the soil with Dragon's Blood grants the blessing of bounty. And so, the guidance of the Dragon has saved us from hardship and guaranteed our glory—" In spite of the glowing details on Crusch's lips, her face did not brighten. Under the silent attention of the entire assembly, she remarked, "Let me ask you. —Do you not think it is shameful?"

The chamber returned to silence with an even greater sense of tension than before. But if one were to compare the emotions of its occupants, the most heated, raw anger was without doubt coming from Crusch, standing before the throne.

"The Covenant guarantees we will be protected from any crisis and any hardship so long as we uphold it. And so, we have descended into softness and depravity, relying now upon a change of leadership for its continuation. To think that you take this for granted."

Crusch's stern lecture spurred one among the Council of Elders to rise, his voice shaking with anger.

"—You go too far, Lady Crusch! I cannot permit anyone to make light of the Covenant! Do you have any conception of the sacrifices the kingdom has been spared since the Covenant with the Dragon long ago...? Are you denying the weight of history itself?!"

"I have already stated that this past prosperity is mostly a good thing. No words have passed my lips claiming that I myself have not been a beneficiary of its blessing. The House of Karsten was born with the kingdom and has shared in its glory. Had a crisis destroyed the kingdom, my house would have shared its fate. Whenever the Dragon has saved the nation, it has saved my house as well." Crusch paused briefly. "However, the future is a different matter. Do you think nothing of the pathetic sight you make at this moment? Have you not ceased to use your minds because you cling to the Dragon and the Covenant? When war, plague, and famine assail the kingdom anew, is there nothing we can do but sing the Dragon's praises?"

"That is—"

"This nation has relied upon the writings of the Dragon Tablet for too long, becoming so soft and weak that it cannot stand on its own power. The nation takes for granted that the Dragon and prophecy will aid it whenever it is shaken. But can you argue that we have strived to avoid such matters from occurring to begin with? A number of calamities in recent years, including the failure of the Great Subjugation fourteen years ago, are things we courted through that weakness."

Everyone held their breath in shock, eyes wide at Crusch's declaration.

Bathed in gazes of shock and anger, she raised a fist and nobly declared, "If the kingdom is to crumble without the Dragon's protection, then crumble it should. A nation too blessed stagnates, that stagnation courts corruption, and corruption brings about its demise. That is what I think."

"Are you... Are you saying you will destroy the nation?!"

"No. If the nation is to crumble without the Dragon, we should become the Dragon ourselves. Everything that the kingdom has relied upon the Dragon for until now should be borne by king, minister, and people. Furthermore..."

Crusch took a deep breath.

"When I become king, I will make us forget about the Covenant with the Dragon until now, come what may. The Dragonfriend Kingdom of Lugunica belongs not to the Dragon, but to us."

"—"

"Hard times await us. Perhaps they will be disasters we averted in the past due to the Dragon's power, or perhaps even greater calamities. But I do not wish to live in a manner that shames my very soul."

Crusch's voice dropped. She shook her head and lowered her gaze.

"I have long harbored doubts about the state of the kingdom. I believe that this course of events is a Heaven-sent opportunity to set it right."

In terms of loyalty to the late king, or lack thereof, it was a blasphemous statement for which one could be cut down on the spot.

Subaru took in all of Crusch's words.

"The nobles are right in theory, but…"

A lot of what she said is hard to deny, he thought to himself. Looking around, he saw he wasn't the only one; no one was willing to raise a voice against the girl's boldly voiced argument. Here was a girl willing to smash the history of the kingdom—the very essence of what it took to be a monarch.

Miklotov, having listened to Crusch's claims to the very end, passed matters along to Ferris, standing beside her.

"Mmmm. We understand Lady Crusch's point of view. Now then, Sir Felix Argyle, is there anything you wish to add?"

Apparently, it was the place of the vassal to advocate for the master.

"Thank you for asking, but I have nothing further to add. Lady Crusch's thoughts are exactly as she says. And history will prove that Lady Crusch's actions are correct. —I have no doubt whatsoever that it is my master who shall become king."

Ferris solemnly bowed at his slender hips as he expressed his immense trust. Then his face returned to its usual fawning expression as he smiled at Crusch.

"Lady Crusch, you're just as incredible as ever. Ferri's swooning—"

"From time to time, I fail to understand what you are saying, Ferris. —But I forgive you. You would never do anything that costs me."

The warm regard for Ferris in Crusch's eyes made the strength of their relationship plain.

With the conclusion of that expression of trust in Crusch, Miklotov briefly set things in order.

"Mmmm, we have finally heard from one person… Mmm, though it seems her opinions have created quite a stir."

To the Council of Elders and the civil officials, the plans of the candidate with the strongest backing were a thunderbolt out of the blue. It was evident the entire exchange had alienated many would-be supporters. But anyone hearing that speech would harbor no doubt that those who supported her held the highest trust in her possible.

Subaru remarked to himself, "I still don't know how they're actually gonna pick someone, though..."

The whole point of this display was to determine how they would go about it. The lack of hard-and-fast rules meant that all he could do was keep watching the debate, mixed feelings notwithstanding.

Marcus, having apparently regained his composure, proceeded.

"Then, let us continue, following with the next in line beside Lady Crusch."

The orange-haired girl stepped forward with an arrogant look on her face.

"Hmph, finally. It's Hyper Priscilla Time, then."

Subaru was in complete shock at the strange combination of words.

"Just now, did she say, Hyper Priscilla Time...?"

Al walked over and stood at Priscilla's side, giving her a thumbs-up like he was taking credit.

"It would seem that the riffraff's eyes are all upon my gorgeous self."

"You used that pretty nicely, Princess. Totally nailed 'em with a big uppercut."

Ignoring the fact that the looks regarded her less as "amazing" than "bizarre," Priscilla thrust her shoulders back in pride at Al's off-the-mark flattery.

"Very well, Lady Priscilla Bariel, if you please..."

"Though it pains me, I shall humor you. I need only demonstrate my majesty to the old fossils and establish that they should simply choose to obey me, yes? A simple matter."

As she spoke, she pulled a fan out of the yawning gap of her cleavage, loudly snapping it open and using it to conceal her mouth as she giggled. Her adorable looks clashed with her evil, sadistic laugh.

"—The Bloody Bride. What gall."

Such words of deep, seething resentment ran across the entire chamber.

Thanks to Crusch's explosive declaration, the atmosphere in the hall was far from warm. The murmurs chilled the air frostier still.

And the prologue of the royal selection had barely begun.

3

Without hesitation, Priscilla cut through the disquiet governing the chamber with a thoroughly wearied voice.

"Such boring, insignificant jeers. I am so accustomed to them that they do not even serve as a lullaby."

She was no doubt referring to the reaction around her moments earlier, including boisterous jeers that called her the Bloody Bride. Priscilla did not let it bother her, nor did she make any attempt to refute them.

Following Priscilla's statement, Miklotov interrupted inquisitively.

"This has been on my mind since well before. Bariel... As in, Mr. Lyp Bariel? Mmm. Now that I think of it, I have not seen any sign of Mr. Lyp. Where is he...?"

"That lewd old man suddenly went senile half a year ago. He remained unable to tell the difference between dream and reality, and passed away but a few days later."

"What, Mr. Lyp has...? Mmmm. Lady Priscilla, what does that make your relationship to Mr. Lyp?"

With Miklotov expressing surprise, Priscilla dully commented on the death of her partner.

"I suppose it makes me his widow. He had not touched me with so much of a fingertip, so our relationship is, quite literally, in name alone."

Al promptly stated, "Princess, isn't it just a little too harsh to put it that way?"

Priscilla paid him no heed, sweeping her gaze across the crowd as if daring anyone else to complain.

"A meaningless death to end a worthless life. If the life of that old man had any meaning whatsoever, it is in the fact he transferred his entire estate to me. Accordingly, the House of Bariel is mine."

Her stare only increased the discontent in the hall, but no one actually lodged an objection. Even Rickert, having protested against Crusch with such vehemence, apparently lacked the courage to enter a war of words with an opponent immune to logic. And so, Miklotov replied, "Mmm. I understand, then. As Mr. Lyp was an acquaintance of many years, I regret to hear of his passing… But I see that your claim is on firm ground, Lady Priscilla."

"But of course."

As Priscilla arrogantly nodded, Miklotov now shifted the conversation to the vassal at her side.

"Though I would like to press for further details, does the knight beside you have anything to add?"

"*Aahhh… Ah, me?*"

Al's yawning reply did a splendid job of drawing the antagonism all around him. It was as if the servant was cooling off the heat that his master had brough to the hall.

"Yes, you. Your attire is highly unusual. I have not seen you among the Knights of the Royal Guard…and your helm?"

"Oh, can you tell? This was made in Volakia down south. It was a lot of trouble getting it out of there. It's tough, so it's held up for a long while. Also, it looks cool, so it's pretty important."

"A Volakia Empire…? Then, you are not assigned to the Knights of the Royal Guard."

"I've cut all my connections to Volakia. Now I'm a wanderer who goes with the flow… So please, just call me Al. Also, you seem a little upset that I'm not showing you my face… Can you gimme a break on that?"

Al's profusion of rude statements drew even sharper glares. Under so much attention, Al deftly slipped his one hand under the chin of his helmet and began to lift it up.

"*Urk—!*"

Out of the blue, someone let out a pained cry as the helm rose to about mouth level. It was hard to blame him for that. After all, the visible part of Al's face was blanketed with old scars from burns, cuts, and perhaps other sources still.

It was no exaggeration to say his scars were ten times as bad as Subaru's.

"So y'see, my face is a sorry sight. That's why I hope you permit me the discourtesy of keeping my face covered in front of everyone."

Marcus interrupted.

"This may be an even greater discourtesy... If you hail from Volakia with such wounds, were you a Sword Slave by any chance?"

"Hehhh, that's the captain of the knights for you. That Empire likes to keep its secrets, but apparently you know a thing or two about the darker parts of it. Yes, I was a Sword Slave, a ten-odd-years vet at that."

Murmurs spread across the chamber once again as the term *Sword Slave* was repeated on the lips of many a knight. From the words forming the compound, it seemed to mean "a sword-wielding slave."

"I take it you were in a battle or two, then?"

"That's the size of it, bro. I messed up when I was young and lost an arm that way, y'see."

Al, ever playing the fool, didn't flinch from discussing the gruesome experience. For their part, those who had gazed upon him with such hostility moments before were now dumbstruck.

But Subaru was shaken by the impact even more than the rest.

Back in the dragon carriage, Al hadn't said much about his own body. He downplayed the cause of losing his other arm and dodged the subject of his helmet altogether. But Subaru had been subconsciously avoiding that subject, too. After all, just like him, Al had been summoned there from another world—in other words, his experiences hit Subaru very close to home. Losing an arm, having his face scarred up to the point he couldn't show it to anyone else—that was a future Subaru, with countless scars already carved into his body, could easily have encountered for himself.

If the icy chill running up his spine was any indication, Subaru would never have been able to endure it.

Miklotov spoke again.

"Mmmm. Hailing from the Empire of Volakia... Is that why you came to stand at Lady Priscilla's side?"

Priscilla replied, "Not at all. It is the result of a little game of mine.

From the beginning, my becoming king was as good as divine providence. The result will be the same regardless of my vassal. And so, I am free to select the vassal that I like. As a showpiece, this man is sufficiently amusing and then some."

"How did you come to select him, then?"

"What, you want to know?—I caught sight of him in a bodybuilding contest I held on my estate, with the winner to be offered the job of my vassal. It was an amusing sight."

Priscilla gave Al a glance rich in meaning as she replied to Miklotov.

"Mmmm, I see. So he was the winner of that contest, I ta…"

Al corrected him, "Nah, I didn't win it. Life's not kind enough for a one-armed guy to beat a pack of beefy bodybuilders. I was lucky to round out the top five at the victory ceremony."

Miklotov's face registered surprise that Al would interrupt even him.

"My word. Then how did you become Lady Priscilla's vassal…?"

Priscilla straightened with pride as she gave Al's back a hard slap.

"I told you. I am free to pick whomever I please."

Al yelped a loud, dry *Ahhnn!* audible to all, as she continued, "To begin with, my keen eyes allowed me to discern that he is a physical wonder, far more than a collection of dim-witted louts overconfident in their muscle-bound arms. And more than that, only he boasted an escape from Volakia and a birth beyond the Great Waterfalls."

Priscilla briskly concluded her tale, loudly stomping with a high heel as all eyes fell upon her.

"And so, I selected Al to be my vassal. It is providence that my selection of Al, and my path to become king, shall both shine in accordance with my glory."

She did not bear even the smallest molecule of doubt or hesitation. She was so full of confidence it was frightening.

"You say that…Heaven has chosen you…?"

"But of course. After all, nothing happens in this world that is does not benefit me. Furthermore, 'tis I who is worthy of becoming king, and no other. You need only bow before me and serve."

Everyone was agape at her insolent declaration. The only one unaffected by her haughtiness was the man who called the girl his master.

"Princess, what's your basis for all that?"

"'Tis very simple. Serving me means siding with the winner. You may have anything you desire; I allow it. But I shall not permit you to serve anyone else. That is all."

Priscilla brushed her orange hair back, raising her hand in a lofty wave toward the heavens. It was a gesture that meant, *I have said all that there is to say.* With that, she turned her back to the Council of Elders on the dais and walked away. Before turning his back to follow, her knight looked up at the dais and said, "You might not like how she says it, but Princess is on the money. If she wants something, so long as she doesn't change her mind, she gets it. —That's because the heavens themselves have chosen Priscilla. I'm sure you've heard how the old... Er, Mr. Lyp's lands have bounced back lately?"

Al sent a meaningful look in Marcus's direction.

"We have already confirmed this for ourselves. Following the passing of Mr. Lyp Bariel, Lady Priscilla took control of policy within his lands...resulting in the region's unprecedented prosperity."

"Well, don't mistake that as us working hard for the sake of everyone else or something, okay? Princess's guesses are always on the mark like she's a natural. She's just right about everything, no ifs, ands, or buts."

"_____"

"Well, if you're under Princess, you can do whatever you want. If you're gonna bet on the winning horse, I think it's best to do it sooner rather than later, though."

It was as if both master and servant, so full of confidence, had forgotten their humility back in their mothers' wombs. When they returned to their place among the candidates, the tension in the air relaxed as a matter of course.

"A cross-dressing guy and pretty-girl combo, a rich widow and a guy from another world, this is totally genre-breaking stuff here..."

As Subaru murmured, the royal selection ceremony continued on. The next person called by Marcus was the girl with violet hair.

"Next, then, is Lady Anastasia, and her knight, Sir Julius Juukulius. Come forward!"

The girl reacted elegantly, but Priscilla had left vestiges of feverish agitation hovering over the chamber. That was when Julius lifted a hand up to the sky and swung it downward. The dry crackle echoed, forcing an inescapable change in the atmosphere.

To this generous deed, Anastasia said, "Thank you kindly," smiling pleasantly as she advanced. Julius stood at her side.

—Thus the most conventional-looking master and servant advanced to the fore.

Faced with the next royal candidate, Subaru cleared his thoughts and focused ahead once more.

4

Anastasia smiled warmly.

"If y'all expect me to be as intense as those last two, I'm in a bit of a bind. I doubt you'd want me to come on too strong, so I guess my gimmick is that I don't have one."

Her demeanor and pleasant smile relaxed some of the tension in the room.

"Now then, I—Anastasia Hoshin—will speak for a spell. I hope you'll forgive my indiscretion, since I'm an outsider and all."

Julius stroked the front of his hair in an unnecessarily polished motion to draw attention to himself.

"I am Lady Anastasia's knight, Julius Juukulius. Please be gentle with her."

Subaru finally reasoned that the talk about her "gimmick" was a high-level joke. But what he couldn't get out of his head was the contrast of Anastasia's accent. Apparently, Subaru wasn't the only one who noticed, as Miklotov asked, "With that peculiar accent, are you a native of Kararagi, then?"

"Exactly. I was born in Kararagi to the lowest class in the League of Free Trading Cities."

Miklotov's eyes narrowed slightly at that.

"Mmmm. The lowest class—then what is your connection to Lugunica?"

If lowest class meant the same thing there that it did in Lugunica,

Anastasia was born a commoner. Depending on the meaning of the term, it could imply something even lower.

"I was born in the lowest class, but now I have a right proper mansion in the city. I have stores in a host of other cities… That's how I first imposed on Lugunica."

Julius added, "She serves as chairwoman of the Hoshin Company, the most influential company in Kararagi. For many years, this position in her nation was occupied by the Lushika Industrial Company, but thanks to Lady Anastasia's personal commercial genius, it was reconstituted under a new name, the Hoshin Company."

Standing beside Julius, Anastasia's eyebrows peaked as if she were a little embarrassed.

If Julius's declaration could be taken as fact, Anastasia's pronouncement had been humble in the extreme about her exploits. Julius continued, "Accompanying its vast expansion across Kararagi, there was talk of expansion into Lugunica as well. That was the impetus for my meeting Lady Anastasia for the first time."

Miklotov replied, "Mmmm. So in spite of being born to humble beginnings, she established herself as a brilliant young merchant… I must say, this reminds me of the tales of the founder of Kararagi itself."

As Miklotov's lips bent into a smile, Anastasia clapped her hands together, and her eyes sparkled.

"Yes, exactly. I always looked up to that man, Hoshin of the Wastes. When the time came to establish my family name as a merchant, I decided to adopt the name Hoshin in his honor."

Miklotov praised Anastasia's spirit.

"Hoshin is the name of a great man known across the entire continent, revered from ancient times to the present. To name yourself after him… I see, a splendid display of spirit."

Even Subaru had heard of Hoshin of the Wastes. If he recalled correctly, the man was the main character in one of the ballads sung on that world.

Anastasia continued, "One of the great things about Kararagi is how it gave a gal like me a fair shot. It turns out I have a real knack. for sniffing out the scent of gold, and it's fun, too."

Subaru saw that these statements were creating a considerable stir all around. Judging from appearances alone, Anastasia was younger than he was. Given her age and the reaction around him, she apparently had a reputation as a monster in the business world.

Julius remarked, "Lady Anastasia's commercial genius is a divine gift... It is no exaggeration that she rivals Hoshin himself. My own lack of ability in this area leaves me envious of her."

Julius's rhetorical flourish drew a generous nod from Miklotov.

"My, my, she must be quite something indeed for 'The Finest of Knights' to boast of her so."

But Subaru, unable to accept that last sentence, asked the man beside him, "Did I hear wrong? Did he just call him 'The Finest of Knights'...?"

Reinhard replied to Subaru's question matter-of-factly. "That is what they call him. Among the Knights of the Royal Guard of the Kingdom of Lugunica, Julius is second only to Marcus, captain of the guard. There is a vice captain, but it is a ceremonial position that exists in name only, so it's best to think of it as vacant. In skill with a sword, employment of mana, pedigree, and exploits, Julius fulfills all the qualifications of a knight and is second to none. He is without question worthy of being called 'The Finest of Knights.'"

"But when people in the capital talk about the 'knight among knights,' they're talking about you, right? You're really well known, plus you never denied it, right?"

"The qualifications for that nickname are somewhat different. Certainly, in terms of strength with the sword alone, I'm stronger than Julius. I have yet to meet someone stronger than I am."

Just like that, he declared he was mightiest of all.

Subaru wasn't sure how to respond to that, but Reinhard wasn't boasting. If anything, his eyes were filled with envy, his lips pursed taut.

The way Reinhard looked cornered left Subaru wondering what to do, but, faster than he could say anything, the debate proceeded with something that could not be ignored.

Miklotov said, "It is plain that relations between master and servant are very good. Mmmm. Lady Anastasia, there is something I wish to ask you. —You are a native of Kararagi. What is your purpose in seeking to be king?"

"Ahh, so my birthplace really bothers you, doesn't it?"

It was a natural subject to raise. Nations existed in this world, too, meaning that borders existed between states and peoples. Subaru didn't know how high the barriers were, but even in a state of emergency, the throne of your own kingdom was not something to hand to a visitor from another nation lightly.

The entire chamber held its breath as Anastasia, surrounded by the tension, smiled wryly.

"Y'all have such high expectations, it's makin' me nervous. Unfortunately, I don't have any high ideals like Miss Crusch, or Miss Priscilla confidence that she's been chosen for greatness."

"Surely you are not saying...the Dragon Jewel responded to you purely by chance?"

Faced with Miklotov's question, Anastasia stuck her tongue out and replied casually.

"Ah-ha-ha, if it was like that even I wouldn't show my face here. 'Course I've got a goal of my own. —You see, I'm actually real greedy."

The declaration, so at odds with what was expected, made most present doubt their ears.

"I think I've been greedier than normal since I was teeny-tiny. The reason I became a first-rate merchant with a nose for gold is because I want it more than everyone else."

"You want it more?"

"As a maid at the first little company I worked for, I made a couple suggestions to the owner and they were big hits, so I got involved in bigger and bigger deals, and soon I was livin' so large I forgot I what it was like to be low class. It should have been fun, but I found out I wasn't free. I was even less free than before."

Anastasia, counting on her fingers the steps she had climbed, shook her head.

"...Mmmm. And why was that?" Miklotov asked.

"That's the scary part about greed. The more you get your hands on, the more you wanna get your hands on. 'I want this. I want that.' It's not enough. It's never enough—and that's when I realized it."

Anastasia grinned as she pointed toward her feet. It was clear what she was indicating—the palace itself.

"I'm greedy, so I want anything around. But I'm not satisfied yet. I don't know what real fulfillment feels like. So I want a country of my own."

"You are saying, you want this kingdom to weigh your greed?"

Anastasia responded to Miklotov's rebuke with a robust smile.

"Hey, if that smashes my scale to bits, smash away. I'll be real happy to have my fill and be totally satisfied."

In other words, she was announcing that she sought the royal throne out of her own avarice.

"But if gettin' my hands on the kingdom isn't enough... I'll probably use this country as a stepping-stone to get even more."

"And what shall become of the kingdom if you obtain it, yet it holds no value for you?"

"I told you, didn't I? I'm greedy. So once somethin's mine, it's mine through thick and thin. And if I get an even stronger hankering, I use whatever I have to satisfy it. My life in Kararagi, the Hoshin Company, and all the people who work there, they're all part of my drive for fulfillment. I would never throw them away. So..."

Anastasia swept her gaze over the faces of everyone in the chamber.

"—How about you just relax and become mine?"

She looked across the chamber with the same warm, gentle smile she had initially worn.

Her way of thinking was founded on desire, but that made her argument very simple. She wanted the throne for her own desires, and, from the day it was hers, she'd work tirelessly for the prosperity of the kingdom. She wouldn't throw it away, given that her personality demanded she make anything she owned into something greater and grander than before. That was her message.

"Mmmm. Lady Anastasia has surely pressed her claim sufficiently. Do you have anything to add, Sir Julius?"

With his master's speech concluded, it was time for the vassal to make his case. Both had argued beforehand about the master's fitness to be king, but Julius stepped in front and indicated Anastasia with his hand as he said, "Lady Anastasia used the word *greed* to express her desires, but put another way, this reveals the depth of emotion behind her ambition. On the other hand, from a business point of view, she is able to make any decision without emotional involvement, an indispensable quality in a statesman."

"Mmmm. Certainly, it is as you say."

"Furthermore, as I stated earlier, Lady Anastasia is a brilliant businesswoman—something this kingdom desperately needs at this hour. Repeated, serious clashes with neighboring nations—in particular, skirmishes with the Empire—have drained our coffers; with the large famine last year, the finances of the Kingdom of Lugunica are in a precarious state."

Faces went red as Julius abruptly touched upon the nation's dirty laundry.

"I believe such details ought not to be so lightly divulged in a public place, Sir Julius."

"The importance of financial reconstruction to the nation has been common knowledge for several decades now. I do not feel any reason to hide this from those assembled here. Do you not think that the very reason the affairs of the nation have stagnated is because we have averted our eyes from this difficult financial state for so long?"

"So a mere knight speaks to us about political affairs beyond his purview...?"

"That's right. These affairs will affect the House of Juukulius very little. Even if we avert our eyes, it surely will be nothing irreversible for my generation. However, even if my house will emerge unscathed, I cannot ignore the matter of the throne I serve falling into distress."

With veins bulging from the foreheads of the Council of Elders, Julius looked back at Anastasia.

"However, the Hoshin Company has connected us to the extreme prosperity enjoyed in Kararagi, bringing a fresh wind to Lugunica. I have seen for myself that Lady Anastasia is worthy to be king if we continue along this path. What can you call this, if not fate?"

Perhaps Julius had been overcome by fervor, for his tenor rose and his words quickened.

"If Heaven chooses the king, then it has chosen Lady Anastasia. I, devoted to the Royal Family, having pledged my loyalty to the kingdom, hereby declare that Lady Anastasia is worthy of the throne. —I thank you for lending me your ears."

Julius behaved much like a stage performer as he summarized his address for the audience. Those attending, mesmerized by his aura, seemed to come to their senses as they looked back upon master and vassal. Yet, even then, Marcus's calm expression did not waver.

"Sir Julius, may I judge this sufficient?"

Julius, probably accustomed to the attitude of his superior officer, stated, "Yes, thank you very much," and returned to Anastasia's side. "You were splendid, Lady Anastasia. It is indeed a place such as this where your flower may truly bloom."

"Yes, yes, you are very kind. Sheesh, you didn't need to say that. It's so embarrassing."

A red-faced Anastasia fanned herself with a hand as she returned with Julius to the other candidates. Now that the third candidate's camp had asserted its claim, the next in line was—

After a brief silence, Marcus called the name of the silver-haired girl who had kept her silence to that point.

"Then, the next candidate—Lady Emilia."

She was the only candidate lacking a knight of her own. After her name was called, she raised her head. From the side, Subaru could see worry on her pale, beautiful face, but, with a look of strong determination, Emilia replied.

"Yes."

She stepped forward. Her part in the royal selection had now begun. —That was when Subaru Natsuki had a thought.

5

The instant Emilia's right hand and foot moved forward together in her first step to the center, Subaru thought...

I've gotta do something.

On any normal day, he could fully appreciate how adorable she looked—E M P (Emilia-tan's Majorly a Puppy)—but it boded ill under the circumstances.

Somehow, even though Emilia's hands and feet were moving at a normal clip, he noticed that her stride seemed strained just before she reached the center.

The Council of Elders gazed down at her as she stepped forward. And yet, the whispers did not stop. Repeatedly, Subaru's ears picked up the word *half-demon.*

Reinhard moved to soothe Subaru's nerves, raw from the unpleasant atmosphere.

"—It's all right, Subaru. You need not worry."

"Don't read my thoughts like that. Am I an open book here?"

"Foul words are overcome by seeing a person's qualities before your very eyes. Believe in Lady Emilia."

But Subaru should have been the one to assert this. Having Reinhard say them to him left a nameless disappointment in his chest.

Following Reinhard's statement, the chitchat receded like the tide as if to prove him right. Roswaal had advanced to stand by Emilia's side.

Seeing Roswaal next to Emilia, Marcus, the master of ceremonies, bowed his head with a weighty look.

"Then, Lady Emilia, and Lord Roswaal L. Mathers, if you please..."

Roswaal's tone was casual even now.

"Yes, yeees. Myyy, following in the footsteps of all these knights, I feel so teeerribly out of place."

He prodded Emilia with an "Am I?" Of course, he earned no reaction. A normal response may have been too much to hope for given her tension from moments before. Roswaal's insensitivity rubbed Subaru's nerves even rawer.

But he instantly set even those strong feelings aside a moment later. After all—

"Members of the Council of Elders, it is my pleasure to meet you for the first time. My name is Emilia. I have no family name. Please, simply call me Emilia."

Her name, spoken with a voice clear as a bell, seemed to engrave itself upon the very hearts of all present. Her voice did not quaver, and she gazed forward, steady and strong.

Subaru had to wonder where all that anxiety from a moment ago had gone. Emilia, stating her name before the Council of Elders, was not to be outmatched by the other candidates whatsoever.

Roswaal followed, "And I am the humble man nominating Lady Emilia, Roswaal L. Mathers, bearing the rank of Marquis. We are grateful for the Council of Elders' valuable time."

Miklotov stroked his beard while directing where the conversation should proceed.

"Mmmm. So she is nominated, not by the Knights of the Royal Guard, but by the Court Magician. I would very much like to hear the details of why this is so."

Miklotov gave Emilia a penetrating once-over.

To Roswaal, he continued, "Please provide us details about the candidate Lady Emilia, including her lineage."

"Understood. First, though I believe all present are well aware, I shall begin with the circumstances of Lady Emilia's biiirth. As you can see from her lovely silver hair, her skin so pale one can nearly see through her, violet eyes that seem to capture the very soul, and her voice, like a silver bell, one echoing unforgettably in the ears, even in one's dreams. As you well know, these enchanting qualities are proof that elven blood flows through Lady Emilia's veins."

A bald old man sitting among the Council of Elders interrupted Roswaal's explanation.

"And the other half of her blood is human—in other words, she is a half-elf?"

A vein bulged on the large-framed old man's forehead, hatred in his eyes shooting through Emilia as he spat out, "How dare you. Have you no shame, bringing this silver-haired half-demon filth before the royal throne?"

Miklotov countered, "Mr. Bordeaux, your words go too far."

"Mr. Miklotov, do you not understand? A silver-haired half-demon with an appearance matching the Witch of Jealousy as handed down by the old tales! She once consumed half of the world; she leads all living things to despair, chaos, and annihilation! Do not claim ignorance!"

"—"

"How much do you think your appearance and lineage alone makes others tremble? You ask us to place such a being on the royal throne? Inconceivable. Even the commoners of other nations would call us a collection of madmen, to say nothing of the people of the Dragon-friend Kingdom of Lugunica—the nation where the Witch sleeps!"

Bordeaux stomped his foot, his arms wide as he shouted, his tone and manner frayed. Even this act brought no reaction from Emilia. The atmosphere in the hall chilled at once. And then, Roswaal replied, "Master Bordeaux, are quiiite finished?"

"If you ask whether that is all I have to say, then I have not said nearly enough. Do you even comprehend what you have done, High Sorcerer of the Court?"

Bordeaux seemed like he was trying to cow Roswaal into submission.

"I understand veeery much. Master Bordeaux, speaking on behalf of the Council of Elders, expresses that the reaction of the populace upon seeing Lady Emilia would be of conceeern, yes?"

Roswaal raised a finger.

"Howeeever, perhaps you have forgotten, Master Bordeaux? The issue of which you speak has no beaaaring upon the royal selection whatsoever."

"…What do you mean?"

Roswaal lowered his voice as he looked up at the Council of Elders.

"If I may, it is preciiisely as Lady Priscilla stated at the beginning. Even if as a mere formality, there are five candidates, so the royal selection may begin. And if it begins, one need merely see it through, yes?"

Miklotov's eyes narrowed.

"Mmmm. In other words, you are saying that what is important is that the Dragon Jewel chose Lady Emilia, and that her actual suitability to succeed as monarch is…irrelevant?"

"Though it might be a cruuude way to put it, think of her as a stalking horse. Lady Emilia's appearance is very particular. Virtually no human being can look at her and not think of the Witch of Jealousy. She is easily employed as a pawn upon our chessboard."

And just like that, Roswaal denied all possibility of Emilia actually succeeding to the throne.

The sheer shock of it was enough to make Subaru completely forget his anger at Roswaal's earlier intemperate remarks.

He was Emilia's sponsor and backer, who knew just how hard Emilia was striving to be king, and yet he said *that*.

Bordeaux asked, "So the royal selection between five candidates would in actuality be between four?"

"Do you not think that reducing the options reduces the possibility of dissolution? The current lack of a king invites other nations to intervene in our internal affairs. Should we not prepare countermeasures to dimiiinish this threat?"

Roswaal's suggestion sent Bordeaux into deep thought. The other members of the Council of Elders appeared ready to say, *Well, if it's like that...*

To decide to abandon all of Emilia's hard work by the roadside to use her as the stalking horse of the race.

An angry shout reverberated throughout the chamber.

"Don't give me that crap—!!"

As the echoes died, the hall was silent once again.

The only sound left in the hushed chamber was the ragged breathing of the boy who had called out—Subaru.

With his face red with anger, the back of Subaru's mind announced, *Now you've done it.*

But it was too late to back out now. He could not retreat.

Now that Subaru had walked forward out of the blue, Roswaal turned his head and gave him a cold look.

"I did not think you were this obtuse. This is not a place for the likes of yoooou to speak. Apologize and leave."

"Don't give me that crap. I said what I meant. And I'll add this. You all should be apologizing."

Gone was Roswaal's aloofness. In its place was an overwhelming, bloodcurdling aura; just looking at him chilled one to the bone.

Perhaps the wavering of the air around him was from a vast quantity of mana.

"I am all the more surprised—at your disregard for your own life."

Subaru clenched his teeth. The back of his mind knew what to expect—overwhelming power, a vortex of great flame. He recalled the sight of the Urugarum demon beasts in the forest, burned away without mercy or pity.

"If you grovel on your knees this instant, I shall permit you to simply leave. But if you insist on being stubborn…"

The royal selection was the gravest issue for the entire nation. For disgracing it with individual feelings, Roswaal would sentence Subaru to the flame on behalf of the dignity of the kingdom.

The vast danger made Subaru's knees cry out for mercy. The shaking spread from his fingertips; had he not clenched his teeth, everyone would be hearing them rattle by then.

But—

"I-I said, it's not me who should apologize, it's all of you!"

His shrill voice quivered. But even so, Subaru would not kneel. He couldn't kneel, for Emilia had not done a single thing wrong.

"Veeery well. One can do nothing without power. I shall drill this lesson into you. Though it cannot serve you in this world, perhaps it shall in the next."

With his final ultimatum ignored, the power flowing from Roswaal manifested in the form of a flaming sphere, so bright that its light dazzled the entire chamber. The mass of fire on top of Roswaal's hand burned with intensity like a miniature sun, enough that Subaru, standing at a distance, felt his skin start to burn.

"Behold, fire mana of the greatest power. —Algoa."

With one cruel, final word, Roswaal turned his hand toward Subaru. The fireball launched from his palm, with the heat slowly approaching Subaru to burn him to a crisp.

Subaru immediately tried to dodge, but his body simply wouldn't move. Perhaps it was because his legs were shaking, or perhaps it was because the knowledge of impending death had spread from his eyes to the rest of his body.

No.

It was because Emilia was standing behind Subaru.

That was why, that very moment, he could not move from that place...

"—!"

Instantaneously, everyone held their breath at what followed.

The instant the fireball collided with Subaru, it was wiped out by a pale blue glow that covered his entire body. The powers of red and white jostled with each other—and vanished into nothing more than white steam.

And as the onlookers gaped, a voice, clear as a bell, spoke with the same frigid tone.

"—That is enough. I shall permit no further violence in my presence. If you wish to continue this—"

Emilia's resolute voice was followed by a more neutral one.

"—Then I am prepared to wield my power as my beloved daughter demands."

Dubious eyebrows rose at the source of the voice, but the next moment, everyone noticed it—the biting cold spreading throughout the chamber manifesting the Great Spirit's frigid anger.

The little gray cat folded his arms, making a small snort with his pink nose as he slowly floated down. His black eyes were frozen in an expression of unprecedented coldness.

"You lowly humans are saying quite some things in front of my daughter."

"—"

As Puck's emotionless gaze swept the area, the strongest reactions came from the knights. Their swords were already drawn as they raised their guard toward the small cat floating above their heads.

Subaru, left behind by the shift in events, hadn't entirely grasped what was going on.

"—Ah? Er, what?"

It was a moment after he was certain Roswaal would really burn him to death. He had thought he was shielding Emilia, but she stood

in front of him, and everyone was warily eying Puck, poised in a position to defend her.

And their wary gazes also contained something that looked like fear.

Miklotov's hoarse murmur struck the silent gallery like a thunderbolt.

"—The Apocalypse Beast of Eternal Frost."

Upon hearing these words, Puck's ears twitched as he answered the old man.

"Ah, that's right, some people have called me that. Seems you're informed for a youngin."

Though everyone else was tense, Miklotov's razor-sharp wit permitted him to maintain his cool in Puck's presence.

"To be treated like a youngster at my age is an experience I ought to treasure deeply."

Puck responded to the old man's attitude with a pompous flick of his tail.

"You are free to call me whatever you like. But if you want details about who and what I am, you should ask him over there, not me."

At Puck's suggestion, Miklotov called out to Roswaal.

"I suppose so… Lord Roswaal?"

Accepting the call, Roswaal solemnly lowered his head before motioning to Puck and Emilia with one hand each.

"As you have surmised, Lord Miklotov… This is a supernatural being, one of the Great Spirits of yore, known to our forefathers as the Apocalypse Beast of the Eternal Frost. And currently, he is Lady Emilia's contracted spirit."

Bordeaux's fixed Puck with a stare, his voice hoarse from the extent of his shock.

"It can't be! One of the Four Great Spirits in someone's service… and that of a half-demon at that!"

But not even the old man could summon the courage to point at a being capable of turning him into an ice sculpture.

"That youngin included, the lot of you should all be grateful to Lia that I'm not turning this place into a glacier right now. My cute, beloved daughter pleaded to me, so I will behave. —If she wasn't stopping me, you'd all be icicles right now."

The casual way he said it only made the threat seem that much frostier, chilling all those in the chamber to the bone. Faced with his presence, it was all too clear that he was making no boast.

When the lives of everyone present were at the mercy his supremely powerful paw—the sudden sound of an inhalation sounded awfully loud.

"—Ho, ho, ho!"

The sight of Miklotov jubilantly slapping his thighs seemed enormously out of place.

"Even my heart skipped a beat. Allow me to call this a most amusing presentation."

Miklotov's words caused Puck to drop his expression and shrug his shoulders.

"Mm, we're busted. See, Roswaal? I told you it wasn't good to overdo things."

That instant, the cold enveloping the chamber vanished. Amid the bewildered onlookers, Roswaal lightly smacked his own forehead.

"Oh myyy, and I had such confidence… It is so dispiiiriting."

"W-wait…! What in the world are you talking about?"

It seemed only Puck, Roswaal, and Miklotov were in on this elaborate joke. Roswaal finally shifted his gaze to the bewildered Bordeaux and said, "To put it simply—this exchange was the speech from Lady Emilia's camp. I understand that the format somewhat differs from that of the other candidates, but…"

Under Miklotov's gaze, Roswaal raised both hands in a show of surrender.

Subaru stomped on the floor, glaring at Roswaal as the latter adopted his familiar, clownish expression once more.

"So you're saying this was all a performance to show everyone Puck's power and pound into them that he can do more than this?! Is that it?!"

As Subaru shouted the explanation, it was Bordeaux who had the strongest sense of being had.

"That was acting... Acting, you say?! Then all this was a farce from start to finish! Roswaal! Damn you, what do you think this place is?!"

Puck began with an apology.

"Yes, yes, of course you're upset. I apologize. I deeply apologize. Forgive me. Sorry. My bad. —But everything I said was the truth."

The last part, though, made Bordeaux's heart beat louder. The little cat circled around the old man and added, "—The reason I'm not freezing you right now is Emilia's benevolence. Don't forget that."

Puck's voice was tranquil, yet somehow threatening. Bordeaux rebutted with an old man's stubbornness.

"A-and now you make threats. These words and this show of force convey, 'Do as I say or you shall be an icicle.' If this is not blackmail, what is...?!"

Then, Emilia wholeheartedly affirmed his suspicions.

"—Yes, I am threatening you." She continued, "I shall make my case to the esteemed members of the Council of Elders once more. My name is Emilia. I spent a long time in the Great Forest of Elioor, the World of Eternal Frost, and am served by Puck, the Great Spirit that governs fire mana. I am a silver-haired half-elf. The people of the nearby villages called me..."

Emilia paused, surveying the faces of the Council of Elders on the dais.

"...the Freezing Witch, born in the Frozen Forest."

Witch. At that word, the atmosphere in the chamber shifted. Everyone's mouths snapped shut, unable to speak; all save one, Miklotov, who was apparently made of sterner stuff than the rest.

"You displayed your power, and now you state your demands. Truly this is the way of a witch. —Then, what does the Freezing Witch seek in threatening us so?"

"I have but a single demand. —I simply want fair treatment."

"...Fair?"

"I understand I am regarded with prejudice, both for being a half-elf and a witch. But even so, I completely reject that this should rob me of this possibility."

"And so you desire to be treated fairly as a candidate for the royal selection?"

No doubt her memories were filled with the inexpressible malice she had experienced on a daily basis. Surely being persecuted because of the circumstances of her birth had not occurred only once or twice.

"Fairness is an exceedingly valuable thing to me. That is the only thing I demand of you: to be treated impartially. In turn, I shall do nothing unjust, such as use my contracted spirit as a shield with which to usurp the royal throne."

That was surely one option available to Emilia. But she did not choose it, instead opting for a situation that, if anything, put her at a handicap. After all, as she explained, "Compared to the other candidates, I am inexperienced and lacking in too many areas. There is a mountain of things I do not know and that I must study. Even so, I believe my effort to reach my goal is no less than that of any other."

Subaru had seen for himself how Emilia took her studies at the mansion very seriously. That was why he knew the truth behind her assertion more than anyone else present.

He couldn't hide his shaking. It was strange how his throat was so dry, yet his eyes stung, ready to shed tears. He desperately held back from bawling his eyes out.

Emilia continued, "I do not know if my efforts are worthy of the throne. But my desire to make my efforts equal to the task is genuine. I believe these feelings are not unequal to those of the other candidates. Therefore, please look at me with unbiased eyes. Look at me as Emilia, of no family name, and see not the Freezing Witch, nor a silver-haired half-elf. Look at *me*."

The final murmur echoed like a solemn plea. But the strength of the will behind it did not diminish the power of her request.

The chamber fell into silence for a time. It was not that they were at a loss for words. They were waiting.

Finally, Bordeaux, bathed in the gazes of all assembled, sighed at great length.

"My view shall not change. It is unmistakable that your appearance, reminiscent of the Witch of Jealousy, will have ill effects upon the populace. It would place the royal selection in a precarious state."

His low voice had, to that point, argued against Emilia's position. A faint shadow formed around Emilia's violet eyes. But Bordeaux continued.

"However—sentiment is an area where none may intrude. Furthermore, it is something no one can do anything about, no matter what he may think. Even so, I apologize for my earlier rudeness. —No, I deeply apologize for my rudeness, Lady Emilia."

Bordeaux knelt then and there, displaying the greatest respect he could.

"You could freeze me where I stand if I do not submit to your will. Yet, even so, you have not, asking only for fair treatment. —This is an act worthy of respect."

Now that he was speaking calmly, Bordeaux's face was gentle and intellectual; now Subaru could understand why he was on a Council of Elders. His reply drove the shadow from Emilia's eyes, replaced by a brighter, more natural expression of joy at being accepted.

Her lips curled in a pleasant, flowery smile.

Bordeaux, under the full force of her gaze, lost his breath and turned red in the face.

Miklotov redirected the conversation.

"Though that was a rather stormy digression, enough has been said, I believe. Lady Emilia, Marquis Roswaal, do you have anything left to say?"

"No."

"I have not spoken suffiiiciently. What to do, what to…"

Marcus swiftly brought an end to Roswaal's playful comment.

"—Thank you very much, then."

He gave Roswaal's tall back a light pat before Emilia turned toward Subaru, still standing right behind her.

Her violet eyes betrayed a whirlwind of conflicted emotions. Her red tongue poked out of her mouth as if she was about to say something—

From the dais, Miklotov raised an eyebrow and looked down at Subaru.

"Incidentally, what is that young man's position?"

The question, concerning the unmoored Subaru, brought tension back over Emilia's face.

"Ah, err, this is my, ah… Err…"

All her prior composure went flying out the window. And so Emilia had returned to the girl who'd ignited the love burning in Subaru's chest day after day.

Relieved by the sight, Subaru patted Emilia's shoulder as he stepped forward.

"It's all right, Emilia. —I'm ready for this, too."

"Ready for…? Hold on, Subaru, what do you think you're…? Wait a…"

As she called from behind, Subaru boldly stepped forward. Beneath the gazes of the Council of Elders up on the dais, the boy grit his teeth and briskly raised his head. As he had learned by observation, Subaru bowed on one knee like the knights had and opened his mouth, his heart racing as he spoke with the highest respect he could muster.

"Pleasure to meet you, members of the Council of Elders. First, I'd like to apologize for the late introduction. My name is Subaru Natsuki! A servant at Roswaal Manor and knight of the royal candidate, Lady Emilia!"

Subaru, feeling the weight of the hall's silence upon him, grit his teeth to beat back the tension.

"I am extremely pleased to make your acquaintance," he continued.

The out-of-place Subaru had joined the battle to clearly define his own place in the world.

He felt the temperature drop, even colder than when Puck had appeared.

6

Subaru Natsuki had shrugged off Emilia's efforts to stop him and declared himself her knight.

When Subaru made his announcement, the hall became bereft of sound, replaced by a thick, unpleasant cloud. Seeing the conflicted gazes of onlookers, Subaru realized that something was going deeply, unexpectedly awry as Miklotov asked, "Mmmm. A knight, are you. Marquis Roswaal… Who is this?"

"Ahhh, a somewhat ignorant boy, is he not? …This is a poor showing, even for him."

"Indeed, what is the status of Lady Emilia's actual knight?"

"Unlike the other candidates, Lady Emilia currently lacks a knight that she can place her trust in. That is most certainly a matter of concern. Howeeever, that does not mean simply aaanyone can be a knight, particularly one claiming to be a knight of someone who may become king someday."

Roswaal continued to speak in his normal tone, seemingly for Subaru's benefit.

"Fidelity toward one's master is one of the qualifications of being a knight. Furthermore, the power to defend one's liege is required. He must have some special quality enabling him to blaze the path for his master to become king. If he does not, then…"

A voice abruptly interrupted Roswaal's speech, hailing from the line of candidates. All eyes fell on the handsome young man with violet hair—Julius.

"—That alone is not enough, Marquis Roswaal."

Julius elegantly bowed.

"Forgive my intrusion. However, there is something I must ask him."

When Julius indicated him, Subaru scowled, remembering the former's hostility from before the royal selection.

"You need not be so defensive. I have only one question. Once it is done, you may do as you please."

"Do I look tense to you? Why not let me relax a little, ditch the question, and save it for tomorrow?"

"Cease with the clown act. At least, if you truly wish to be Lady Emilia's self-declared knight."

"…What do you mean by that?"

Julius regarded Subaru with exasperation, as if he was a complete dunce.

"It seems you do not understand. Just now, you announced

yourself as a knight before the entire body of Knights of the Royal Guard of the Kingdom of Lugunica."

Julius slowly motioned to indicate the knights lined up behind him. Prompted by his words, the knights in their rows stood at attention without disturbing a single thread of the carpet, saluting with their swords raised.

"Th-that's pretty good stuff there. Did you all practice that just for today?"

Subaru was sniping to keep his wits under the pressure, but Julius's calm composure did not falter.

"Indeed we did, for we are highly aware we embody the dignity of the kingdom on a daily basis. We train in body and spirit, including how to behave in a ceremonial place. Are you prepared to learn all this?"

Only then did Subaru truly appreciate the true intent behind the question posed to him. Julius was asking him if he was prepared to shoulder the weight of the title of knight, like the Knights of the Royal Guard behind him did.

Subaru had called himself a knight to demonstrate that he was Emilia's supporter and the person who held her the foremost in his thoughts—to her rival candidates, to the knights, to the Council of Elders, and everyone involved in the royal selection.

"I…I want to…make Lady Emilia king. No, I *will* make her king."

"Do you have enough resolve, and enough strength, to do this?"

"Resolve isn't everything, and I know I'm not strong enough. The feeling in my heart may not be the same loyalty and fidelity that other people have…but my answer won't change."

Subaru took a deep breath, wet his tongue, and braced himself as he stepped forward.

"—I'll make Lady Emilia king. I'll make her wish come true."

"…Do you not think that this is an exceptionally arrogant reply?"

Dismay entered Julius' expression, as if he were listening to a tale of an empty dream.

"Do you understand? People are divided according to their birth. Perhaps it is best to use the term *capacity*. Nothing is gained by attempting to surpass one's own capacity. Furthermore, you will never gain what you seek in doing so, especially not the title of knight, which falls so frivolously from your lips."

Julius drove the scabbard of his own sheathed sword into the floor with a thump. On cue, the knights assembled behind him produced the same sound a moment later. The hard, heavy echo displayed that he had all the knights behind him.

"Those who pursue knighthood require loyalty to lord and kingdom and the power to protect their liege by force. No one may call himself knight without either one of these things. —Can you still say there is the will, the power, the resolve within you?"

"Don't get all high and mighty on me with your buddies. I know I don't have the power to follow through on how I feel as I am now…"

"You say that you accept your *current* lack of power? I see; that is a precious thought. If you had not acknowledged your weakness, I might have been forced to reduce myself to your disgraceful level."

Subaru was helpless to respond as Julius, unable to conceal his contempt, heaped scorn upon him.

"You understand that you are lacking in strength? Did you declare it so loudly in expectation of a reward? Weakness is a matter of shame, not pride."

"—!"

"Next you will no doubt say your feelings will carry you through. I see. Your emotions conquer all. Fine and well. Did you strive to earn the right to stand in this palace with the might of your strong and lofty *feelings*? Did you come here in an effort to insult us, the Knights of the Royal Guard, to the highest degree possible?"

The stern words bit into him. But even then, Julius did not sheath his verbal blade.

"Only those of certain birth may be recommended for entry into the Knights of the Royal Guard, the pinnacle of knighthood. This is not out of deference to lineage, but because their ancestors have displayed their loyalty to the kingdom, down to the very blood that flows through their veins. I do not accept that you, nor the mercenary calling himself Al, have any qualifications to call yourselves knights."

"Bloodline… It's not like a person can do anything about something like that…!"

"Indeed. It is just as I have said. People are separated by birth. It was the same in your home. Just because two people have been born does not make them equal."

"—"

"Of course, not all born to knightly households become knights. Many lack the will. A knight eternally strives for greater heights, ever willing to cast his life aside, coughing up blood, to protect whatever greatness stands behind him. That is the ultimate honor of those qualified."

With classical nobleman's thinking, Julius stomped on Subaru's feelings, rejecting the essence of his very existence. And every knight there felt the exact same way.

Not a single person in that place acknowledged Subaru as a knight. And yet, he replied, "—Even so, I'll make Emilia king."

"I do not understand. In the face of such rejection, why are you still even here?"

Cold glances from throughout the chamber watched Subaru's recklessness with scorn and contempt. But Subaru couldn't feel any of that.

He felt something far stronger—the gaze of the silver-haired girl behind him. He felt Emilia.

He couldn't look back. He didn't have the courage.

Feeling her presence, he hesitated for a brief moment, and then answered.

"—Because she's special."

That was his answer.

Julius's eyes widened slightly in apparent surprise. However, the surge of emotion was immediately concealed when his face calmed again.

"You are obstinate. I accept that you have a reason for standing here regardless of whether you are qualified or not. In that case, I have nothing more to say to you."

Julius turned his back to Subaru as if he was returning to the line of candidates. But his very first step halted, and his head alone turned back toward Subaru.

"—However, do not think that I accept you as a knight, or ever will."

"What are you…"

"I understand that you esteem her enough that you wish to protect her. However, your thoughts are… No, it would be ugly to elaborate deeply upon it."

Julius shook his head, pitying Subaru.

"A man who brings such an expression to the one he wishes to stand beside…is not a knight."

Subaru's thoughts shifted behind him. Everything felt cold.

He wondered what kind of look was on Emilia's face.

He was too frightened to find out.

That was why the next thing out of Subaru's quivering lips was a transparent attempt to get in the last word.

"Y-you're saying that whether you can be a knight or not is settled from birth? What, every one of you was a golden child, the best at everything? Don't make me laugh. You're not the one who gets to be called the knight among knights around here. Don't think anything you say can get to me."

It was a cheap insult. But Julius did not display his emotions as he casually replied, "Subaru Natsuki, you said? You should know that speaking such cheap insults to others diminishes not only your own worth, but damages the worth of everyone around you. Subaru Natsuki. —There is no beauty in it."

And so, Julius summarized Subaru's words and actions to date, rejecting them, and him, in one fell swoop.

That single remark made Subaru realize that he, and his own conduct, had hit rock bottom.

The candidates gave Subaru blank stares. Behind the dignified Julius, many of the knights seethed with resentment at Subaru's rude statement.

For their part, the rows of civil officials had no love lost for Subaru, who seemed unable to make any argument not based on sentimentality. He didn't even have the courage to look up and see what the Council of Elders thought of him.

Even if it meant making an enemy of the whole world, he'd be in Emilia's corner.

Until that moment, his resolve for that part, at least, had held strong, but…

Before Subaru summoned the nerve to look back, a voice, clear as a bell, moved around to his front.

"Subaru, that's enough."

The trembling of the hand touching his shoulder shocked him enough that even he wanted to look away.

Emilia took hold of Subaru's wrist as she bowed her head to the Council of Elders and said, "I apologize for the waste of your time. He will leave immediately."

The words *waste of your time* sliced into Subaru's heart sharper than any razor.

But he could say nothing.

He had indisputably taken his resolve, determination, and himself, and trampled on them all.

Subaru did not resist as he was led away from the stage by his arm. As Emilia pulled him forward, he still couldn't look at her face.

From the dais, Miklotov sounded hoarse, yet mysteriously, his voice carried far.

"I judge some of this to have been time well spent, Lady Emilia."

Neither of the two stopped walking as Miklotov continued.

"He showed us that, at the very least, you are not a half-elf like the one the world fears. —You have a good vassal."

Emilia paused and looked back.

"—Subaru…"

She was watching the Council of Elders on the dais. Subaru, standing beside her, was not in her field of vision whatsoever. But when she turned, he could clearly see her face.

Her expression was frozen over. Her eyes were frigid with the readiness to emotionlessly cast something aside, when her tranquil, clear voice stated plainly—

"…is no vassal of mine."

Thus, she spurned Subaru's words and feelings up to that very moment.

7

Subaru wandered around in a corridor outside of the chamber, completely rudderless.

He didn't remember much after he'd humiliated himself in front of Emilia and a huge audience. All he remembered was that the captain of the knights had permitted his departure and had left his fate to Emilia's judgment.

It would have been wrong to say he was there because he didn't want to cause Emilia any more trouble. The reason he'd fled, even after he had gone against her instructions to reach the palace in the first place, was far simpler.

—He couldn't bear Emilia's frigid eyes any longer.

Subaru was mentally berating himself as the guard who'd escorted him to the castle's waiting room gave him a concerned look.

"Did something happen to you?"

He hadn't seen Subaru's humiliation because he'd been stationed outside the huge double doors. Furthermore, his demeanor showed respect toward someone he believed to be involved with one of the royal candidates.

"It's…nothing. Sorry for all the trouble in the middle of a really important job."

"I don't mind. Inside the throne room, they're deciding the future of the entire nation. Even if I'm not qualified to be inside, I'm proud just to be on the edges of it."

The irony of the words, spoken with a clear voice, left Subaru with an uncomfortable awkwardness. Here was a guy full of pride for what he was doing at the edges of the selection of the next king.

What of Subaru? Could anyone take pride in what he had done?

No one would. And the one person he had wanted to acknowledge his efforts had rejected him.

"—"

Unable to stand still, Subaru shifted his gaze when he suddenly noticed a ruckus at the end of the corridor. Just as he turned his head to look, a guard popped in, apparently in a hurry.

"Pardon, open the way! We've captured an intruder. We need orders from the captain!"

"Wait, they're still in the middle of the conference! Hold the intruder in the barracks until..."

"The circumstances do not allow us to do that. Either way, we cannot make this decision ourselves!!"

Ignoring the urgings of his comrade, the guard shouted back down to the corridor. Several men were dragging forward the intruder that'd snuck into the castle.

Subaru, wondering what was so bad they needed to interrupt the royal selection, glanced at the intruder. Then...

Regret stronger than anything else that day struck Subaru Natsuki.

"—Ah?"

He stared dumbfounded as four men dragged the man along by his hands and feet, desperately trying to move forward with a balding old man Subaru knew well.

It was Old Man Rom, who had no business being there whatsoever.

"—"

He'd left a message at the fruit seller's place for him to wait. What was Old Man Rom doing there—

Subaru's mind went blank, but then, for once, he instantly found the answer to his question.

"W-wait... Don't tell me, he..."

He followed me. At first, Subaru doubted himself, but then certainty welled within him.

If Old Man Rom had tried to sneak into the castle there and then, the trigger could have been none other than the message Subaru had left at Cadmon. The sharp old man had deduced that Subaru had reason to think Felt was at the royal palace. And he'd tried to enter by any means necessary.

No doubt Old Man Rom's own clumsiness had led to his discovery and capture. But Subaru was the one who'd brought that result about. Subaru knew how precious Felt was to Old Man Rom. He should've known Rom might lose his head over it…

"—!"

The guards passed before his eyes. By the time he reached out, Old Man Rom was already too far away. Subaru froze in place, watching them go in silence.

If he spoke to the guards then and there, he could explain to them who Old Man Rom was. But that also meant admitting that Subaru was connected to an intruder who'd attempted illegal entry of the palace.

It wouldn't end just with Subaru. It would make him an even weightier ball and chain on Emilia's ankle.

That was as far as he got before he did a mental double take.

When he considered the possibility he'd leave Old Man Rom to rot, using Emilia as the reason why, he felt filthy.

"Hey, wait a…!"

Subaru called out to stop them, but a foul-mouthed shout buried his words. Quietly, his eyes went wide as he realized the torrent of insults was coming at him from Old Man Rom himself.

"Ha! You high-falutin' nobles have some awful taste! Is one bumbling old captive something to stare at?! If you're going to laugh, laugh, you filthy-minded youngin!"

Old Man Rom, watching Subaru holding his breath, made a disgusting grimace with his bruised face.

"If you wanna stare, take a good, hard look at this dirty old man from the slums!"

One of the guards, offended at the rude words from the intruder toward Subaru, a VIP, swung his fist down in punishment.

"—Watch, your, tongue!"

"Ugh!"

Subaru countered, "Wait, please! There's no need to go that fa—"

Rom replied, "You are very kind, young one. Heeey, how about it, knights? Your beloved master's giving you an order. Why don't you just wag your tails and do what he sa—ugh!"

"Haven't you said enough, vagabond?!"

The knights responded to Old Man Rom's continued verbal abuse with even harsher strikes than before.

For a moment, the boy's gaze met Rom's, and Subaru understood his intent.

—Even in that place, Old Man Rom was covering for him, because if Subaru said too much, it would only put Subaru in a worse position.

"—Don't butt in, youngin."

The small, faint murmur was followed by insults like those from before for the benefit of the guards. Subaru alone realized the true meaning of Rom's words.

And that sentence left a very deep scar in Subaru.

Subaru had reached out, only to have his hand rejected, his assistance refused, just like in the chamber. No matter what he tried to do, the person concerned didn't need, or want, his help.

"—"

Subaru fell into silence. The guards saluted, dragging Old Man Rom with them once more. Their destination, the throne room, lay ahead. He wondered what treatment Rom would receive at the site of the royal selection.

He shook his head, driving the images off. Rom had a much better chance at a pardon without Subaru opening his big mouth. Besides, there were three people present that knew him, with one practically a relative. Nothing bad was likely to happen to him.

Probably nothing. Almost definitely nothing. His judgment shouldn't have been wrong, but—

"What am I...doing this for...?"

8

Murmurs spread through the throne room. The cause of this exchange of whispers was obvious. The uproar had begun when Marcus, receiving a report from the guards, dragged a vagabond who had infiltrated the castle into the throne room. At first, many doubted the judgment of the captain of the guard, but one look at the intruder made numerous participants understand the reason for his decision.

And then…

"I told you, let Old Man Rom go. That's all I'm asking."

"—Unfortunately, I cannot comply."

In the center of the chamber, a tense deadlock continued, with Felt and Marcus squared off against each other. A vein bulged on Felt's forehead at the way Marcus dismissed her demand.

Reinhard raised his voice in an attempt to mediate.

"Captain, I believe that explanation is insuffi—"

But Marcus rebuffed his intervention.

"Silence, Reinhard. I understand you wish to support the master you have sworn your sword to, but her acceptance of your sword is premised on her willingness to become your king. During the proceedings of this conference for the royal selection, Lady Felt publicly announced she has no intention of participating in the selection process. Abandoning her qualifications means abandoning any right she might have to give commands to us Knights of the Royal Guard… Do you understand?"

Marcus laid out the logic of his refusal to comply with Felt's demand. His words brought a scowl to the former thief's face as she furiously clawed at her own blond hair.

"This is getting annoying, so let's sum it up, 'kay?—In other words, you won't do as I say because I don't wanna do this royal selection thing?"

"—That is indeed the crux of it."

"Ohhh, I see. I get it… You are so annoying."

Felt's catlike eyes glared fiercely at Marcus. Marcus easily maintained his usual poise under the pressure of the young girl's near murderous gaze.

Then the old man, having kept his silence up to that point, made a plaintive yell that echoed throughout the chamber.

"Never mind all that…!—Hurry up and save me!! Felt, it's me! The Old Man Rom you lived with in the slums! I don't really get all this, but you can save me now, right? Then save me! I don't wanna die!!"

Kneeling on the carpet spread across the floor, the old man made the most amicable smile he could as he pleaded to her. The shameful display left Felt speechless. Even the attendants showed hints of disgust at the miserable old man.

"I always saved you when you were in trouble! Many, many times over! Pay those favors back, now! Now, I say! Quick, quick!! Do something, will you?!"

The old man sent spittle flying as he cried out for a quick rescue, flailing around with self-serving logic. It was such a mean and disgraceful sight that even those predisposed to sympathy and compassion would be sorely tempted to walk away.

In a brief span of time, the old man had made enemies out of most occupants in the hall.

Reinhard, sensing danger in the old man's behavior, instantly began to step forward.

"This is bad—"

The red-haired knight instinctively realized the old man's true intent and judged he needed to adapt to the circumstances.

"—Do not move, Reinhard. 'Tisn't good to do anything untoward here..."

But his efforts were frustrated from the outset by Priscilla, smiling craftily as she hid her mouth with her fan.

"Why do you act in such haste, Reinhard? ...It almost looks as if you wish to silence this elderly man before he says something troublesome for you. Simply frightening..."

She got me, thought Reinhard, clenching his teeth as he realized his mistake. Priscilla shrugged her shoulders in a manner more typical of her. Around them, people seemed to recover from their stupor, whispering about what they had just seen—an old man pleading pathetically for his own life.

"Did you see? How unsightly."

"And that face is even worse. I cannot even feel sympathy. It is the spitting image of a thief."

"He shouldn't be released, though Lady Felt defends him..."

Even the knights hoping to have the crime dismissed began to faintly scowl at the old man.

"Lady Felt was raised in the slums...where people like *him* live?"

"Even if she really does have royal blood, can someone with such an upbringing handle royal duties…?"

"We need to rethink this. Or just do what the Dragon Tablet says in name only…"

Reinhard bit his lip as the spreading murmurs confirmed his worst fears. He had been too late, denied any opportunity to refute the words putting down the girl he revered as his master.

Then, with the knights' murmurs all around her, he watched from behind as the girl slightly lowered her head—

Finally, unable to listen to any more, the young girl let loose with a high-pitched, foul-mouthed shout, "—Would you all *shut up*, you ball-less jerks!!"

A wave of shock plunged the chamber into silence. Attendees looked at one another, seemingly unable to believe what their ears had heard, when the girl, her shoulders slumped, marched forward. The giant old man was kneeling, and she was a little girl, but she still had to look up at him. Her red eyes filled with grief.

"What's with you here? That's the worst-looking, most pathetic plea for your life, ever, and I really, *really* hate it."

"—"

The old man's amicable smile at her approach froze over.

"Hey, Old Man Rom. We people from the slums, there's no help for us, right? We know the people above us look down at the poor lives we lead, and we all have rotten personalities, me included. It's a terrible place to live."

Having rated so many things so lowly, including herself, Felt paused for breath and added, "But…

"Yeah, we're a pile of garbage at the bottom of the trash heap…but even if we do live in a place like that, we've come this far by having at least a smidgen of pride in ourselves. No matter how lowly other people see us, we don't lower our heads."

"Felt…"

"I wish I could show you your face in the mirror right now. Looking all meek and submissive, wagging your tail and eager to please, just to save your life… You can't call that *living*!"

Many of the attendants gravely nodded at Felt's words, with Crusch among their number. The ideas Crusch had voiced were very much in tune with Felt's words.

The small girl put her hands on her hips and bluntly stated, "If you wanted me to spare your life, you went about it all wrong. There's no way I'd give up my right to run from a crummy place just to save you, if that's how you're gonna be."

The red-haired young man watched. Her declaration meant she was abandoning someone very close to her, abandoning her right to issue commands—and refusing to participate in the royal selection.

"...Lady Felt."

Reinhard couldn't bear the pain that her declaration sent running through his heart. He'd seen it coming. He'd guessed what reaction the proud girl would display when she saw the old man's behavior. In that sense, she was playing right into the hands of Priscilla and the old men—no, of one old man.

Now abandoned, the old man's shoulders fell, bending forward onto the floor as if all strength of will had left him. But Reinhard did not miss the faint, instinctive slackening of the old man's lips. This was a display of neither despair nor regret; no, he was filled with a sense that his actions had achieved their intended result.

The old man had gambled his very life, and had succeeded in grand fashion.

Truly, Reinhard wanted to expose the old man's scheme even then, to tell Felt that she needed to change her decision. But Reinhard could do no such thing—His hands were tied, precisely because of who, and what, he was.

Marcus, watching the old man hang his head before the girl, must have decided the discussion was over. The knight pulled on the old man's manacles, sending the clink of the chain echoing through the chamber.

"I deeply apologize for causing this uproar before the throne. I shall immediately remove this—"

Suddenly, Felt interrupted Marcus's apology and attempt to leave.

"Or something like that, I guess. I was waiting for someone to jump to conclusions…"

Marcus's mouth closed with a rare look of shame. Seeing his solemn facade crumble, Felt beamed, feeling very proud of herself. She twirled before the dumbfounded audience.

"Sooo, get his hands loose, captain. Those shackles are way too small for him. It hurts just to watch."

"I have already informed you several times over, Lady Felt, I cannot comply with your comma—"

"Because I didn't wanna do this royal selection thing, right? Then it's simple. —I'll do it, the royal selection. I just gotta try to be king, right?"

"—!"

The declaration, accompanied by a laugh showing off her snaggletooth, sent a shudder throughout the entire chamber.

Many of the onlookers seemed aghast at how lightly she made such a critical decision. But naturally, the old man's reaction was even greater, his feelings about her announcement plain on his face.

"Wh-what are you saying, Felt? I-I accepted it. What you said is right. You can't live by losing your pride. Having you cut me loose couldn't be hel—"

"Cut the crap, you shitty old man. What, you've lived this long without knowing you can't act worth a damn? I've been with you long enough to know all sorts of things about you, like—when you tell a lie, the swirl on your forehead turns backward!"

Felt raised her cheeks and drew a little pattern on her head to demonstrate. Her gesture made Old Man Rom's face go pale. He cried out, "You're lying!" and touched his bound arms to his own head in haste.

Felt watched him and said, "Yep, I'm lying. Wow, do you look stupid. No sympathy from me."

"—Ah?!"

Old Man Rom was beside himself at falling so easily for her trap. Felt shook her head.

"So there you have it. Get those shackles off him. Everything up to now was just the wild fantasy of a senile old geezer."

Marcus dragged his feet even then.

"We cannot simply let him go on such flimsy grou—"

"—This old man's my family," Felt resolutely stated. "Let him go, *now.*"

Hearing these words, Marcus's face registered surprise for a brief instant. The next moment, the hesitation vanished.

"As you command."

Marcus stood at attention and let go of Old Man Rom's shackles. Then, he ordered the guards behind him, "Unlock the manacles." But Felt raised a hand to stop them.

"Too slow—Reinhard!"

"Here."

Reinhard responded instantly to the girl's sharp voice, his tall frame advancing to the chamber's center. As the red-haired young man stood at Felt's side, Felt didn't even look at him. Instead, she crossed her arms and motioned with her chin.

"Do it."

It was the world's shortest command.

"Yes, my Lady—"

Reinhard raised a hand up to the sky, fingers straight, slicing down through the air like a knife. The old man's wrists were bound by metal shackles, but the knight's hand sliced through them as if they were paper. The manacles, cut clean in two, slid off as if they melted, falling to the floor. A high-pitched clink echoed in the chamber. In a true sense, this sound announced this was the moment the two had become lord and vassal.

Felt remarked, "So this all went the way you wanted, didn't it?"

"Not at all. This was guided by the hand of Fate."

"Ha! Fate again. What, are you a slave to fate?"

"No—I am, more than anything, your knight, Lady Felt."

Felt seemed to yield in the face of his unrelenting support as she murmured, "You're no fun..."

Old Man Rom was still prostrate as the two bantered right in front of him.

"Why, Felt... I— I wanted you to..."

Felt replied, "I have a pretty good idea why you said all that embarrassing stuff and what you were after— You saw how I hated being here so much I couldn't stand it, right? So you thought you'd give me a helpful nudge."

"If you understand that, then why—"

When the old man tried to pose the question, Felt broke into an awkward laugh.

"What, you think I can sneak back into the city after abandoning my own family? There's no way I could be that shameless."

When Old Man Rom heard these words, his face broke into an expression different from bitterness. He turned his back to her, rubbing an arm over his face to hide it.

"I-I've lost! And all because…"

Old Man Rom looked up to the heavens, his hoarse voice quivering with chagrin and something powerful and inexpressible.

"…I raised her too well—!!"

9

Rom's plaintive cry about how he had raised the girl resounded in the hall. Miklotov, perhaps moved by the lament, cleared his throat, seeking to clear the air in the process.

"Well, then, Lady Felt, Sir Reinhard, may I conclude that you both intend to participate in the royal selection?"

"Sure, go ahead."

"Yes, as my Lady wills it."

Felt's behavior was insolent to the end, with Reinhard following her. The lenient sage let the incongruity pass without comment, quietly replying, "Understood," as he nodded. He continued, "Though there have been some minor uproars, I judge that all the preliminaries have concluded. Lady Felt, do you have anything else to add?"

Surely he thought it proper to give Felt the same chance to give a speech that the other candidates had received.

She answered the prompt with a, "Hmm," and thought about it a bit. "One thing, then."

Landing on a proposal, Felt raised a finger and looked up, bathed in gazes from the dais. Her red eyes flared as they surveyed the faces of those assembled. Finally, she took a deep breath and smiled buoyantly as she swept one hand toward the Council of Elders.

"—I hate nobles."

She kept that smile on her face as she pointed at the Knights of the Royal Guard with her other hand.

"—I hate knights."

Then, with both arms still spread wide, she said, with a spectacular smile and maximum venom...

"—I hate this kingdom!"

She continued.

"—I hate all of you in this room, I hate the structure you built, I hate every little thing here. That's why I think I'll break it all. How 'bout it?"

Felt inclined her head. For a single moment, her behavior brought time itself to a halt. Then, the chamber exploded.

"Wh-what is she saying?!"

"This is where the king is selected, and she says she'll destroy the nation?!"

"What have we spent all this time for!!"

Felt blew off the vociferous, angry shouts of the onlookers all at once.

"Ohh, where's all your high-and-mighty talk now? What about that proud history? Now look, when I become king, I'm breaking all of it. I'm smacking down the lot of you knuckleheads who still can't see the floor crumbling underneath. You all need a breath of fresh air."

The speech of the bright-faced girl threw the hall into chaos like never before.

Miklotov, listening to the proclamation that was reckless without precedent, nodded generously, his expression unchanged as he glanced at the knight standing beside the girl.

"Your lord is quite a feisty one. Having heard her words, what do you think of them?"

"—Truth be told, I believe Lady Felt's wishes are, unfortunately, still in the realm of fantasy."

"Hey, you!"

"However, someday, Lady Felt's words will reach everyone. It is my duty to give her my full support until that day comes."

Miklotov countered, "But Lady Felt counts you among those things she intends to destroy, does she not?"

Reinhard bowed deeply on one knee toward Miklotov, showing no sign of relenting.

"Surely after destruction, there will be renewal. If she will have me, I have no greater desire than to be at her side during that time."

Felt furiously scratched at her hair as she watched his chivalrous profile.

"So in the end, which one are you, my ally or my enemy here?"

"Your ally. Yours, and yours alone."

"…Fine, then. I'll put you to good use."

With her acceptance, the final candidate for the royal selection declared them lord and vassal.

Miklotov dipped his head as he gazed at the radiant row of royal candidates.

"Finally, all the candidates have been assembled. I ask the Council of Elders, do we have a consensus?"

As Miklotov closed his eyes, the atmosphere around him shifted. The old man's voice carried the power of a strong will.

"—My brethren, I ask for your consent to announce that this royal selection shall begin with the five candidates assembled to date."

"—By the authority of the Council of Elders, I assent."

"And I."

"I assent as well."

One by one, the members of the Council of Elders agreed to Miklotov's proposal with solemn nods. Listening to them until the end, Miklotov finally rose from his seat, walking beside the empty throne before opening his eyes.

"—Then, I shall announce the rules for the royal selection!"

Crusch Karsten, lord of the House of Karsten.

Crusch's foremost knight, the Blue Knight, Felix Argyle.

"The candidates are Crusch Karsten, Priscilla Bariel, Anastasia

Hoshin, Emilia, and Felt. All of these five bear the qualifications to be Dragon Maidens!"

Priscilla Bariel, the Bloody Bride.

The mercenary Al, one-armed wanderer from another world.

"The day shall be one month prior to the Dragonfriend Ceremony in three years, renewing the pact with the Dragon!"

The young company president from a foreign nation, Anastasia Hoshin.

Anastasia's foremost knight, the Finest of Knights, Julius Juukulius.

"The selection shall be made according to the guidance of the Dragon via the radiance of the Dragon Jewels and the combined will of the nation's people!"

Felt, of the lost royal bloodline (unconfirmed).

Felt's foremost knight, Reinhard van Astrea, the Sword Saint.

"Until the appointed day, all candidates for the throne shall work to uphold their own lands and the kingdom to the greatest possible extent!"

The silver-haired half-elf, Emilia, the Freezing Witch.

And absent from that place, her self-declared knight, Subaru Natsuki.

"With the minimum conditions fulfilled, I hereby announce the royal selection has begun—!"

Miklotov's great shout filled the chamber with an incredible fervor. No one spoke, but they all were unable to contain their heartfelt cries.

Miklotov, feeling the waves of excitement rolling against him, straightened from his stoop and declared—

"Let the royal selection—commence!!"

CHAPTER 5

SUBARU NATSUKI, THE SELF-DECLARED KNIGHT

1

—Subaru learned of how the tale had proceeded in his absence thanks to Reinhard and Ferris, who had shown up together in the castle's waiting room.

"And so the meowgnificent royal selection began," Ferris concluded. "Subawu, you're going to serve as Lady Emilia's knight, huh? Good luck to both of us."

Ferris wrapped up his summary, but the sarcastic twist of the knife at the end was very sharp indeed. He'd been in the chamber from start to finish; surely he knew quite well what kind of mental state Subaru was in. But Subaru had no time to pay the jab any heed. The royal selection details were crucial, but at that moment, there was an issue Subaru had to find out about even more than that.

Seeing how Subaru was too timid to properly ask, Reinhard answered his unspoken question.

"—The old man is unharmed. His safe release has been secured through Lady Felt's kindness."

"—!"

"I didn't think he'd come in through the same corridor without you seeing his face, and I knew you two know each other. It was easy to guess why you were anxious."

When Subaru lifted a finger, Reinhard moved quickly to assuage his concerns. But even he didn't know the true source of Subaru's sense of guilt.

The instant Subaru had let himself leave Old Man Rom to rot, a dark cloud formed at the bottom of his heart from which there was no salvation.

Ferris chimed in, "That's wonderful. You should thank Reinhard and Lady Felt because it's all thanks to them. Now you don't need to make any excuses at all, Subawu!"

"—"

An icy shudder ran up Subaru's spine. He looked up and turned to face Ferris. His amber eyes glittered like they could see right through Subaru, all the way into his soul.

Having someone look inside him felt deeply unpleasant. So Subaru forced his stiff face into motion to cover it up.

"Y-yeah... I'm so glad! Totally like I figured! It really was a good idea to leave it all to Emilia-tan and Felt—better than anything I could've done... Right? That's right, isn't it?" Subaru spread his arms wide as he gave both a dose of deliberate, exaggerated, clownish behavior, his next words even hastier and more flippant, "But man, Felt really set her heart on winning the royal selection 'cause of me, and that means one more strong rival for the throne. Emilia-tan might give me a real scolding for this one."

In different ways, the expressions on Reinhard's and Ferris's faces changed in response to Subaru's sudden shift, but in the end, they chose not to press the point.

Both knights were showing him pity. Subaru, painfully aware of the fact, ignored his crippled heart's pleas.

"So now that the talk is all over, where is Emilia-tan and everybody?"

"The candidates remained in the chamber to discuss the fine details of the royal selection process. During that time, I said I would go to check on you, and Ferris came with me," replied Reinhard.

Reinhard's actions made sense, but he couldn't stop wondering why Ferris was showing his face, too. Thus, Subaru asked the latter, "Thanks for checking up on me, but is this all right, not being by your master's side?"

"It's totally fine. Lady Crusch is much stronger than Ferri, so it's perfectly safe!"

"Just laying that out there like that… How's a slacker like you in the Knights of the Royal Guard, anyway?"

Ferris gave Subaru a sidelong glance and wagged a finger at him. His fingertip glowed with a blue light.

"Mew know why. Ferri's got a special talent that's in high demand."

"Uh… Why do I feel lighter, like my shoulders, knees, and hips aren't working as hard anymore…?"

"Subawu, your body's aching all over like an old man."

"That's your selling point, eh…? Right, I heard you're a really good water mana user."

In the first place, the reason Subaru was allowed to go with Emilia to the capital was to improve the poor physical condition he was in. The one who was supposed to heal him was none other than the cat-eared man before his eyes.

Reinhard replied to Subaru's comment, saying, "The words *really good* do not suffice, Subaru. It is fairer to call Ferris the greatest master of water-type magic on the continent. It is not for nothing that he bears the title of 'Blue,' standing at the pinnacle of those who share his magical affinity despite his young age."

Reinhard's praise prompted Ferris to push his chest out, displaying not the slightest shred of modesty.

"*Meow*, the title came from all Ferri's fans."

Given that he really was a healer as good as his title, Subaru saw his numerous admirers in a new light. It really put into perspective that this person was treating him.

Subaru's tone was heavy and pained as he arrived at the answer he'd expected.

"—So Emilia-tan really did…"

"So Lady Emilia indeed organized it," Reinhard concluded.

Subaru could only guess at the back-and-forth that arranged for his healing. That was why he couldn't stop the heavy melancholy rising deep in his heart.

Asking Ferris, in the Crusch camp, to treat his body meant relying on a political rival on the very eve of the royal selection. In other words, Subaru had been deadweight for Emilia…again.

He asked, "Hey, why do I have to accept the treatment no matter what?"

"Because she already paid. If Ferri doesn't heal you, Subaru, it'll mean Lady Emeowlia went through aaaaall that effort for nothing."

"What's this payment? If it's just some object, you can hand it back, ri—"

"It's not an object, and once you know it you can't give it back. So Ferri has to say no to your request, Subawu."

Shot down at point-blank range, Subaru could only put a hand to his forehead and cradle his head.

Even though Subaru didn't want to be a liability, it seemed that was all he had been to Emilia. He wanted to help her. That was Subaru's whole reason for being there. It was the one and only reason that gave his existence there any meaning.

A tranquil voice echoed through the waiting room. The speaker was neither Reinhard nor Ferris, but a man with refined features leaning against the open door—Julius.

"—If you curse your own lack of strength so much, I believe you have one choice you can make."

Subaru's face shot up like it had been slapped.

"What? Oh, it's you."

Subaru scowled with resentment. Julius received his gaze with a calm, composed look.

"I would rather you did not make such a disagreeable expression. I did not expect a warm welcome, but letting your emotions get the better of you…"

"The better of me… So what?"

"…It brings the character of those who stand with you into question. Strive to remember this."

"Ugh…!"

Subaru's throat constricted with anger. It wasn't the words themselves, but the sensitive places they jabbed.

He maintained his silence as Julius strode past him toward an open window.

"Now, I suppose you wanted to ask me what I am doing here?" The knight turned his back, surveying the grounds beyond the palace, narrowing his eyes as a breeze blew. "Naturally, I came to see you. I would like you to accompany me for a brief time."

How about it? Julius asked with a wave of his hand. The man's sharp gaze even then implied this was not some friendly suggestion.

"Just so you know, I'd never say yes to something like that, not knowing the place or what it's for, even on one hour's sleep."

"The place is the parade square. The objective... Yes."

In response to Subaru's seemingly casual but extremely biting words, Julius looked down in apparent thought. Then, with an arrogant smile, he spoke with as much venom as Subaru had.

"How about...teaching you a lesson or two about reality?"

2

Some ten minutes after that precariously sarcastic exchange, Subaru was standing atop tightly packed, sandy soil.

They'd moved from the waiting room of the castle to the knights' garrison adjacent to the castle. The tamped-down reddish training ground was ringed by stout walls that gave off a strong sense of the place's history.

The area was perhaps half the size of a high school campus, providing plenty of space for running around and crossing swords.

Subaru tested his footing, then casually began stretching.

Reinhard, standing at the entrance of the parade grounds, tried to get Julius to relent. "Julius, you should stop this. It isn't like you." The expression on his face was not one of haste or anger, but pure concern for Subaru's well-being. He continued, "I accept it was a petty thing for him to say, but it was nothing that couldn't be settled by a retraction. Normally, you would judge as much yourself, no?"

"That is precisely so, my good Reinhard. Normally, I would."

Julius was removing the ceremonial decorations from his Knights of the Royal Guard uniform one by one as he looked back at Reinhard, his eyes betraying no emotion.

"Had it not been this day, and had I met him in a different place, I might have simply let him be. However, it was not meant to be. My good name was sullied before those connected to the throne, and he spoke lightly of chivalry itself. Furthermore, he has not only failed to apologize but has heaped on additional insults."

Just like that, the faint murmurs that had filled the parade square fell silent.

"—I shall now chastise the base ruffian who has besmirched my knightly honor! Any objections?!"

"—!!"

Abruptly, a wordless typhoon roared through the air over the training grounds. The gathered knights and guardsmen shouted, their voices creating the gale. No doubt they saw things very simply: Julius was their representative against Subaru, the man who had disrespected them all.

Never in his life had Subaru stood before so many people directing such hostile emotions at him. He remarked, "Odds are about seven hundred to zero with no one betting on me. I'm so unpopular, I could cry..."

Truthfully, it chilled him to the bone; his body was filled with an overwhelming urge to fall to his knees. Yet, his heart was calm, and though his limbs felt heavy, they did not shake.

It was not that he had resigned himself to his fate. Subaru really didn't understand the mental state he was in when Julius spoke up again. "Now then, before we begin, I shall ask once more: Do you intend to apologize for your earlier impropriety and ask for forgiveness? If you make a full apology for your repeated transgressions here and now, I shall pardon you."

"Repeated transgressions, huh. I can't think of any... And apologize how?"

"Put your forehead to the ground with tears in your eyes. Or, if you find it more fitting, roll onto the ground and show me your belly to curry favor like the good lapdog you are."

"Neither choice is very elegant, so if you don't mind, I'll pass on both."

No doubt he'd never expected Subaru to accept. "I see," Julius murmured to himself curtly as he finally handed his knight's sword to one of his fellows standing beside him. He accepted a pair of wooden swords in its place.

"Properly speaking, it would not be strange for a man to cut you down for your foul tongue. However, you are Lady Emilia's vassal, whether she desires it or not. Accordingly, I shall face you using these wooden wasters."

Any objections? asked Julius's eyes. Subaru answered with a curt wave of his hand, signaling there was no problem. Concluding that his opponent had accepted from his gestures and expression, Julius nodded.

"The referee shall be—Ferris."

Julius glanced sideways at him, while Ferris casually lifted up his palm and waved back.

"Sure, suuure."

He'd easily accepted the role of referee. There was no way to know what he thought on the inside. Unlike Reinhard's hope to put a stop to this, Ferris seemed all too eager to get things under way.

"Have at it, you two. No matter what horrible wounds you suffer, Ferri can patch you up as long as you don't actually die, Subawu, so good luck!"

"Why say that to just me? Worry about the other guy, geez."

"*Meow*, what strong resolve! Hear that, everyone? All right, one, mew, three!"

Turning to the onlookers, Ferris raised both hands high and brought them down. At his signal, the parade square erupted in uproarious laughter, pouring scorn on Subaru's reckless words.

Bathed in laughter, Subaru stepped forward and turned to face

Julius. When Julius offered him one of the practice weapons, he gripped the hilt firmly, as if he was used to it. Similarly, Julius gripped the other waster and announced the start of the mock duel.

"At least you are enthusiastic. Shall we begin?"

Subaru, his skin crackling with the electric energy of the audience, poised the wooden sword and pulled back, then twirled the waster in his hand around as he complained, "Ah, time-out. The feel of this doesn't seem right."

"Is that so? I do not think they differ much, but you may use this one if you prefer?"

"Sorry, sorry. I'm a child of the modern era, so I don't wanna use something that doesn't feel right."

As he spoke, he accepted the wooden sword Julius offered with one hand. In its place, he offered Julius the sword handed to him just earlier—

"Oops."

"—"

Subaru's hand let the wooden sword go a moment before Julius's fingers could take it. Naturally, gravity caused the waster to fall. Julius instantly bent forward as his hand chased after it. The knight, his body curved forward, had lost his height advantage over Subaru.

"...Hmph."

Subaru stepped forward and flipped the waster in his hand from down to up, aiming squarely at the tip of Julius's chin. Simultaneously, his left hand thrust straight forward, tossing the sand he'd covertly picked up during his warm-up exercises toward Julius's eyes—a classic blinding, two-step surprise attack.

—Got him now, thought Subaru, smiling with malicious satisfaction at his little trick. The next moment, he heard a voice right against his ear.

"It seems that you truly have no shame— It must make the vulgarity easy to come by."

Simultaneously, a blow struck Subaru. He felt a sharp, hard jab right to the solar plexus.

The shock to his torso shuddered through the rest of his body. He felt weightless; just after his feet left the ground, his face slammed hard into the earth. Sandy dirt smeared his face, mixed with vomit forced out by the blow to his solar plexus. Pain and heat struck his brain with equal force. The next moment, the parade square erupted in boisterous cheers at how Subaru, the fool who did not know his place, received what he deserved.

The boy curled into himself on the ground as the pain caught up, screaming into the sky above the parade square.

Higher, higher. Farther, farther.

3

"Reporting. Currently, Sir Julius and...Lady Emilia's vassal, Sir Subaru Natsuki, are engaged in mock combat with wasters in the parade square."

"...Eh?"

Upon hearing the guard's report, Emilia's thoughts slipped out in a breathless whisper.

Stay calm, stay composed, the voice inside her kept saying. She didn't know what it meant.

"Wh-why would they be doing such a...?! The parade ground, you mean the knights' building next to the royal palace, right? Julius and Subaru are...brawling there?"

Emilia could not conceal her bewilderment. The guard, however, could not let one part go uncorrected.

"Pardon me, but it is a mock combat. It is no brawl arising out of a personal grudge, but a matter of Sir Julius's honor."

His manner, on the verge of open disrespect, shook Emilia all the more deeply.

She thought back to the war of words between Subaru and Julius in the throne room. Neither had a good impression of the other, and if that was the reason for a private duel...

"Anyway, I need to stop this immediately. Lead me to this parade square..."

Emilia was about to rush off to the square to talk some sense into them when a high-pitched voice interceded—Anastasia's.

"Ah, I think you oughta let them be."

When Emilia turned, she saw that Anastasia had raised a hand, gathering attention on her. Having moved from the throne room to a conference room, the candidates were seated, with their associates at their side.

Naturally, everyone else had heard the report as well. Anastasia continued, "I want to make sure of somethin'. Who proposed this mock combat?"

The guard replied, "I understand that Sir Julius did. However, because Sir Subaru Natsuki accepted, we are in the present situation—"

Anastasia gave the guard's reply a generous nod before looking back at Emilia.

"Ahh, that's fine, that's fine. I just needed to know it was Julius's idea— Since Julius started it, I'm against stopping it."

Anastasia's reply put her squarely at odds with Emilia.

"Your knight and my...my friend, are clashing. Aren't you worried?"

"Worried? About what? That Julius might go too far and make me pay to heal your boy?"

Anastasia tilted her head a little as she replied, looking mystified. Emilia was at a loss for words.

In the half-elf's place, Priscilla poked a small smile out from behind her fan.

"Certainly. From what I saw, he is an incorrigible fool. I imagine he is having his face rubbed into the dirt for a second time today out of excessive stubbornness."

Anastasia added, "Perhaps. Back in the hall, he had some nerve. Makes you wanna look up to him—since someone probably threw him across the room."

The ill-natured smiles the two were trading left Emilia unable to believe her eyes, her voice quivering.

"D-don't you have anything else to say...?"

But only adding to her shock, Crusch broke her silence and announced her own opposition to Emilia's view.

"If Emilia's vassal had requested a duel, I would agree that it is correct to stop them. However, since it is Sir Julius who requested it, and Emilia's vassal who accepted, I believe stopping them is a mistake."

"Why? I mean, Subaru isn't my..."

"If you do not understand, no explanation shall suffice. Besides, though his temper was quick, this is a necessary thing."

Crusch cut Emilia off with a strong tone that did not allow further discussion. Crusch, too, had taken a hard stance that Emilia should not get involved.

The stalled conversation brought a sour expression to Felt's face before she raised her voice in annoyance. "So why did that guard come to tell us about this, anyway? I mean, it's one thing if you're gonna report before they start, but why get all weak-kneed in the middle of it? Just wait for them to finish fighting and tell us what happened after."

Felt's question, posed with arms crossed and a bad attitude, made the soldier's face visibly blanch. Marcus, sensing from his demeanor that something was amiss, stepped in front of his subordinate and broke his silence.

"Report."

"S-sir! I have come to request orders because...the mock duel between Sir Julius and Sir Subaru Natsuki is excessively one-sided!"

"...What do you mean, one-sided?"

"Sir Julius is surely holding back...but it does not appear that way."

The guard seemed distressed, as if he'd seen such a miserable sight that he couldn't bring himself to look in Emilia's direction. That announced to all present just what a terrible spectacle was occurring.

That news was the last straw for Emilia, who threw her indecision to the wind and rushed out of the room.

"I have to stop them...!"

She ran down the corridor toward the knights' garrison and the parade square within.

Once Emilia left, the room seemed on the brink of an uproar when Al raised his hand and suggested, "So, how 'bout we follow the lady and take a look, too?" he motioned toward the open door and shrugged his shoulder to Priscilla, standing beside him. "You like this sort of thing, right, Princess? Watching a ferocious beast toy with a weak critter."

Priscilla lightly turned her back away from him as her charming laughter shook her bountiful breasts.

"Do not cast aspersions upon me with your petty delusions, Al. Well, I do enjoy it... Very well. I wanted a break from this dreadfully long-winded talk, anyway. Looking down upon a variety of fools and laughing at them is good for the soul."

The haggard guard broke out in an icy sweat as Priscilla thrust the tip of her fan toward him.

"Lead us to this parade square—I command it."

4

Blood from Subaru's head wounds seeped into his eyes. He raggedly wiped at them to clear his red-tinged vision.

He'd already lost count of how many times he'd been knocked to the ground. His left eye was already swollen shut; he tasted too much blood to tell if it was just his lip, or if the inside of his mouth was cut, too.

He didn't really feel the pain.

He wasn't sure if the aching had become so great that he had grown numb or if it was the adrenaline soaking his brain. It was probably a number of things.

But what was driving the pain from Subaru's mind was pure *anger*.

The strength of Subaru's spirit, so deviant from the norm, earned him exasperation from Julius, not praise. "How about you finally acknowledge your own limitations?" His handsome face was still untouched by a single speck of dust or a single drop of sweat as he calmly swayed the tip of the frayed wooden sword he had used to beat Subaru to a pulp. He continued, "Surely by now you are painfully aware of the difference between us, and how grievously you insulted me by treating the word *knight* with such casual contempt?"

It was not an attempt to appeal to Subaru's heart, but to smash it to pieces.

Julius was only pounding on Subaru to show him what being a knight meant. Subaru was only recklessly, stubbornly resisting the reality Julius was drilling into him. There was no room for anything to grow between them. And nothing did, no matter how long their confrontation continued.

Julius said to him, "I believe going any further may put your life in jeopardy."

"...Like this much is gonna kill someone. Don't talk about it like you know."

"You sound as if you have prior experience."

"I know more about it than any man in this world."

Since Subaru had set foot upon that land, he had perished a total of seven times. There was no one in that whole, wide world that had faced death as many times as Subaru.

People used words like *hurts enough to die, mortified enough to die, enough to die, enough to die*, but he knew that people did not die of these things.

Shaking his cut, throbbing head, Subaru sluggishly lifted up his weapon, raising his voice as well. The instant he brought Julius into range, the tip of his wooden sword cried out as he raised it for a swing—

"There is no beauty in you."

A moment before Subaru was about to unleash a downward strike, a blow struck his right wrist—his sword hand. The sharp smack sent his wooden sword flying, and Subaru's eyes instinctively followed it. The next moment, he was bowled over by another blow to the solar plexus.

His breath caught, and, unable to break the fall whatsoever, Subaru rolled onto the ground, the earth and sky trading places about five times before he ended up flat on his back, arms and legs spread wide. Subaru literally coughed up blood.

The knights and guards were still gathered to watch Subaru's public whipping at Julius's hands. But there were no cheers any longer.

Subaru was the villain who had belittled the very nature of knights at the royal selection that would determine the kingdom's future. And so, Julius rose to represent the Knights of the Royal Guard and rebuke him, making him taste pain until he apologized—That was the scene they had come expecting to see.

Indeed, when it had begun, they cheered heartily in delight, or laughed in mockery at Subaru's pathetic display, unreservedly supporting their comrade, Julius. What had changed was that everyone now understood this was a beating, and nothing more.

There was a vast, yawning chasm in ability between Julius and Subaru. Unskilled in attack and wide-open in defense, the boy was knocked down over and over.

At first, derisive laughter rang out each time he went down. The exasperated sighs began when the number exceeded ten. By the time people had lost count, everyone wanted to avert their eyes. *Just end it already*, they thought. Anyone could see who had won and who had lost. They had learned all over again that knights were superior. Beyond that, this was a meaningless dispute.

But Julius continued to beat Subaru and showed absolutely no sign of relenting.

As referee, Ferris had the authority to stop the fight at any time, but made no sign of stopping, regardless of how hurt or injured Subaru became.

And Subaru himself betrayed the knights' hopes, standing up again.

Everyone understood. This no longer held any meaning, any significance. It was nothing more than a pathetic display of senseless stubbornness. Therefore, in the end, it was the least they could do to watch Subaru be bullheaded to the bitter end. They did not leave, because those who watched the spectacle unfold had become part of it, and shared responsibility for it.

"—"

Subaru's quivering upper body sat up before the eyes of the knightly onlookers. He picked up the waster that had fallen beside him, using it as a crutch to prop himself up. He coughed violently, spewing a large volume of blood.

The somber sight confirmed everyone's thoughts. As if by nature, they understood—

The next exchange would be the final blow in this pointless dispute.

5

—One more hit and I'm done.

Funnily enough, Subaru had managed to reach the same conclusion as the onlookers watching his absurdity. But he no longer cared about what anyone saw. Inside Subaru, there was no one but him and Julius.

He wouldn't get up after the next blow. Even if Subaru's sword miraculously made contact, Subaru would be unable to continue.

Why challenge him, then? If the end result would be the same either way, why even try?

He couldn't see the answer. He had lost his original reason for starting the fight, filled purely with hatred for Julius standing nonchalantly in his swollen field of vision. And so he decided he'd put everything he had into one final blow, aiming to break the bridge of Julius's nose.

"—"

His lungs ached simply from breathing. Exhaling made his mouth hurt that much more.

Pushing the agony away with his threadbare consciousness, Subaru collected his remaining strength and waited for his chance— hoping Julius would let his guard down for even a moment. He couldn't let this opportunity slip away.

—Painpainpainpainpainpainpainpainpainpainpainpainpainpain painpainpainpainpainpainpainpainpainpainpainDIE.

"—!"

Julius's gaze seemed to drift for an instant. In his tattered state, Subaru took his shot.

He heard nothing. He left everything behind, lifting his sword up with all his spirit.

Julius, having taken his attention ever so slightly off Subaru, hadn't reacted yet. Something had attracted his attention, but every cell of Subaru's brain was devoted to thinking about that single blow.

"—!"

He thought he heard something—something in that world without sound, where only he and his target existed.

"—ru!"

He heard a voice. Someone's voice. Someone's voice in his ears.

His mind was being pulled away. But everything was forgotten, drowned out by his furor.

That moment, his eyes trained on the single thing that gave his existence any meaning.

"—baru!"

The voice became clearer. It began to hold meaning.

If he heard it clearly, there would be no going back.

That was why Subaru brushed everything away, to escape from the overwhelming fear that pursued him still, right on his heels. With every ounce of his being—he shouted.

"—Subaru!!"

"—SHAMAAAAK!!"

Betraying the clear-as-a-bell voice in his ears, Subaru chanted the incantation at the top of his lungs.

A black cloud erupted, dying the reddish-brown soil of the parade square black, blotting out everything.

A realm of oblivion unfolded. Within it, Subaru rushed forward, shouting in his guttural voice. In this space where reason held no sway, his brain commanded his arms to swing down. The dark cloud swallowed the limbs stretching in front of him, ignoring all else to do as they were commanded, so that the tip of "something" might reach—

"So this is your secret weapon, then?"

Clear as day, Subaru heard the voice in a world that should be soundless.

The black cloud brightened— And from within the source of light, a wooden sword cut through the air, mercilessly slamming Subaru's body down to the ground.

The voice flitting his way from above sounded surprised rather than hurt.

"I did not expect that you would use Dark-type magic. I admit you caught me by surprise."

Subaru, lying on the ground with his limbs splayed, gazed up at the sky in a daze as he faced reality head on.

"However, your training is deficient. Such low-level magic can only work on someone of lower ability than you, or perhaps an unintelligent beast. Such a plan would not work against a single Knight of the Royal Guard." The voice seemed to carry pity. Pity that crushed Subaru's heart and told him to give up on everything.

He had thought he could change his situation. He thought that even he could accomplish something.

"You are irredeemably powerless. You have no place by her side."

Those words, at least, he wished to refute—words that denied that his life held any meaning. Subaru moved his neck to glare at the man, trying to get him to at least take that part back…

"_____"

…but instead, he caught a glimpse of the silver-haired girl with violet eyes.

She was leaning over a terrace on a floor midway up the royal palace wall that overlooked the parade square. Behind her were girls he recognized, each one coldly surveying the results.

The thoughts behind her blanched face no longer mattered.

Subaru no longer cared what anyone at all thought of him.

Or rather, that would have been true if the person standing there hadn't been the absolutely last person in the entire world he wanted to see him in this state.

"_____"

Inside him, Subaru heard a sound like a thread snapping.

That was the last thing he knew before his consciousness began fading far, far away.

With his mind, distinct until that point, cut loose, the world quickly lost its color. This time, Subaru's mind truly left anything and everything behind as it plunged to the bottom of the abyss.

"—Subaru."

He thought he heard a murmur he should have been unable to. Then, it vanished along with the rest.

6

When Subaru awoke, his brows furrowed as he stared up at an unfamiliar ceiling.

To Subaru, who usually woke up more quickly than he liked, the brief period of mental vagueness between sleep and fully waking was precious time. For several seconds, Subaru immersed himself in this boundless, nebulous state as his mind groped for its memories, such as what he'd done before sleeping, what that place was…

Subaru felt his temple throb painfully. That ache brought everything rushing back.

"I…remember…"

He remembered the disgrace he had endured before he ended up where he slept.

He raised a hand to his forehead, but his eyes were drawn in by the discovery of a serious scar near his wrist that he didn't remember. He immediately realized it bore the traces of healing magic.

And that he could feel the traces of wounds on his body meant—

"—I didn't…die."

Touching his presumably cracked forehead and most likely fractured wrist, he let out a sigh, lamenting that the healing had removed all physical pain. If not for the smoldering feeling of humiliation in his chest, he'd almost think the whole thing had never happened. No—

Now that Subaru had regained consciousness, the betrayed look *she* gave him was something no spell could heal.

"—Subaru."

Emilia sat on the side of the bed, her violet eyes full of melancholy.

For no reason he could discern, she'd folded the white robe she'd been wearing over her lap while watching over Subaru.

The rays of the western sun filtering through the open window made Subaru guess it was several hours later on the same day.

The first thing on his lips was harmless and inoffensive enough.

"—The royal candidate discussion's over already?"

Emilia apparently waited for him to make some kind of excuse before she opened her eyes a little wider, caught off guard by how he tried to pretend nothing had happened.

"Yeah, it's finished… Most of what everyone wanted to say came out in the throne room, so the rest was mainly working out the minute details about the royal selection. Most things were settled by Roswaal approving them."

Emilia shook her head, a subtle lament in her voice at her own powerlessness. Subaru realized he took comfort in that—Emilia, regretful she couldn't do anything in the royal selection, was somehow sharing in his misery.

Subaru tried to hide it from himself by making an attempt at being glib.

"That so. Then you probably wasted a lot of time waiting for me while I overslept. Anyway, let's get straight back to the inn. Gotta pick up Rem and work out plans for the royal selection, right?"

"Subaru."

"Here in the castle you don't know who's watching or listening, so best to save the deep talk till we're back at the mansion, right? Or do you have to talk with high-ups in the capital here first?"

"Subaru…"

"Errrr, maybe it's best to make non-aggression pacts with some of the candidates here instead? It's tough when you don't know who's coming at you and when…"

"—Subaru!"

Emilia sharply shouted Subaru down amid his rambling, cutting off his excuses. He turned his averted gaze back toward her.

She spoke to him quietly, but gravely, not be swayed.

"—Let's…talk."

Emilia rose from her seat, her arms tightly hugging the fabric of her folded robe. The stiffness of her cheeks conveyed better than any words that the coming conversation was not about anything good.

"There are things that I want to ask you… Truly, many things."

Her lips quivered, as if in hesitation, groping for exactly what subject she should broach.

"…Yeah, I, suppose so."

Subaru had a pretty good idea why she was hesitant. Everything Subaru had done until then had been completely unexpected. —Therefore, Emilia was seeking the right way to ask about Subaru's true intent behind his actions that day.

He had only a single, unabashed reason to give. But the question on Emilia's lips was not what he wanted.

"Err, then… Why did you…come to fight with Julius?"

This answer was much harder to come by. What significance *did* that battle have—?

"You had a reason for it, didn't you? It's you, so I'm sure you had an important…"

Already beaten down, Subaru had been waiting in the corridor when Julius appeared before him. When Julius invited him to the parade square, Subaru immediately deemed it would be payback for the rudeness he had shown in the throne room.

He certainly tried to appreciate the difference in the power Julius wielded compared to him.

He knew from the start he had no chance of victory. And yet, Subaru had taken the wooden sword, challenged him to the hopeless battle, and had been pounded into the dirt.

Why did he do all that? The answer was—

"I wanted…payback."

"…Ah?"

Subaru lifted his face. Looking up at the bewilderment in the silver-haired beauty's eyes, he continued, "I wanted to show him that…I'm not something to throw away on the side of the road. I thought I could pay him back, and show him I could…stand by guys like him even if only a little."

His words were all jumbled. He resented himself for not being able to put it more clearly. If not for the emotions smoldering in his chest, ramming against his heart, he wouldn't need to endure such conflicted thoughts.

"Subaru..."

"I was...stubborn. I hated him. For saying I'm disgraceful, powerless, how I'm in the way...how I'm not worthy of you, how he tried to push me away from you... So I took him on."

He figured the last one was the straw that broke the camel's back.

Yes, Julius had been sternly rebuking Subaru, telling him he wasn't worthy of Emilia. But he didn't even have to say that. Subaru himself knew that more than anyone. To gloss that over, he had desperately worn a mask, feigning ignorance, but that man had easily called his bluff. So unable to forgive him, Subaru had taken him on, leading to the inevitable result.

The boy's listless reply, spoken with a hung head, made Emilia's breath catch a little.

"That's...why you...?"

No doubt it was not the concrete reply she had been searching for. Whatever lofty ideals she had held onto, the truth behind Subaru's banal stubbornness betrayed them.

Subaru listened to the trace of disappointment slip past her lips.

"...Emilia...tan, you..."

Her quivering words had scolded the powerless-feeling Subaru into a confession.

Emilia hadn't intended to do it. She did not understand how cruel and relentless her act was. That was why, as Subaru spoke with a frail voice, he was unable to even look at her.

"—You just don't understand."

That was what he said.

The moment he said it, Subaru realized he'd been lashing out. To deny that someone understood was the worst kind of excuse, cutting off that person from your heart.

Subaru was unable to keep his face raised when he heard a breathless-sounding voice.

"—You're right."

Her agreement, spoken almost like a sigh, made it sound like she grasped what he had said, that she was agreeing not to push the issue any further.

Her reaction made Subaru's shoulders ease with a sense of relief. That was when she said, "Tomorrow, Roswaal and I will be returning to the mansion. You will remain in the royal capital to focus on medical treatment."

Subaru couldn't make sense of her words

"Huh?"

When he tilted his head in confusion, Emilia strove to hide her heavy emotion as she turned toward him.

"That's what we agreed to in the first place, yes? You came to the royal capital so that your depleted gate can be healed. Ferris agreed, so you will be healed by him, then recuperate."

"W-wait a minute."

Emilia stated the plans for Subaru at a rapid clip. "While staying in the capital, you will be in Ferris's...or rather, Lady Crusch of the House of Karsten's care. Rem will be staying with you, so you won't need to worry about a thing."

Subaru, realizing that his intent had been completely missed, called out to her in a desperate voice.

"I said wait!"

His fingertips immediately reached out, taking hold of her sleeve as if that would stop her from pulling away.

"Why are you...all of a sudden...I..."

In reply to Subaru's frail voice, Emilia looked away as she said, "... You push yourself too far when you're around me. Don't you?"

Subaru held his breath at her words. Emilia's expression was unreadable. He strained, trying to get her to look at him.

"You don't have to...put it like that..."

"I'm not wrong, am I? It was like that when we first met, and like that at the mansion. And it was like that today... All of it's because you were together with me, wasn't it?"

Her way of speaking was thick with discontent.

Faced with negativity and cynicism that was all too out of character for Emilia, Subaru could only shake his head.

"That's not what I was trying to say... I just..."

"Just?"

"I just did those things...because I wanted to give you something..."

"For...me?"

When she echoed his words back, Subaru sent a determined nod back her way.

He had earnestly struggled against destiny for Emilia's sake, and hers alone. It was that feeling, above all others, that he wanted her to understand.

...That was why the next words out of her mouth left Subaru in complete shock.

"—It was all for your own benefit, wasn't it?"

"—"

Beyond the silence, Subaru's brain was a complete blank.

He didn't know what to say. He didn't know what he *wanted* to say.

"I...I just...wanted...to give you..."

Sadness? Suffering? Regret? Anger? Sorrow?

—I want to give you happiness.

—I want to help you get what you desire.

—I want to protect you from everything that makes you sad.

Those were the pure feelings Subaru had for Emilia that formed the foundation of his every deed.

He had acted in the belief that his efforts would convey his feelings stronger than any words.

But that had been his conceited assumption, made without any consideration for other people's feelings.

"—Mff!"

The dazed Subaru yelped in surprise at the sudden impact of soft fabric on his face. When he immediately pulled the material away, he realized it was the white robe with an embroidered hawk that Emilia had been holding in her hands and that she had struck him with it.

But he couldn't associate Emilia with such a violent action. Even if he accepted that, logically, Emilia had thrown it at him, he could not emotionally accept it.

After all, the Emilia Subaru knew was always kind, filled with motherly affection, and, though she was not consciously aware of her own stubborn streak, she was a soft-hearted girl who couldn't stop helping others if she tried.

Why, then?

Emilia's violet gaze quivered with a wave of emotions. Her face was tense as she bit her lip, which seemed to tremble from fierce emotion. He'd never seen either before.

Neither her expression nor her gaze fit the girl he knew whatsoever. Yet, both were aimed at him, of all people.

He understood how out of place the sentiment was, but he thought that she was...beautiful, like this.

The wave of emotions turned to tears that filled her purple eyes.

"Stop lying about doing all these things for my sake—!"

With a small shake of her head, she seemed to be venting about every last thing eating at her.

"Coming to the castle, fighting with Julius, using magic... You're saying it was all for me? I didn't ask you for any of those things!"

"—!"

"All I wanted was for you to do the things I asked you to do!"

"_____"

"Hey, do you remember? What I asked?"

"I-I..."

Hearing her reject his actions so clearly froze Subaru's mind with terror. That was why he couldn't produce an answer to her question from within his jumbled head.

With Subaru unable to answer, Emilia firmly closed her eyes.

"I asked you to stay at the inn with Rem and wait."

"_____"

"Using any more magic would be very bad for you, so I asked you not to use magic."

He remembered that she'd used the word *please* for both.

Both times, Emilia had strongly urged him to behave out of concern for his health. But Subaru had trampled on her words each time based on his own selfish delusions. Somewhere deep down inside, he had thought of things so frivolously, as if good results would always let him smooth over his broken promises. But as a result, Subaru had not only disregarded her pleas, but didn't have a single proper thing to show for it; indeed, he'd only disgraced himself and held her back.

But even so, he at least wanted her to understand that the underlying motivations were genuine.

"I'm sorry I didn't listen to you. I'm really, really sorry. But! But you're wrong, I, I didn't do them for my sake…"

But Subaru's tongue cramped like it had gone numb, rejecting his efforts to put feelings into words. As he flailed for words, Emilia stared at him with sadness.

His words were unforgivably selfish. He never should have said them.

"Emilia, don't you…believe me?"

Someone who had just denied that she could understand him had no right to say any of it.

"I want to believe you… I want to believe you, Subaru."

She sounded like she wanted to cry. She might have already been crying. But Subaru didn't have the courage to find out. He couldn't bring himself to look at her, even though she might be in tears; even though he might have been the reason why she was in such a state. Subaru had continued running forward trying to avoid that, but at the most critical moment, Subaru Natsuki just—

Her emotions exploded.

"I wanted to believe you…but you're the one who stopped me, Subaru!"

Though she had sometimes lost her calm and logical demeanor to anger before, this was the first time he had seen her cast them aside, like shackles on her emotions. Freed of those restraints, Emilia poured her overflowing feelings into words.

"You didn't uphold a single promise, did you, Subaru? You… *promised*, but you broke them all like they were nothing and ended up here, didn't you?!"

He'd trampled on the promises they made together—in other words, her trust.

His claim, that he had done it all for her, was moral justification that only held meaning for Subaru himself.

Emilia carried on, saying, "You haven't kept your word, but then say you want me to trust you...? However you ask, I can't do that. I can't..."

No!, he wanted to cry out in a loud voice. But in reality, Subaru's trembling throat made no sound; his head felt as heavy as lead, too heavy to lift from its lowered, face-down position.

In front of the crying girl, whose emotions he had toyed with, who sought an honest answer from him—Subaru chose to turn his back to her, and thus, continue to betray her.

She asked him, "...Hey, Subaru. Why do you want to help me so much?"

It was surely the doubt nestled in Emilia's mind that kept her from asking many times before. Seeing Subaru running around covered with injuries, forcing himself to smile all the while, or watching him endure great pain and leap into the jaws of death, she must have entertained those doubts for some time. Thus, it was inevitable she would press the issue now.

If Emilia didn't let it all out there, if she kept her misgivings forever deep inside, not understanding why Subaru kept doing his utmost for her, it would only bring her more pain.

The question was Emilia's final offer of salvation to Subaru. He had thought that, having so lightly treated his promises, there was nothing he could say that could reach her, but even so, she was asking him to honestly tell her.

—Why did Subaru work himself to the bone for Emilia?

—Why had he tenaciously clung to her since arriving in that world?

"I want to do everything I can to help you because you saved me..."

"I...saved you...?"

"That's right."

When he had been suddenly invited into another world, he was at a complete loss, not knowing right from left, with unavoidable violence threatening him; for all he knew, that world would have been the end of him.

He continued, "I don't think you understand how...much you helped me. But that...saved me, more than words can express."

What Emilia had saved back then was not his life, but Subaru himself.

It didn't start with Subaru. The first time, it was Emilia who did the saving. Everything he'd done since was nothing more than repaying her for what she had given him.

"Subaru, I don't understand..."

"That can't be...helped. But it's true. You saved me. That's why I tried to...pay back the favor...but now, it's..."

It's not just that, were the words that should have followed. But Emilia exploded in emotion, her silver hair violently swaying as she shook her head, so the words never arrived.

"—I told you, I don't understand!! I saved you? I did no such thing. The first time I met you was at the loot cellar. I'd never seen you before in my life!"

"No, listen to—"

"If I'd met you before that, if that was true, I'd... I'd...!"

Burying her face in her hands, Emilia rejected Subaru. She would listen to him no longer. His words did not have the strength to stop her from fully retreating into her shell.

He had no idea what kind of sore spot of hers he'd brushed up against. He didn't know, but he had to keep talking. That's why Subaru quickly pulled himself together and said, "Maybe you don't understand, but listen to me anyway. It's the truth! The first time we met when I came to this world—"

Instantly, the scene ground to a halt, and Subaru realized he had brushed against the forbidden. This was the world where time was frozen and everything stopped.

He could no longer hear even the furious beating of his heart. Emilia's voice, which he had heard until that very moment, grew distant. Even the high-pitched ringing sounds vanished without a trace as the world of silence beckoned.

Subaru could not contain his anger, both at himself, and at the enforcing shadow with no respect for the mood—the shadow that inflicted unending pain upon Subaru when he spoke about his peculiar trait.

After the warning from the halted world that he had nearly violated the taboo, time began to tick once more.

—With a thump, Subaru realized his entire body had broken out in a cold sweat.

By the whim of the shadow, he had not received a painful penalty. He remembered that. If he kept talking like he had just been about to, the shadow would mercilessly torture his heart in the frozen world.

The words he would have spoken tumbled back down his throat. The sincere thoughts he wanted to share had no place to go, a millstone Subaru's shoulders had no choice but to bear.

Emilia said, "...Once again, you're not saying anything."

Her cold, hard voice battered his eardrums. It sounded like despair—like she'd given up. The uncharacteristic anger, the surge of sadness within her chest that had no outlet—what could he do about them? Even if he tried to tell her how he really felt, she wasn't listening to him anymore. And if he tried to tell her everything, that accursed shadow would get in his way to stop him.

He asked, "Why...don't you understand...?"

"...Subaru."

"I thought, you... You of all people would understand..."

"The me inside your head is really something, isn't she?"

That one sentence was filled with enough distance and isolation to make him cry.

When Subaru lifted his face, astounded, Emilia averted her eyes and faced away from him.

He wondered whom the lonely smile that came over her lips was meant for...him, or her?

She continued, "She understands it, all of it, without even having to ask. Your pain, your sadness, your anger—she feels all of them as her own."

"......Huh?"

"—If you don't say it, I can't understand, Subaru."

He'd been rejected. He'd been smashed to bits. His illusion crumbled into dust.

The one thing he truly thought he could believe in since falling into that world vanished.

"I…"

He'd risked his life, endured the pain of being bitten all over, wiped away his tears and surpassed them, all to continue to protect the idol he had erected in his mind.

And so, his arbitrary utopia, one that had never existed, crumbled without a sound.

His lips quivered. His eyes were hot inside. His tongue was twitching. His heartbeats were so fierce he could hear them.

"Everything…I've done…"

He lifted up his face and met Emilia's violet eyes. They were filled only with sadness. When he saw his own face reflected there, it was truly pitiful and beyond salvation.

He raised up his shrill voice in anger, so much that the room seemed to shake with it.

"—You got this far because of me, didn't you?! Like at the loot cellar when your crest got stolen! I saved you from that uber-dangerous serial killer! I put my body on the line! All because you're important to me!!"

His fingertips trembled as they gripped the sheets. His nails dug into his palm and slowly drew blood. He continued, enumerating every deed to his credit that he could think of as he tried to chase after her shadow, far in the distance.

"Like at the mansion! I barely hung on there! My skull got cracked, my head went flying, but everyone in the village got saved anyway, didn't they?! And things turned out the best way possible with Ram and Rem, I'm sure of it! That's because I was there, right?!"

The fact that he had saved everyone at the loot cellar, and at the mansion—all that had been possible because of him. These were the deeds Subaru ought to be proud of, and rewarded for. He'd come that far. He'd done so much. He added, "You have to owe me something for everything I've done for you—!!"

He shouted because the meaning of all his actions, and the thoughts behind them, had been refuted. Subaru's vainglorious search for praise, his gnawing desire for satisfaction, and his egotistical wish to be wanted, had been the unconscious extremes that had led him down his path.

And all were summed up in a single, defining word.

With a halting, shaky voice, Emilia said to Subaru, who was breathing roughly with sweat on his brow, "…Right."

Her words had a tone of acceptance, of resignation, of resolve—in other words, it was the end.

"Subaru, I owe you a huge, incredible debt for many things you've done, so…"

"Yeah, that's right. That's why I—"

"So I'll repay it all to you. Then we can end this."

Her statement, incredibly clear, raised Subaru's face like he'd been kicked. And when he saw that Emilia's gaze was even hollower than before, he realized that his hasty words should never have been spoken.

In a childish tantrum, he had trampled even his purest thoughts underfoot, throwing it all away.

"—That's enough, Subaru Natsuki."

If the relationship between them was only about repaying favors, that relationship would end as soon as the debt was repaid.

That was the only conclusion the situation could reach, now that he'd tallied up the things he'd done in the hope of giving her something without the slightest thought of a reward.

Ever since their first, intimate encounter, she had called Subaru by his first name. He understood all too late that he could not recover the affection he had lost.

She stated, "Rem will come later. Do as she says. Everything else, I will arrange afterward, so…"

He couldn't even reply. Nor was there anything he could ask of her.

Emilia began to walk, putting distance between them—physical distance, but an emotional distance that was far greater. In that moment, Subaru lacked the courage to reach his fingers toward her back, or even to watch her as she left.

When Emilia reached for the door, she abruptly stopped and murmured.

"I..."

She spoke in a soft voice, like she wanted to say it less to Subaru than to herself.

"...got my hopes up. I thought, just maybe, you...*you* wouldn't give me special treatment, Subaru. I thought you could look at me like an ordinary person, like an ordinary girl, the same as any other..."

This was the girl that had demanded fair treatment in the chamber at the royal selection.

The fact she was a half-elf must have caused her intense and prolonged suffering for her wish for something so meager. But...

Subaru replied with a faltering, quiet murmur of his own.

"I can't...do that."

Emilia hadn't spoken as though she sought a response. Therefore, Subaru's own murmur was not a reply, but a statement for his own benefit.

Mulling over Emilia's words, Subaru weakly and limply shook his head.

"Even if you tossed out every other person in the whole world, I couldn't do that. I can't look at you the same as everyone else, I just can't."

That, at least, was the unmistakable truth.

He heard the door close. The air became still again.

Left alone in the room, Subaru curled up on top of the blankets, his gaze wandering.

Abruptly, he pulled himself to the corner of the bed. He saw the robe that had fallen on the floor.

He reached out, pulled it close, and embraced it. As he hugged it, he felt like a trace of human warmth remained in it when all others had vanished. Subaru squeezed it against his chest, as if trying to bind that warmth to himself.

—That day, for the first time in that other world, Subaru Natsuki became truly alone.

EPILoGUE
KNIGHTLY EXPECTATIONS

1

"So do you have anything to say, Sir Julius?"

"No, nothing at all. Everything is in accord with the report."

Two men spoke in the darkness of a room untouched by the sun's rays. The space belonged to the captain of the guards in the knights' garrison, adjacent to the royal palace. Marcus was sitting at his official desk, with Julius standing ramrod straight in front of the table.

"I could offer no complaint if you were to banish me from the Knights of the Royal Guard for my breach of conduct. Do as you will, captain."

Julius pulled his sword out of the scabbard at his hip and offered it across the top of the desk. The sight of Julius offering up his sword drew a deep sigh out of Marcus.

"So during a discussion about the royal selection, you detained a man related to one of the candidates, led him to the parade square, beat him senseless, and sent him off to be healed. Judging from the contents of this document alone, I cannot simply let this pass with a slap on the wrist." But the better question was what in the world the "finest" of knights was thinking when he did such a thing. Naturally, the knightly blood was not so thin in Marcus that he could not hazard a guess. He continued, "I am at liberty to take circumstances into account. Many of your fellow knights at the parade square have entreated me to show leniency. Having said all this, you indeed went too far."

The wounds endured by the young man at the parade square far exceeded what was tolerable for mock combat. Marcus asked, "Did you find his tarnishing of your knightly pride unforgivable to that extent?"

"Glossing this over will only give rise to personal grudges. My personal shortcomings are solely to blame. Please, captain, do not waste any more words for my benefit."

Julius did not relent, meekly awaiting his punishment to the very end. Marcus lowered his eyes, considering what words to use in light of his unyielding stance. Then, Ferris opened the door, entering the room with his well-worn guard uniform and a casual attitude.

"Hi, sorry to keep you waiting. Your dear Ferri has returned!"

Seeing Marcus and Julius facing the other, Ferris put a hand to his mouth and smiled mischievously.

"*Meow*, did Ferri come at a bad time? You're sharing such passionate looks..."

Marcus replied, "...Cease that idle prattle and report, you precocious brat."

"Ohh, captain, your true colors are showing."

"I suppose I should behave before my men the same as in public... Well, fine. Make your report."

With Marcus shooing him off, Ferris stood right beside Julius.

"As per the captain's orders, Ferri went all meowt healing Subawu. His wounds are closed, his bones mended, even his teeth have been restored. He'll be all right."

"Well done. You didn't miss anything?"

"If Ferri missed it, it couldn't be found in the first place. There's no problem with his body... Though, the same can't be said for his heart."

Ferris's cat ears twitched as he shot Julius a teasing sidelong glance.

"You really are a softie, Julius. How many girls have you made swoon with that thoughtfulness and devotion? You're even making Ferri's heart flutter."

"I do not know what you speak of, Ferris."

"You don't need to keep playing tough. That girl with good instincts already noticed, and it still worked wonders on the guy who didn't, so why worry? Or maybe dear Ferri comes off as an airhead who won't notice what Julius and the captain are thinking?"

When Julius held his silence, Ferris's eyes narrowed in even greater delight.

"Tee-hee, you're so cuuute when you're quiet. But don't worry. —Because you put him through so much torture, we don't need to worry about other people going after him that don't know how to stop."

"_____"

Ferris's teasing words dragged a faint smile out of Julius. Marcus, having listened to their conversation in silence, nodded and indicated he understood Julius's decision.

"The young ones were no doubt on edge from how the brat's statement demeaned the knightly class. Being assigned to the royal guard means great skill with the sword and pride to match."

The knights' discontent, created by Subaru's conduct at the royal selection conference, had been in search of a place to explode. Marcus continued, "Had someone else run off and started a confrontation, the lad might well have lost his life for his insolence."

Ferris picked up where Marcus left off and pointed out what Julius had concluded.

"So a knight had to smack Subawu around before that could happen. If it wasn't for Julius, Ferri might have had to take care of it…"

Julius explained, "It's using the right person for the right job. We can't have you becoming his enemy when you have to heal him. Besides, it seemed more natural if I was the one to do it. I could also say…I was confident that I could pull it off the best."

Marcus commented, "It was no doubt correct to leave a weaker opponent to Julius's hands. Practice with your sword more often, why don't you?"

"Nooo! Swinging swords around makes you all sweaty and gives you callouses. *Meow,* Ferri could never show these pearly white palms to Lady Crusch again!"

Marcus, seeing Ferris so casually brushing off his captain's commands, sighed with a resigned look.

"Sir Julius Juukulius, this is your punishment. —For five days, you are suspended from your duties and forbidden to enter the garrison or enter the royal palace. I shall retain your sword until that time has passed."

"—As you command."

Julius, closing his eyes as if digesting the stated punishment, handed Marcus his knight's sword. Marcus, accepting the weapon that was the very symbol of his pride as a knight, quietly shook his head.

"Sorry. Properly speaking, this was not a burden you should have had to bear."

Julius rebutted, "Captain, you always strive for the best possible outcome. The Knights of the Royal Guard were once disbanded, but today, they boast the strongest and most gallant of men because of you."

Ferris chimed in, "That's right. Ferri would never say this to anyone besides Lady Crusch, but have more confidence in yourself, captain."

Marcus bluntly replied, "If you're going to say things like that, put on a proper man's clothes!"

Ferris shrugged his shoulders as if to say, *That's the one order I'll never obey.* Marcus laid Julius's sword on top of the table with care before sitting back down in his chair.

"The matter is concluded. There are other duties I must attend to. Dismissed."

Marcus's formal words announced he had returned to his public persona.

When the other two left the room, the atmosphere became tranquil once more. Marcus, now alone, leaned back into his creaking chair and glared up at the ceiling. The affair on his mind was separate from the mock combat, and concerned a report he had received from the castle guards after the conference's conclusion.

"'Should an intruder in the castle bear the family crest of the hawk, let him pass'..."

So read the order issued to the guards at the palace gate. That order was why the guards had requested instructions from Marcus after they captured the old man related to Felt.

In other words, the appearance of an intruder was set in stone from the very beginning.

When the clownish visage of the man who had issued the command came to mind, Marcus ground his teeth.

"Damn you, Roswaal. What the hell are you planning...?"

His stony face burned with irritation as he pondered what the eccentric might be up to.

2

"*Meow*, the captain's not too smooth, either. He saw the whole thing through, so why couldn't he just drop it altogether?"

"Allowing such an act to go unpunished would be unacceptable even under these circumstances. I wouldn't wish for that, either."

Ferris was gazing at the side of Julius's handsome face as the two walked down the corridor of the garrison side by side.

Ferris's lips pouted at how Julius looked so satisfied.

"So, Julius, what are you going to do meow?" Ferris asked.

"Naturally, I will follow my captain's command and spend time at the mansion. I will explain the situation to Lady Anastasia... My only concern is whether she can take it easy in the meantime."

"But you like that about her, don't you? Ferri can tell!"

Ferris's cheeks puffed up as he put his own spin on Julius's words. Julius then looked at his cat-eared companion as if he'd just remembered something.

"Incidentally, Ferris, about the boy from earlier..."

Before the question was even fully posed, Ferris replied, all warmth draining from his lips.

"He's with Lady Emilia right now. After…he'll be staying at the Karsten mansion to convalesce."

Accepting the reply, Julius closed his eyes and pondered for a time.

"Convalesce…is it? It would seem he has suffered an injury far graver than any seen from without."

"Mew didn't hear one word about that from your dear Ferri."

Ferris's behavior, however, made the situation clear as day. Julius could guess what had happened since handing Subaru over to Ferris. The wise young man soon arrived at his answer.

"—It is truly in Lady Emilia's nature to cause pain in others."

"Are mew thinking, 'Even though she could live a much wiser life'?"

"No. That very nature is what allows her to live as nobly and beautifully as she does. I do not deign to wish her to change. Thus, all I can do is hope that she lives more righteously, more genuinely, without anything to be ashamed of."

Julius lifted his face and resumed his walk. Ferris followed half a step behind, hands crossed behind his back, leaning his body forward as he looked up at Julius.

"Does that go for the boy, too?"

"It goes for everyone, Ferris. It is for that very reason I wield a sword."

—He will probably break, thought Julius.

If he was going to break, breaking him then and there would be a mercy.

But if—just if—all that was not enough to break him, then…

"It would not be such a bad thing to trade swords with a fool full of idealism once more."

"Well, even if that's what you think, Julius, Subawu might not wanna do that again after the public beating you gave him. Hey, hey…"

"What is it?"

"Lots of things came together to cause that duel, but he got on your nerves juuuuust a little, didn't he?"

With Ferris's words seeming meant to test him, Julius stopped and looked over.

"Ferris, you wound me. I am a knight. However imperfectly, that is the precept I live by."

Julius, deeming his own conduct to have nothing to be ashamed of, looked straight at Ferris.

"As for an annoyance…perhaps he was that, a little bit."

"Well, he got on Ferri's nerves quite a bit, mew know?"

The two exchanged laughs as if it was the funniest joke they'd ever shared. They finally arrived at the entrance to the garrison and shook hands. Julius said, "Well, then, we must part. I deeply wish that you and your lord remain in good health."

"Lady Anastasia will probably complain, so good luck with that, Julius… You can just leave all the mopping up to Ferri."

Ferris casually waved before turning his back and walking off.

Julius watched from behind as his friend departed—and an enemy took his place.

"Lady Anastasia shall succeed as king."

"Nuh-uh. Lady Crusch is the fittest for the throne."

And so, the knights exchanged their declaration of war before returning to their respective masters.

The rays of the setting sun poured down from the evening sky, dying all who dwelled in the royal capital equally red.

—In so many ways, the royal selection had now begun.

AFTERWORD

Hiya, Tappei Nagatsuki here! Also, Mouse-Colored Cat! That is an alias!

You know, it's a real pain to have more than one name, but don't worry. Back in the second year of middle school, I had not three names, no—I had *six*. Two were names drawn from my previous lives. As for my true self— Stop! Don't open up that dark history! You'll wake the Id!

Now then, we're now into the Return to the Royal Capital arc, which was the third chapter in the web novel. Until now, *Re:ZERO* had a limited cast in cramped quarters, but the regular members suddenly doubled with this volume!

In particular, the girls ended up so visually gorgeous that you almost hate them for it. With Otsuka putting his mad design skills to work, when we were done fiddling with them I was like, "This is fun, damn it!"

All that aside, work on the fourth volume was extremely rough. It was like a death march at my day job, too, so I did most of my work on it at a family restaurant near where I live. Lately it's to the point that when it's time for "Thank you for your patronage!" and for the bill, the staff are always calling me by this nickname they've pegged me with. They call me Vegetable Juice.

So Tappei Nagatsuki, Mouse-Colored Cat, Vegetable Juice, and my real name is… No! You'll wake the Id!!

Having gracefully arrived at my punchline, I will now proceed with the established practice of giving thanks.

First, thank you, Mr. Ikemoto, for getting through this hellish schedule together with me. When I was e-mailed at four in the morning, I was worried they'd say "Mr. Ikemoto has passed away." Thank you for your hard work.

Also, thank you, Otsuka, for all your design work without a single hint of a grimace, even with the cast of characters doubling between Vol. 3 and Vol. 4. You did a truly splendid job with each and every one. It makes writing scenes for them a real joy.

Kusano is a magician, and his illusions have captivated me one more time. Thank you once again for persevering to the bitter end and for your passion in making this the finest piece of work that we could.

This work was supported by many others, including proofreaders, managers, bookstore owners, and so on and so forth. Truly, thank you very much.

And more than anyone, it is thanks to all of you who have purchased this fourth volume who are responsible for my being able to write what I want. Thank you very much.

Well then, let us meet again for Subaru's suffering in Volume 5.

Tappei Nagatsuki
May, 2014
(Getting a cold shoulder from store employees
after having stayed for over twelve hours)

AFTERWORD

Before I knew it, Vol. 4! The royal selection starts in earnest so there's a ton of new main characters.

RUMBLE...

DAMN YOU, BARUSU...

SNEAK

STAAARE...

High-End Black Tea

There's some characters I didn't get to draw, though. There was no place for Ram or Beako so I'm borrowing this space to draw them here!

Shinichirou Otsuka

AL

"So, Princess, we've gotta do this next volume preview thing so, what are we gonna do?"

"What a foolish question, Al. I shall take pity upon the foolish, mediocre, common rabble with an act of compassion. Seeing them bow before a display of my majesty should be amusing, yes?"

"In other words, you're just gonna do it, huh? Well, that's a relief. So about what's in this next volume here…"

"The foolish commoner, abandoned by the cheeky half-demon, remains in the royal capital, wallowing in regret, irritation, and gloom, feeling out of place and in search of an outlet… Yes?"

"Man, my bro there has a life filled with suffering."

"He is a fool, and a common fool at that. I cannot possibly understand the unsightly struggles of a life such as his."

"Wonder what happened to make ya say all that. Why don't you just read the manga or something?"

"The comic version serialized in *Monthly Comic Alive*, the short stories from Deka Bunko, and so forth. These are for the little people alone."

"Well, there's the serialization starting up in *Monthly Big Gangan*, too. There's a new *Re:ZERO* project every time you blink, and there's even more in the works that haven't been unveiled yet. Man, it sure ain't gonna be boring."

Priscilla

"Ha, but of course. At the very least, it is sufficient to attract the eyes of the public until *I* appear in earnest, at which point the ignorant lot may bow before me."

"Your spirits are as high as ever, Princess."

"This world is formed solely for my convenience. —It is providence."

"So I wonder what's gonna happen to my bro there, with providence turning its back on him?"

"You can read all about it in *Re:ZERO -Starting Life in Another World-*, Vol. 5, to be published in October… That is some time from now, is it not? Al, do something."

"Princess, according to what you said, this has to be providence, and something that's convenient for you somehow?"

"I see, that certainly has the ring of truth. It seems that you know your place in the world quite well, Al. I expect much more of it for my sake in the times to come."

"You got it… You know, when I see you taking the helm like this, it's kinda cute, well, in one sense…"

"That goes for the rest of you foolish commoners reading this, too. Struggle, work to the bone, all for my benefit. This is your duty to me as part of the common rabble."